I0578664

DEWEY BELONG TOGETHER

GREEN VALLEY LIBRARY BOOK #7

ANN WHYNOT

WWW.SMARTYPANTSROMANCE.COM

COPYRIGHT

This book is a work of fiction. Names, characters, places, rants, facts, contrivances, and incidents are either the product of the author's questionable imagination or are used factitiously. Any resemblance to actual persons, living or dead or undead, events, locales is entirely coincidental if not somewhat disturbing/concerning.

Copyright © 2021 by Smartypants Romance; All rights reserved.

No part of this book may be reproduced, scanned, photographed, instagrammed, tweeted, twittered, twatted, tumbled, or distributed in any printed or electronic form without explicit written permission from the author.

Made in the United States of America

Print Edition: 978-1-949202-34-2

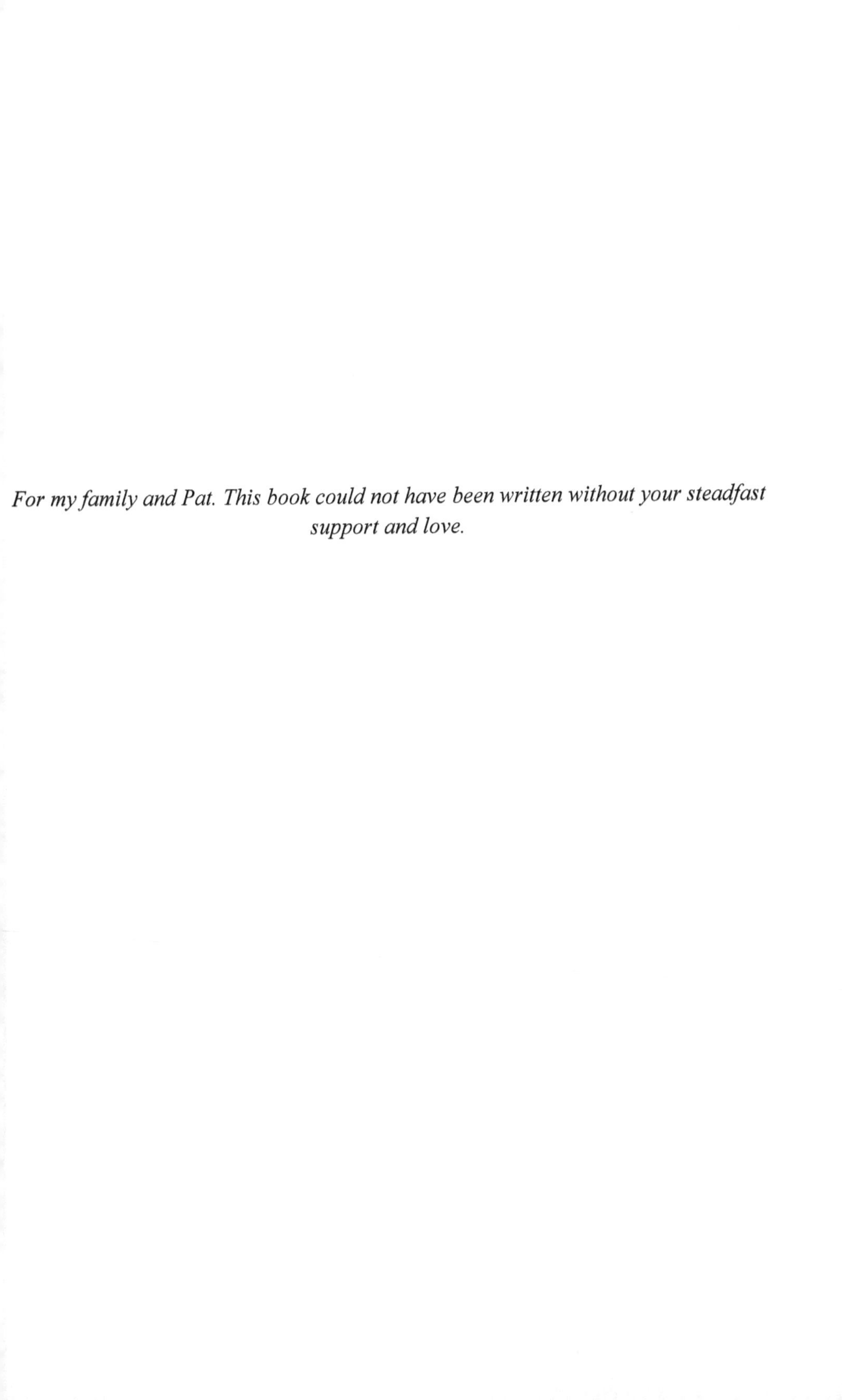

For my family and Pat. This book could not have been written without your steadfast support and love.

CHAPTER ONE
MAXINE

"A game is an opportunity to focus our energy, with relentless optimism, at something we're good at (or getting better at) and enjoy."

— Jane McGonigal

I must have been crazy when I agreed to host a dozen strangers from an online game in my hometown of Green Valley, nestled in the Great Smoky Mountains of Tennessee.

In person, I was the furthest thing possible from a social butterfly. I am what might be called a basement dweller. Like all underground creatures, I prefer depth and darkness to the shiny world above. Above the basement floor of the Green Valley Public Library, that is. And okay, so I don't inhabit the basement as much as catalog there. This is my ninth year of creating, polishing, and publishing records in all their metadata glory for several counties—an honor given to the Green Valley branch because of, well, me. I can say without an inflated ego that I am probably the best cataloger in the state, due to my meticulous nature and the fact that the beauty and structure of the records appeal to me as a librarian far more than interacting with the patrons, or other staff, upstairs. I swear, half the time the other librarians forget I'm even down there.

More than once I've come upstairs after working a bit late to find the library locked up tight.

Sound a little boring? Sad? Well, strap in because I am not just Maxine Peters, ace basement cataloger. Unbeknownst to those who know me in "real life," I am a *warrior*. As Maximus_Damage, I am a fighter in the eternal battle of good versus evil, a vanguard against might makes right, a last bastion against … well, you get the picture. I am, and have been for the last eight years, an avid player of the massive multiplayer online role-playing game *League of Magecraft*. What I love so passionately about *Magecraft* is that I get to be, from behind my computer screen, tough, sassy, strong, and fierce. I get to tap into a part of myself I never let out offline. Have fun, complete epic quests, and make friends along the way.

It's not that I don't have "real" friends here in Green Valley, I do. But they know me as a buttoned-up cataloger who works in the library basement. The perpetual wall-flower at the few Friday night jam sessions I venture out to at the community center. The woman who overindulges at Daisy's Nut House and who often gets runs in her stockings and has lipstick on her teeth. Offline Max's idea of fun is hosting monthly book club meetings for three friends—two of whom also work at the library—or sipping wine and watching a Hallmark Christmas movie. In June.

Online Max? She tells Alexa to slam on Black Veil Brides, sticks her hair up in a messy bun, and logs in to a fantasy world of mages, demons, knights, and warriors. She throws on her armor, picks up that ginormous sword, and kicks major ass. I've earned a bit of a reputation in the game as a badass of epic proportions that you do not want to cross weapons with. I'm also a leader of sorts, as an officer in the largest and best guild on the continent. See, *Magecraft* isn't only a game, it's a vast social network that connects people from around the entire world, organized into guilds—associations of players committed to helping each other build friendships and reach both peak fun and potential in the game.

And this year, several of my fellow guild members, aka *guildies,* are descending upon Green Valley like a plague of locusts.

Okay, scratch that. I did invite them, after all. It all happened so fast; some of the officers suggested a meetup offline for folks in the South after the success of a Midwestern gathering. After a lot of hemming and hawing over the location, I suggested my little town in autumn with all its riotous colors. And what do you know, it turns out no one else wanted to organize the thing anyway. So the invitations went out, and before I knew it, I was arranging activities and accommodation for a gaggle of geeks for four entire days.

This is how I wound up standing in the airport in Knoxville holding a sign with their names: "Deathdrop, Carebear, Nedris, and Wrath." So perhaps I used the word *gaggle* a little liberally. To both my consternation and relief, after a dozen RSVPs, people began to drop out of the gathering one by one. Some had family obligations, couldn't get time off work, or perhaps they couldn't face their crippling social anxiety to meet in meatspace. We were down to five, including me, the others all due to arrive within the next two hours.

I paced the terminal feeling a bit like an alien in blue jeans, red Converse, and a tight red T-shirt that read "Got Geek?" with illustrations from *Firefly, Lord of the Rings,* and *Game of Thrones.* I never wore clothes like this in public, preferring to hide under a lumpy cardigan and an ankle-length skirt or something else that screamed frumpy business casual. The truth is, I had fretted for weeks over what to wear during the gathering. Did I show them the Maxine Peters who yawned her way through life in Green Valley, or did I embrace my inner extrovert and present myself how I had always wanted to be seen? During a night in which wine may or may not have played a big part, boxes from the back corner of my closet were dug out and jeans, T-shirts, tank tops, and sneakers I hadn't seen since college were unearthed. The extrovert screaming inside me begging to be let free won, and I was going to let myself be seen. Not only in jeans, but socially, through the activities and events I had planned around town. For the first time in a decade, I was going to cut loose in public, not only in my gaming room.

Not since I was fresh out of my library and information studies master's program— almost ten years ago—have I been my truest self offline. The main reason being that I was assaulted by a pair of Iron Wraiths one evening as I was fixing a flat by the side of the road. The Iron Wraiths were Green Valley's local biker gang-slash-menace, and most of the members were unhinged in one way or another. That night left me in the hospital with my jaw wired shut, unable to talk. Even after I healed, I didn't talk very much. I didn't feel like it. But online? I could speak fine with my fingers. And in gaming, a newer hobby of mine at the time, I had discovered that beating up on virtual bad guys gave me a sense of satisfaction, helpless as I was to do much about the actual bad guys in the picture. The official story was that I didn't get a good look at their faces, and that's how I'd wanted it. I didn't want retribution against me or my mom if I had pressed charges. I didn't want to be looking over my shoulder all the time. The Wraiths were not known for being kind to their enemies. They could all go to hell as far as I was concerned; lately it looked like they were halfway there already. With their leadership in jail and their numbers plummeting, their demise seemed imminent. I'd try not to shed a tear, bless their hearts.

And to give Julianne MacIntyre credit where credit was due, she didn't hesitate to hire me back then, bruises and all. It probably didn't hurt matters that I'd given up on my dream of being a children's librarian and decided cataloging in solitude was more my jam. After the attack, being around so many people had become frightening to me, and I was well-suited to the cataloging world.

I saw some passengers coming through the arrivals entrance and rechecked the itinerary. First to arrive were Carebear, Deathdrop, and Wrath on a flight from Jacksonville. I inwardly seethed. I couldn't believe Wrath had the gall to show up, knowing I was the organizer and host. Of course his name wasn't really Wrath, but we didn't do real names in *Magecraft*. Our guild placed a high value on privacy. I played as a male dwarf—it's all about the beard—so everyone in-game basically assumed I had a dick. Speaking of dicks, that brings us back to Wrath. If everyone in the world is destined to have one mortal enemy, one great nemesis that follows them through time and space, Wrath would be mine.

The feud between Wrath and I had been going on for a decade, following us from one game to another. We had been leaders of opposing guilds in an earlier online game, *Guilds of the Ages*. Back then, Wrath had been the very definition of a competitive, petty little shit. If my guild had something, he wanted it. If we hosted an event in *Ages*, he had to have one bigger, rowdier, better. And as for me, personally? At this point, I'd like to introduce the word *griefing*. To grief another player is essentially to go beyond the code of fair play and be as big of a pain in their posterior as possible. And Wrath and his guildies griefed me in spades.

I could have sworn that Wrath's very existence hinged on giving me grief.

Ages went the way of the dodo when *Magecraft* was released, and I thought my days of alternately avoiding and being annoyed by Wrath had come and gone. Not so. Turns out we both applied for and joined the same *Magecraft* guild, and the game? It was still afoot. Only now, because we were technically on the same side, it was psychological warfare and pranks galore. Just last month, "someone" had taught the parrotling in our guild hall to say "Maximus is a jackoff" every time someone walked nearby. The same parrotling that was in the dead center of the hall and could be heard for miles. Very funny. It took three days for the guild leader to figure out how to get the damn thing to shut up without killing it (which I may have floated first as an idea).

Let the record show that I am not as well liked as our virtual parrot made up of code and rendered in pixels. Killing Pollywoggy? Not an option.

The crowd was starting to thin, and I still hadn't spotted my guests. I knew Carebear used a cane, but I hadn't seen any women with one yet. As for Wrath, who the heck knew. I was expecting every terrible gamer stereotype come to life, right down to bad odor. As I scanned the assemblage, my gaze stopped on what was possibly the finest male specimen I had ever laid eyes on. He was standing against a pillar fiddling with his cell phone, his long, sleek black hair pulled into a ponytail that reached mid-back. He was at least 6'2" and had shoulders that made my lady parts tingle and take notice. I was glad of this as they hadn't taken notice of much of anything for a long, long time. I could see tattoo sleeves poking out of his T-shirt. And his face! Beautiful cheekbones and a neatly trimmed but not too short beard. I did love a man who knew how to maintain attractive facial hair. Suddenly, he plunked the cell into his pocket and gave a visual sweep of the room before advancing in my direction. He looked younger than me, maybe late twenties?

"What, he couldn't be bothered to pick us up so he sends his mousy girlfriend?" came out of the perfectly shaped mouth, a duffel thudding to the floor at his feet. In that instant, when he looked at me and rolled his eyes, I knew. Wrath. The hottie was *him*.

Gritting my teeth, I lowered the sign and stuck out my right hand. "Maximus. Good to meet you, Wrath. I see you haven't picked up any manners lately."

He reared back. "Max?! You're a ... chick?" he asked, his mouth agape, his arms hanging uselessly at his sides. I held my hand firm, giving him time to recover and adjust his worldview to one in which his worst nightmare had two X chromosomes. After it became apparent that Wrath lacked any social graces, I dropped my hand and shook my head.

"Have you seen Carebear?" I asked, ignoring the odd look Wrath was giving me. It was downright unnerving. At least when the rest of the group arrived, I would have some potential reinforcements to balance out Wrath's assholery.

"Geez, madame hostess, haven't you been checking the guild chat? Before I boarded, Carebear bailed. Her kids' babysitter flaked. And Deathdrop and Nedris are out too.

Their mommies took away their permission slips or something equally lame. Looks like it's just us, sweet cheeks," he said with a broad grin.

Just us? *Just us?!* I reminded myself to breathe, and not to get distracted by the gorgeous face staring down at me. Didn't they say Lucifer was the most beautiful of the angels? And what in the holy hell was I supposed to do on my own for four days with *Wrath?*

First things first. *Start as you mean to go on*, my mom always said. I looked up at him and growled, "Call me sweet cheeks again, and I'll acquaint your testicles with my kneecap." I heaved his duffel onto the luggage cart I had procured earlier, then looked him in the eye and said in my sweetest Southern voice, "Welcome to Tennessee."

CHAPTER TWO
JONATHAN

"I'm a Knight of the Realm. We have a code to uphold, you know."

— Wrath

As my plane descended into Knoxville, I stared out the window, my left knee shaking rhythmically and probably bothering the bejesus out of the person next to me. The stranger, I should say, sitting where my best friend Deathdrop was supposed to be. I hated flying, even more so when I had to do it with someone who fell asleep on my shoulder as soon as we hit cruising altitude and then drooled on me as we flew north. It was only lunchtime and already this day was turning into a shit-show. My anxiety levels were at a peak, and I needed to get in touch with Deathdrop, like, yesterday. I was about to meet Maximus_Damage, for Pete's sake!

"All passengers are requested to remain in their seats with their seat belts fastened as we approach the gate. Mobile functions on devices may now be used." I sighed in relief as the crackling voice of the flight attendant gave us the all clear to use our phones. I fished my cell out of my pants pocket and frantically dialed Deathdrop. He picked up on the second ring, his voice positively jovial considering the stew I was in.

"Wrath, my man! Toss a coin to your Witcher, beotch. I totally slayed another nerd for you and cleared the way for you to have four whole days of lurve alone with Maximus."

"Dude, where the hell are you?" I whisper-yelled. "Why is there an elderly lady next to me instead of your sorry carcass?" Oh, this had better be good. Someone had better be dead for this to get a pass. Deathdrop loved to hatch schemes, and if I was caught up in some stupid plan of his, I was going to be beyond pissed.

"Look man, I thought about it, and after I saw that Carebear was out, I messaged Nedris and told him the weekend was off. I messaged you that I'd meet you at the airport after spending the night at Mindy's, but I stayed home. Think about it, bro. You are about to see the love of your life after ten years of crushing hardcore. Some things a man has to do alone."

"Alone?" I almost shrieked. "If there was ever a time for a wingman, this is it, you ass! I have never been attracted to a guy before, and here I am about to see one live and in person that I have these crazy strong feelings for, and where is my best friend? Off picking his toes in a swamp!"

He laughed. "I don't know man, you thought Jason Momoa was pretty hot in *Aquaman*. And I keep telling you, they are ingrown toenails. It's not my fault I get picky."

"Jesus, Norman, would you quit it with that? No one wants to hear details about your toes. And it was his tats that I thought were awesome. I wasn't mooning over his luscious locks." God, again with fraking *Aquaman.* I let out a huge, frustrated sigh. "This conversation is going nowhere, and we've stopped at the gate. Man, all I can say is, you suck."

Before I could hang up, I heard him laugh again and say, "Not as much as you will—"

This was great, perfect really. I was about to take the biggest leap of my life and go after someone I'd been interested in since I was seventeen, and dammit, now I was doing it alone. And not just anyone, a *guy*. It was true that I'd never been into dudes, but Max's personality is so damn bold and bright it never failed to draw me in. From the day we first met online, I knew there was some kind of spark between us, and I did all kinds of foolish things to try to win his attention and show him I was worthy of it. I was eighteen when after a very excellent day of verbal sparring with Max, I knocked on my mom's bedroom door and cried in her arms as I told her I was interested in a guy, but I didn't really think I like-liked guys, so was I gay or what? She held me and rocked me back and forth while she prayed to Jesus that I would be led down the "right path" for my immortal soul.

Luckily, my mother believed in mental health professionals almost as much as she did her Lord and Savior. She took me to see Tom, a therapist, to help me try to sort out the spaghetti-like tangle of gay panic in my brain. Tom helped me understand that I didn't need to slap a label on my sexuality if I didn't want to, and that it wasn't crazily uncommon to be attracted to one special person of the same sex. He also told me that there are all kinds of orientations out there, like people who are attracted romantically to someone, but not sexually. Or not sexually until a strong romantic connection is forged. I liked how that sounded because it explained so many things, like why I only liked looking at the ladies in porn but I loved talking to Max. Maybe I was one of those people that needed a strong romantic connection first, and my physical attraction to Max would develop over time. Or maybe I was one of those people who thought that a person's body simply wasn't nearly as important as their mind, heart, and soul. Yeah, I liked that.

With Tom's help, I got fairly comfortable with the idea of Max and me. In theory. So comfortable that at twenty I told my best friend, Norman, aka Deathdrop, about my feelings. After laughing for a solid fifteen minutes over how much Max hated me—which had to be impossible—he slapped me on the back and offered himself up as a test case to see if making out with a guy really did anything for me. I learned two things that day: one, a mouth feels pretty much like a mouth, no matter what genitals it is eventually attached to; and two, when your best friend tries to slip you the tongue, shit gets awkward, fast.

Despite our weird make-out session, Norman and I were cool. Except this stunt. This right here put him in the category of traitor to the realm.

So why had I kept my feelings secret from Max? Long story short—plain and simple terror. Tom and I had worked on my crushing fear of rejection, but I still hadn't worked up the courage to put myself out there with Maximus. I know, glaciers moved quicker than I did when possible romance was involved. But when I read the message on the guild forums about this gathering, I knew I would beg, borrow, and steal to get the time off work and the money together for a trip to Tennessee. Finally, this was my chance to tell Max directly how I felt.

Breathe, I told myself, *just breathe. Be mindful of your body and let your feelings wash over you. Focus on staying calm. Nobody accomplished anything by playing it safe.* After a few breaths and a few more platitudes, I thought, *Screw deep breathing, hello pharmaceuticals.* In my pocket were two little white pills, each one capable of calming me down before I had a full-blown panic attack on the tarmac. I took one of the lorazepam and let it melt under my tongue. I was grateful my slower exit from the back of the plane would give me a bit more time to let the fast-acting medication work. I didn't exactly like relying on antianxiety meds, but desperate times and all that. Not that I thought taking medication was a desperate measure, just not one that I enjoyed. Especially considering what my daily dosage of various meds already looked like, all piled up twice a day.

After I deplaned and grabbed my duffel from the luggage carousel, I saw a pillar and leaned against it, pretending to use my cell phone while I searched for Max. Would he be tall? Short? Would he think my tats were cool? Dammit, I was acting and thinking like a swoony teenage girl. And why was it suddenly so hot in here? I collected myself and did a quick scan of the room until I saw a woman holding a sign with our names on it. And sweet Lord of the Rings, she was beautiful; tall and voluptuous, with bangin' curves and a pretty face. She looked kind of like that model on Instagram, Ashley Graham, but a bit bigger. She was wearing a cute T-shirt, jeans with a few rips, and red Converse like the Tenth Doctor which made me smile a little. Her light brown hair was done up in a retro style in a red bandana, and she was also scoping out the thinning crowd.

Then it hit me like a raining iguana—this must be Max's girlfriend. I was lusting after Max's girlfriend when I should be focused on Max. And oh my god, he has a *girlfriend.* I hadn't even considered this possibility. I assumed that anyone who played a video game as much as Max did had to be single, at least most of the time. I didn't let the fact that this was a blatant stereotype deter me in that assumption. Disappointment and irrational anger wrapped around me like a blanket. I tried to be nice. I really did.

"What, he couldn't be bothered to pick us up so he sends his mousy girlfriend?" I was almost shocked by what came out of my mouth. I didn't know this girl, and it wasn't her fault I was crushing on Max. And calling her mousy because she looked a bit uncomfortable wasn't fair.

She looked jarred for a moment but quickly lowered the sign and stuck out her right hand. "Maximus. Good to meet you, Wrath. I see you haven't picked up any manners lately."

I felt like I'd been struck by lightning, and my head reared back. "Max?! You're a … chick?" I asked, my mouth gaping like a codfish, and my arms limp at my sides.

There was probably a loading bar hovering over my forehead as it all sunk in. Max is a chick. A girl. A woman. A *woman*, for the love of Pete! I've spent nigh on ten years sexually confused over being in love with a *girl*. I didn't know whether to laugh, cry, break dance, or throw something against the damn pillar behind me. All of that angst, all of it for nothing. I mean, okay, I did learn a lot about myself going through counseling. I know if Max had been a guy, I would still try to pursue something because I had come to believe that what resides at the core of a person was far more important than the packaging it came in. But faced with this strange new reality, my resolve wavered. If Max was a girl, didn't that make him—er, her—a liar of epic proportions? It wasn't only me, everyone thought Maximus_Damage was a dude. There's no way she could be ignorant of that. And she what, just rolled with it? The Max I knew had integrity. It was one of those noble qualities I admired but that sometimes annoyed me about him. *Her.*

Argh, this was a total mess. I suppose a part of me was relieved that Max was a woman, despite the deception. I wouldn't have to face the judgement of being in a same-sex relationship, should I be able to convince girl-Max that I was worth taking a chance on if she happened to return my feelings—please, God, let her return my feelings. Not that I gave a shit on an average day what others thought of me, but being in a gay relationship in my hometown? Not recommended. Mom could finally stop praying for my immortal soul. Plus, other than that one ill-thought kiss with Norman, all of my experience had been with women. I was on much firmer footing on the seduction front with girl-Max.

I fumbled through a few words with her, trying to sound cheerful and not like a dick. I was in shock, that was it. Plain shock. This beautiful woman, holding her hand out to me, was the one I thought of as the love of my life. How would I move forward from here? There's no instruction manual or game guide to tell me what to do because no strategy had ever been dreamt up for this situation, I'm sure.

After having my testicles come under what sounded like a viable threat, we made our way to Max's car, her stubbornly insisting on pushing the luggage cart even though I knew my bag was heavy as all hell. Conversation between us had come to a standstill, both of us probably lost in thought as we made our way through arrivals and to the parking lot. I mean, besides all my inner drama over the discovery of Max's gender, what do you say to someone you know because you talk to them every day, but you don't really *know*?

"So this is a bit weird, huh, princess? Seeing someone from the game in person?" I asked, floundering around to make conversation. I wondered how discombobulated she was that it was just the two of us. I knew I was having a hard time processing that I had four days to get Max to return my affections, or by some miracle, be with her if she already did,. Maybe Norman had done me a favor after all.

"It's a bit strange, yeah. I've never met someone from the internet before. Not a big Tinder user. Um, I've organized a bunch of group activities, but we can always ditch the itinerary if you'd rather hang out and game while you're here. I have a PS4, a Switch, and a spare laptop," she replied, like she was trying to be hospitable but was uncertain how to proceed.

I thought about the work she had probably put into this weekend and felt a twinge of guilt at being happy it was crumbling to pieces around her.

"No way!" I replied. "We'll stick to the itinerary you made up. We can game on our own anytime. How many opportunities will we have to unplug together?"

"Not too damn many, I hope," she mumbled, exhaling loudly. I decided to interpret that as a sign she was tired from pushing the luggage cart, and my fingers itched to take over the chore from her.

"Max, I can push around my own bag," I said, moving closer to the cart.

"I've got it!" she said, sending me a glare which spoke of fire raining from the sky if I didn't leave it alone. But then I rarely left things alone when it came to Max.

"I know, but it would be easier for me to push," I explained, getting into position to take the cart from her.

"Why, because you're a guy? You think I'm weak now that you know I'm a 'chick'?" she asked, bringing the cart to a standstill and cocking her head to one side, looking straight into my eyes.

Okay, whoa. I wasn't touching that with a ten-foot pole even if she may have been technically correct in that I did think I was stronger than her. I stepped to the side to grant her more room and gave a little flourish with my hand, saying calmly, "As you wish. I was just offering because my mother raised me right."

"And I'm pushing because *my* mother raised *me* right, and you don't let a guest take care of their own bags. Honestly." She let out a puff of air and kept pushing.

We finally stopped by a blue Jeep that looked like it was literally held together with duct tape and glue. I wondered how Max had planned to squeeze everyone in there, had the others arrived. Since it was just the two of us, my bag was tossed in the back, and I grabbed shotgun. As we peeled out of the parking lot, I watched Max from the corner of my eye. She really was beautiful, and I'd be lying if I said I was anything but gobsmacked. She had shiny, light brown hair, green eyes that kept flashing annoyance, and a cute, round chin.

After a few minutes of trying not to be obvious about watching her, my curiosity could no longer go unsatiated. I had to address the elephant in the Jeep. "So, Max, are you going to tell me why you're a lying liar who lies?" Yikes, even I inwardly cringed at how that came out.

"Excuse me?" she replied, sounding offended. "I'm not a liar. What have I ever lied about?"

I let out a snort. "You know exactly what I'm talking about, princess. Your gender. You've been lying to the gaming community for a decade, pretending to be a guy."

"I never once stated I was a man," she defended, and I tried to recall if that were true. "You gamer guys are all the same. You assume anyone that's any good has to have your kind of junk. Like a girl couldn't possibly rise to the top of the ranks."

I didn't bother to correct her because I didn't want to get stuck on a tangent about sexism in video games. I knew, from reading the game forums, Max could and would talk about it at length.

"You may have never come right out and said you were a guy, but you've been actively concealing that you're a girl. You've never joined in on the guild voice chat. You always let the other officers take point on everything. There's a rumor that you're mute! You could be better than good, you know, you could be a great raid or arena leader if you'd stop hiding and step up." Voice chat was essential to parts of the game where tight team coordination was needed. In my opinion, Max's lack of vocal participation has held her back from rising to the leadership of the entire guild.

She blinked rapidly and stuck the tip of her tongue out of the right-hand side of her mouth. I'm going to guess this was her thinking face. It was also cute as all get-out.

"I'm not *hiding*. I did play as a girl for a little while in *Guilds of the Ages*. Before I was Maximus_Damage, I mean. I made the newbie mistake of uploading myself into one of those websites where you reveal your real face and character name. Do you know what it was like gaming as a girl back then? Guys would message me asking for cybersex or virtual lap dances. Random dudes would shower me with gold or presents I didn't ask for and then expect me to owe them some kind of relationship. My looks were made fun of on the forums—called fat, which may be accurate, but they meant it as an insult—and my skills were ridiculed even though I was damn awesome. People accused me of expecting a handout or a free ride because I was a girl despite never asking for anything from anyone. It was …" She trailed off for a minute, as though grappling for the right words. "Not fun. And it's a freakin' game, it's supposed to be fun, right? So I re-rolled as a male warrior and no one asked me if I was a girl. Suddenly, all that crap was gone. And every time you call me sweet cheeks or princess, you remind me that you're the type of guy I was trying to escape from."

Huh. And ouch.

"And do you even *remember* Gamergate?" She shook her head in frustration. Oh, here we go. "Because I sure as hell do. I was very vocal on my personal Twitter about it, and on the game forums as Maximus. Coordinated harassment of women, doxing, even threats of rape and death, for the love of the gods. Is it any wonder that after years of playing a male dwarf I wasn't keen on having some kind of coming out party? Although I guess that's what this weekend is, in part. I'm not a total idiot. I knew when I agreed to host that my grand plan to deceive you all for years would come crumbling down the moment you saw me," she said, her voice dripping sarcasm. "You know what, how about I turn on some music and save us from more of this conversation." I hummed in agreement, needing some time to digest her point of view.

I found it hard to believe it could be that bad for girl gamers. I kind of remember guys talking about some of the girls we played with in unflattering terms. Saying crude things. That was just harmless guy talk, right? But then how could it be harmless if a player as well-known as Maximus had concealed who she was for nigh on a decade? That had to mean something, especially when she could probably make a living playing games and streaming it online. Plenty of girl gamers hosted their own channels and had hordes of subscribers. But maybe those women got harassed too? My intuition told me that despite everything she said, there was still another reason why Max had concealed her gender online, and I was going to Sherlock it out before the weekend was over.

I swear she spun the dial up to eleven, blasting "Mother Superior" by Coheed and Cambria, surprising the pants off me. "This is from *No World for Tomorrow,* right?" I asked, only slightly surprised that our tastes for prog—progressive rock—matched.

She nodded. "It's their earlier work, and I gotta say I love it."

I loved it too. Hearing the familiar music calmed me in addition to the lorazepam now soothing my brain. I decided to stow my hurt at her deception for a little while and see how things could go between Max and me. I had to say, she made some excellent points. And though I occasionally gave her a bit of hell in the game, she was also rarely wrong. I extended an olive branch to mend the weirdness between us. "I have their music on my playlist in my shop," I said, giving her some real-life info about me, the kind of stuff we didn't talk about in-game. "I build computers with my best friend." Norman and I owned a fairly successful online business and had built a reputation for making crazy custom builds. The "shop" I'd referenced earlier was really my garage, not that I was going to mention that.

"You build computers with Deathdrop? Cool beans. I built my own system," she replied, then went back to bopping her head and mouthing the words. When the chorus hit, she burst out into song, and I had to quickly stifle a laugh. The incredible Maximus_Damage couldn't carry a tune in a bucket, though her enthusiasm was contagious. I thought, to hell with it, and joined in. We sang together in excruciating harmony for the next twenty minutes to Green Valley.

CHAPTER THREE
MAXINE

"Do you want to live forever? Get over that ridge!"

— Maximus_Damage

After a half hour in the car, I felt as though I was driving through an apocalyptic hellscape, one in which Wrath was the only other person to survive. I couldn't think of any other reason why we would be cheerily singing together unless the end of days had arrived. But no, that didn't make much sense: Who sings their way through the apocalypse? As he belted out another verse, I thought, Wrath and I, that's who. As much as four days alone with Wrath might be my own personal hell, I had to find a way to get through it, sanity intact. I'd take car karaoke and whatever other agreeable moments as they came.

I was still hopping mad as hell that I was in this position to begin with. I stuck my neck out for the guild organizing this meetup, and when it came down to it, a dozen people flaked on me, leaving me alone with the very last person on this planet I wanted to host until Sunday.

And who the heck was he to call me a liar? Simply because a segment of people, obviously including him, had assumed I was a guy didn't make me responsible for their assumptions. They needed to self-examine why they thought that in the first place rather than Wrath's implication that I should be checking my head over why I "misled" the gaming community for a decade. Should Wrath out me as a girl and the proverbial shit hit the fan, it wouldn't be hard to understand why I had made the choice I did. The guys I played with assumed I was a guy because I was in what they perceived to be *their* space, and I was kicking ass in it. Period. I had nothing to feel badly about. So why did I feel … bad? Because I had come face-to-face with someone I had "lied" to?

As we sang, I decided to be a good hostess and keep the peace. I drove my trusty Jeep named Stiles to the Dew Drop Inn, a bed and breakfast where I had originally reserved a block of rooms for the gathering. Though cozy, the Dew Drop Inn was in a rather sorry state, making it cheaper by miles than the popular Donner Lodge, but the guild budget wouldn't stretch very far, and needs must and all that. I already had sorely disappointed the proprietor, Mrs. Potter, by canceling one room after the other over the past few months, but now she was surely going to throw a hissy fit when she saw me come in with one lone guest. I was going to have to stop by the Donner Bakery in the near future and bring her a banana cake or some lemon custard tarts by way of apology.

We both hopped out of the Jeep—a minor difficulty for Wrath because of the tricky door handle on the passenger side—and as we walked up the steps of the inn, he casually said, "You know, paying for a room for only one person for three nights seems excessive, and a waste of the guild's money. Don't you have a guest room I could crash in? Hell, even a couch halfway comfortable? I'm not picky."

I almost threw up in my mouth a little. Wrath had been behaving himself for the most part—other than calling me a few sexist names and a liar—but there was no way I was going to let him stay with me, for four days or four minutes. Besides, my spare room was my game room, and I wasn't keen on letting anyone see that. It was my inner sanctum. But there *was* an extra bed in it, and he had a point about the waste of guild funds. The guild didn't charge dues or anything, but people voluntarily chipped into a pot for events or gifts or prizes. We were given a slice of that for our gathering, and I did want to use it as responsibly as possible. Dammit! I hated it when Wrath had a point. By now I should be used to his critiquing some strategy I'd dreamt up. Despite his other faults, he was far from stupid. I could say from experience that it's hard to loathe someone who has a knack for pointing out the weak points in your plans.

I stopped on the stairs and let out a huge breath, the thought of Wrath staying at my place creeping through my brain. Wrath sleeping in my game room. Wrath sharing my bathroom, eating my food, touching my things for four whole days. Almost everything in me rebelled against the idea, except the phantom voice of my frugal mom protesting against the waste of money and lack of hospitality. Well, that and the appeal of Wrath potentially walking around naked wearing nothing but a towel. Gah, where had *that* image come from? I mean yes, he had a nice body and a beautiful face. Piercing brown eyes, silky looking black hair. Okay, so he was hot. But his appearance was not going to factor into my decision-making process. I was more disciplined than that. What if he was a serial killer? How would I know, considering they looked like everyone else? Okay, maybe that was a stretch. No more true crime documentaries for a while.

"I confirmed the rooms with her ages ago," I explained. "I have to pay cancellation fees on one more room as it is, and now you want me to cancel the entire reservation?"

"Are the cancellation fees cheaper than the rental fees?" he asked, crossing his arms.

"Yes," I replied with dismay, letting out a large sigh. I could see where this was heading, and I didn't like it one bit. Okay, maybe one teeny bit that was attracted to him physically, but that was simple biology, I was sure.

"Then there's our answer," Wrath continued. "Let's save the money and do something fun with it instead. Or give it back to the guild. Expensing this room is ridiculous. Look, I get that you might be a tad shy to talk but I can—"

"Hold up, I am not shy!" I protested. Okay, maybe that was a wee bit of a fib, but for this weekend at least, shy had flown out the window. I was going to be as badass offline as I was on. And where had he gotten the impression that I was shy? I never shut up when I'm online. Maxine Peters might be reluctant to cancel on Mrs. Potter, but Maximus_Damage? She got shit done. And for the next four days, online or off, I was Maximus.

We ascended the staircase, and I held the door open for Wrath, noticing the pleasing scent that wafted from him. Well, there's another stereotype he didn't fit. People tended to think hardcore gamers had abhorrent personal hygiene, but this certainly didn't apply to Wrath. His scent evoked sandalwood, cut grass, and sunshine. It made me want to snuggle him and breathe in that delicious, manly smell over and over. The jerk. Of course he would just happen to smell like catnip for my ovaries. Before

I had a full grasp on my bearings, Wrath had steamed ahead of me to the check-in desk and performed a transformation spell right before my eyes because he was suddenly oozing charm.

"Hello, ma'am," he said, tipping his head at old Mrs. Potter as though he was tipping a hat. "My name is Jonathan Owen, and I was scheduled to be a guest in your beautiful home this weekend. I'm friends with this little lady here." He gestured to me, and I realized he had avoided using my name because he had no clue what it was. "Now, she's run into a spot of trouble involving a gentleman suitor, and I'd feel a lot better about things if I could stay with her while I'm in town. A bit of a nasty guy, if you catch my drift. I hope you'll understand and accept the cancellation fees for the block of rooms. My other friends couldn't make it. There was a death in the family, bless 'em."

A death in the … now who was the lying liar who lied?! Jonathan Owen, that's who, the big hypocrite. The big hypocrite with the big shoulders, currently leaning against the check-in desk, his T-shirt tightening over his back. Jonathan Owen, Jonathan … hmm. I mulled it over and decided I liked the name. At some point I had better tell him my real name too.

"Oh, goodness me!" Mrs. Potter said, actually clutching at her pearls. I hoped we wouldn't need to whip out the smelling salts if she took on a full case of the vapors. "Of course, such a strapping lad as yourself must stay with her if her safety is in jeopardy. Maxine, dear, I didn't know you had men buzzing around you. It's about time, you know, if you want to have children. You're not getting any younger, and your poor momma, well she'd love to have some sweet young thing to spoil. Let's only worry about the cancellation fee for one room. I don't feel right about taking the full amount when there's been a death and you're in a spot of bother. Though I daresay the trouble isn't from this gentleman."

I inwardly bristled at the jab about my age, and the failure on my part to provide grandchildren. My family fell somewhere in the middle of the Green Valley hierarchy, I would say. My mother had come from money, but she married my father, a humble sheriff's deputy, and they built a life here. Until it all fell apart. My mother suffered from agoraphobia ever since my father's death, but people remembered her and occasionally dropped by with a casserole or for a visit. It was one of the things I loved about living in Green Valley. People gave a damn about their neighbors.

Wrath had been in town for all of ten minutes and had already swindled old Mrs. Potter out of a cancellation fee that was rightfully hers, plus he had planted the seed of me being some kind of secret hussy. Mrs. Potter was in the church choir, and every single member would be hearing about my supposed dating life at their next rehearsal. Knowing it would be both fruitless and rude to protest her generosity, I elbowed Wrath out of the way and paid the cancellation fee. I thanked Mrs. Potter profusely, discreetly asking her if she liked bananas and wondering if I could get the guild to pay for one of Jennifer Winston's banana cakes.

* * *

"A DEATH IN THE FAMILY?!" I said to Wrath as we walked back to the Jeep. "How creative of you." I seethed.

Wrath shrugged but had the decency to look sheepish. "I was thinking on my feet," he said defensively. "Look, how was I supposed to know she wouldn't take the full amount of money she was owed? I was just trying to cancel the reservation and leave your good name intact. I wasn't *trying* to fleece her."

I threw my hands up in the air. "And yet you did it so well! From now on, I do the talking, okay?"

"Aye, aye, captain," he replied with a mock salute. I eyed him suspiciously and shook my head. Wrath tended to get mouthy at inappropriate times—we'll call what happened back there Exhibit A. I could barely remember a raid party where he hadn't picked an argument with someone. A raid was when twenty-five or more guildies grouped together to take on an otherwise undefeatable enemy in the game. Like any social event, it had rules, both implicit and explicit. When all the rules were followed, the fight was like a dance and I was the choreographer, providing the instructions and strategy in advance and then listening as they were implemented by a fellow officer over voice chat.

Wrath liked to step on other people's feet rather than do the Viennese waltz.

"Max," he began when we were back on the road.

That was as far as I let him get. I was as angry as an armadillo stuck in a screen door, and I did not want to hear more of his voice at the moment. I held up a hand in his direction, and he quieted instantly and looked contrite. I flicked the stereo on, and we drove, this time neither of us singing. I felt humiliated, but mostly I felt stupid. How had I trusted Wrath to know how to behave in public when he didn't know how to behave in-game? Some people said the game was like a mirror for life. If you were kind in the game, generous, giving of your time and skills and all that, chances are you were that sort of person. Well, here I was, figuratively chained to someone who had shown me over and over in-game that they were a douche of the highest order. Was that a real reflection of who Wrath was as Jonathan? I didn't have enough data to decide, but it was looking that way. I thought of that easy charm and repartee he had demonstrated with Mrs. Potter and wondered why it was never directed at me. But then, that was like an in-game interaction as well, wasn't it?

I detoured on the way to my place to the Piggly Wiggly so we could buy some extra groceries since I'd have one more mouth to feed and my supplies were running low. I grabbed a cart and asked Wrath to get enough snacks or things he liked to last a few days and excused myself to the restroom. Ducking into the bright, clean bathroom, I grabbed my cell out of my carpetbag of a purse—seriously, there might be a lamp and a potted plant in there somewhere—and dialed Lois in New York City. After two rings, during which I chewed on my finger nervously, she picked up.

"Max? What's wrong? Aren't you supposed to be entertaining half a dozen nerds right now?"

"Oh, so just because you quit gaming you're allowed to call us nerds now?" I teased, already feeling on firmer ground at the sound of her voice. Peily—or Lois, I should say—and I met ten years ago in *Guilds of the Ages* when I still played as a girl. She was another girl gamer I could talk to, and we formed a tight bond. I was sad when she didn't join *League of Magecraft* with me, but getting married, working, having a kid, and getting divorced didn't give her a lot of solo recreation time. We stayed in touch though, and she enjoyed hearing about my guild.

"Seriously though, what's up? Can I help? Lose anyone to boredom yet?" Lois's voice pulled me from my spiraling thoughts.

"No, it's worse than that," I moaned. "They didn't come! Three of them bailed at the last minute. And the only one to show up? Wrath! And he did some kind of mind wizardry to me because he logicized his way into staying at my house—in my gaming room!" I was huffing a little bit by this point, my breathing going ragged as I felt anxiety sweep through me. I hadn't let myself feel anything but a simmering anger or bitterness since the airport, my previous excitement for the weekend already stripped away. But now that I was with a safe person, my real feelings were bubbling up.

I wasn't pissed, I was scared. At least I wasn't scared of having a stranger come to stay—I didn't really consider Wrath a stranger. We talked every day, and hordes of people knew he was coming to see me, so that stray serial killer thought earlier really had no merit. I was scared because I didn't know how to behave around him, and a little scared that he might be offended that I hadn't told him I was a girl before now. I hated unintentionally offending or hurting people.

"How'd he sweet talk his way in there?" Lois replied, both curiosity and mirth in her voice. She loved to hear about anything that could be deemed a misadventure.

"He Jedi mind tricked me, Lois! That's the only explanation. And he lied to old Mrs. Potter. If Mom ever finds out about *that*, I'll never hear the end of it." I let out a long, deep breath, trying to calm down. "I just wanted to do something fun with some of my friends from the guild. Show them around, have some laughs. I knew Wrath was coming but I didn't know there would be no buffer between us whatsoever."

Boy, how I had counted on there being a buffer. Carebear in particular was someone I had been looking forward to meeting, and she would have thwarted any tension in the group with her cheery outlook and mothering ways.

"What you have to do is let go of the idea of what kind of weekend you were going to have, accept what's happened, and make the best of it. That's the Max I know. You hate him? So what? He might not hate you, and who knows, he could be decent company if you give him a chance."

I snickered. "Oh, trust me, he hates me. Wrath has always hated me, you know that." And here it comes, like clockwork. Lois and her wild theory.

She had this crazy idea that Wrath actually liked me, and his annoying the hell out of me at every available opportunity was his misguided way of trying to get my attention. I had dismissed this theory because Wrath thought I was a guy, and I had seen him join in the guy talk enough in the guild chat to know that he was definitely interested in women.

Now, I was enlightened enough to know that it was possible for someone to be attracted to people of any gender or biological sex, so his history with women didn't preclude him from being interested in a guy. Plus, he had shut down homophobic talk a few times. Had he been personally offended? I recalled, after one such an incident, the perpetrator of such dastardly language called Wrath gay and Wrath had replied that he wasn't into dudes but he also wasn't a jerk, which was why he wanted the idiot to shut up. That was cool of him, and I was glad that douche had been given a public dressing down before I had the pleasure of booting him from the guild.

But if he wasn't into dudes, that pretty much shut down Lois's theory about a secret crush, didn't it? I didn't let myself contemplate for too long what he thought, now that he knew I was a woman.

"You know I don't agree with that, Max. I think he likes you—like, a lot—and doesn't know how to show his feelings. Some of the stunts he's pulled sound an awful lot like peacocking."

I visualized an elegant bird blasting its tail feathers upward, kind of like that scene in *Jurassic Park* where the dilophosaurus reveals itself to be venomous. That was a much more fitting image.

"Okay, we are not going down that road again," I said, glancing at my Fitbit to see the time. "We can discuss your little theory once the weekend is over, hmm?"

"Sure thing. Are you going to be okay, Max?" she asked, concern filling her voice. "You know I would fly down there in an instant if I didn't have Elsa to look out for. But as she is my spawn, I gotta put her first."

"Yeah, yeah, love you too," I replied, smiling. We hung up, and I filled my lungs with some deep, calming breaths, then headed back out to find Wrath with a half full cart of mostly veggies and practical meal choices. I was surprised, expecting a pile of junk. I nodded in approval at his choices, and we checked out.

The drive home was a bit livelier, with me turning on the sound system again and Wrath immediately jumping in on vocals. Not to be outdone, I proved I knew as many Beatles lyrics as he did.

We finally pulled up to my modest, two-bedroom cottage near the outskirts of town. It was not in the greatest shape, but I did my best to make it feel homey. Fall had been in the air for a while, so my flower gardens were no longer in bloom. On the front step, I had two bright pumpkins brought to me by one of my colleagues and member of my monthly book club, Naomi Winters. Folks said she was a witch—like the kind that flew around on a broom—and she had suffered for that idiocy. The trees around the house had turned wondrous shades of orange and yellow, and while the yard might need raking in some people's opinions (and I'm not saying my nosy neighbor Mrs. Howser's name, but I'm thinking it), all in all, things were looking suitable for company.

Wrath jumped out of Stiles and I hadn't even brought the Jeep to a full stop-and-lurch. Before I could protest, he'd grabbed his own bag and lugged it toward the house. He did at least fall in step behind me and had the courtesy to say, "Nice place."

I unlocked the front door, and we were instantly greeted by my twin black cats, She-Ra and Catra. I had read online that black cats were less likely to be adopted and also more likely to encounter violence in their lives due to superstition. My grandma had been the most superstitious woman in the South—which was really saying something —but thankfully my own head was free of such thinking. When I found the pair at the local cat rescue, it was love at first sight. I made sure to keep them inside and away from any harm, especially around Halloween.

Catra and She-Ra rubbed against our ankles, and we fought against their affection as we struggled to take off our shoes and hang up our jackets without tripping. And damn, there were those tattoo sleeves I'd spotted at the airport and those perfect arms and shoulders. Wrath reached down to give scritches to both cats around their ears, making baby-talk noises at them while doing so, which made him more attractive. Stupid hot Wrath and his stupid hot body and face and voice and hair.

I unleashed a virtual bucket of cold water on my head when I reminded myself that this was Wrath, the guy who once followed me around in-game for a half hour shouting, "This is my boomstick!" when he was lucky enough to win a cool weapon. Wrath drove me up the wall. And he wasn't nice either. He played on the edge of cheating sometimes. He and his minions griefed me in *Guilds of the Ages*, he'd even opposed me going up for guild officer in *Magecraft*. The Dark Side would be so lucky to have him!

"And aren't you just the cutest kitty cat there ever was. Yes you are, yes you are!" I concealed both my surprise and a smile. He was currently rubbing She-Ra's belly, and the cat was purring loudly while Wrath talked to her. I stood there for a few minutes, mouth agape, while Catra got similar treatment. When Wrath was done, he smiled at me, pushed his ponytail off his shoulder, and shrugged. "I like cats, what can I say."

Not to be distracted, I walked into the main room of my open-concept cottage and swept an arm around. "This is it. Home sweet home," I said. The main room was my personal library, with built-in bookcases on practically every available wall space. Wrath whistled as he looked around the room, taking in the multitude of volumes. From there he could also see the smallish kitchen and the cozy configuration of sofa and chairs in front of the fireplace made of river stones. I waited a bit nervously for his judgment, which I didn't fully understand. Why did I care what Wrath, of all people, thought of my home?

"So you've got cats, ten thousand books, and are a huge geek. What are you, a librarian?" he asked, snickering.

I instantly bristled. "See, this is a prime example of why I hate you. You say *librarian* like it's the lamest thing ever, when in fact, I am very proud to be a librarian in this community, Wrath. More than ever, libraries are essential in rural areas." I knew I sounded like a PowerPoint, but I didn't care. How dare he mock my profession and stereotype me.

Color literally drained from Wrath's face. I saw him turn pale before my eyes, and I reached for him instinctively in case he had suffered a sudden drop in blood sugar or some such. But no, he yanked himself away from me.

"You … you …" he started, clearly at a loss. "You hate me?"

For some reason, his voice was one of utter disbelief, like this was new information. Interesting. And then, to my immense surprise, I saw the Hindenburg explode in his eyes.

"You flippin' *hate* me? We've known each other for … I've been gaming with you since I was seventeen! Almost ten years, Max. I know I can be an asshole, but you've always given as good as you got."

"I really haven't," I said softly, defending myself against such slander. I had never lowered myself to Wrath's level, I was certain of it. He looked stricken, and I honestly didn't know what else to say.

I bit the index finger of my left hand and closed my eyes for a moment. It was a teeny coping mechanism that I relied on too much, but hey, it got me through a lot. Confidence wavering, I thought back to when I'd first met Wrath online. He said he'd only been seventeen. Seventeen! I'd been twenty-two. He'd probably been a high school kid, and I, having graduated early at sixteen, had just earned my master's degree. We were only five years apart, but we'd been in completely different places in life.

I'd be lying if I said I hadn't let those first few years color our entire relationship. But now, all of the talk he'd smacked back then seemed so long ago. So irrelevant. He'd been *seventeen*. And I still hated him. I wondered what in tarnation that said about me, other than having inherited the Peters' ability to hold a grudge.

But wait a minute!

"Hold up. *You* don't hate *me*?" I asked Wrath, my voice full of suspicion. The truth would out, surely, and maybe we could put this farce to bed.

And again, he surprised the pants off me. "I would rather not discuss how I feel about you right now," Wrath replied cryptically, bitterness detectable in his voice.

I wracked my brain as I made a slow approach to the sitting area and sat gingerly on the sofa. He hadn't known I hated him. He thought we were what—acquaintances? Or, horror of horrors, friends?

I turned my body toward Wrath, but before I could open my mouth, he said, "So, what exactly will we be occupying ourselves with this weekend, oh mighty Maximus?"

He crossed his arms and looked at me with a smirk. To be honest, it looked like a half-hearted attempt at a smirk, but there it was. I didn't get how he could go from stricken to bitter to smirking in twenty seconds flat. The Wrath I knew was a proud guy, and now that I thought about it, that smirk was probably a front to hide his true feelings of … what? Hurt? Did I have the capacity to hurt Wrath? It would appear I did, and I didn't know how I felt about that.

"Well, our first event was supposed to be a friendship-speed-dating thing. We were all going to swap tables at a restaurant and ask each other questions as quickly as possible to get to know each other better offline. Since it's only you and me, we can definitely skip it."

"Skip it? No way. We can do it right here over some stiff drinks. What kind of booze do you have?"

My thoughts strayed to the lone box of white wine in my fridge. Did I want to get wasted with Wrath on boxed wine? Did I even want to admit to owning boxed wine? I decided I did not. Worse than that, I had a jug of moonshine in the pantry gifted to me by another book club member, Cletus Winston. Cletus's family went way back here in Green Valley, and there was always one or three of them around somewhere. Cletus wasn't a hardened criminal moonshiner or anything, but he liked moonshine eggnog and had brought the shine to me last year as a holiday gift so I could mix up some of my own.

Under no circumstance would I tell Wrath any of that. I already felt a bit like a hill-billy next to someone from Jacksonville. Suddenly, inspiration struck. "We can go out for a drink, and get some dinner too. There's a bar not too far from here."

"Now Maximus, you're not going to drag me to some two-bit honky-tonk out here in the sticks, are you?" The thought had merit because that's almost exactly what I was about to do, though locals might argue that Genie's Country Western Bar was at least a three-bit kind of place. It could get rowdy, but it was only Thursday, so I was sure we'd get a booth.

"Just you wait and see," I replied, keeping the charade going that everything was okay between us when I had the distinct feeling that something was rotten in the state of Denmark. Why wouldn't he own up to hating me, too? I essentially had verbally bitch-slapped him, and he was all creepy smiles. "If you want to freshen up first, I'll show you your room, and you can get settled and wash the travel off, if you like."

He got up and flashed me a tight smile. "That sounds delightful."

CHAPTER FOUR
JONATHAN

"Hey Maximus, do you wanna quest with me? I bet we could take down a whole pile of dragonkin and get the treasure under the lava waterfall. I see you walking away! Is that a no?"

— Wrath

She hated me. Maximus_Damage, the best player I have ever seen, the funny, smart as a whip, genius strategist, take-no-prisoners Max, loathed me. All of these years I thought we were having fun, and she probably thought I was that annoying kid who wouldn't leave her alone. Who pranked her. Who made her time in the game—which, in her words, was supposed to be fun—miserable. Lovely. I knew now that any chance I had been holding on to that Max returned my feelings was strictly in the realm of fantasy or delusion.

Almost as bad was the fact that Deathdrop had been right. Freakin' Norman. I'd never hear the end of it from him. The last time he'd been right about something, I heard about it for three months.

I thought of the other pill in my pocket but refused to give in. I could wait until tonight to take my regular cocktail of meds. Taking another one now would also mean I'd have to come up with some reason why I couldn't drink at the bar. Why had I suggested it to begin with? I knew drinking was reckless for me, considering all the prescriptions I took, and yet at that moment, in the face of Max's hatred, I wanted to say screw it all and be irresponsible.

I followed a nervous Max down the short hallway past three doors before stopping in front of one with a small Hello Kitty poster on it. She let out a long sigh and stood there with her hand on the knob so long that I thought she was never going to open the door. Then she dropped her hand and turned to look at me.

"There are a few things you've got to understand," she began, looking almost green. "This is my game room. It's a sacred space to me. It's where I can be myself in this town. Ever since my, um, accident I've been someone else in public. Mousy, like you called me at the airport. I tried dressing differently, carrying myself differently, and yet I couldn't shake that particular attribute. Maxine Peters, mousy basement librarian."

"Max—" I started, wanting to stop her from putting herself down, and curious about what accident she was referring to.

"No, let me finish. I am who I am. Try not to judge me too hard and keep the snarky comments to yourself after you see inside. And if you aren't comfortable staying in there, I'm sure Mrs. Potter would love to have you back at her place."

"Uncomfortable? Why would I be …" A wayward thought struck me. "Max, is that room painted red?"

A burst of laughter bubbled out of her, exactly the reaction I was hoping for. Something had to break this awkward tension between us. "No, you fool. Let's just go in. You'll see what I mean."

She opened the door and stepped back, ushering me inside. I held back my initial laughter and gazed around in amazement. I'd been expecting sex swings from her warning, but instead found myself in geek heaven—or geek hell, depending on your point of view.

"It looks like a comic book store, an anime convention, and an art gallery threw up in here. But in a good way," I said. Maximus's inner sanctum was rockin,' and my heart was hammering in my chest as I moved deeper into her private world. Of course the first thing I noticed was the computer. It looked like a custom build, and with three huge monitors, it was kind of hard to miss. I was itching to sit in the enormous desk chair, log on to *Magecraft,* and tell everyone that I was in Maximus_Damage's gaming room.

Shelves completely lined one wall, and they were packed full of action figures and statues, miniatures and plushies; everything from *Steven Universe* to *A Song of Ice and Fire* to *Batwoman* was represented. Along the bottom shelves were cardboard comic book boxes, labels placed with obvious care on each box. Against another wall were tubs of what I presumed were Legos, considering the size of the sprawling Lego city built on a long bench. In a corner was a round chair, with gauzy stuff hanging down from the ceiling, and little white lights brightening the cozy reading space. Towering potted trees were in the other corners of the room. And the walls! Every inch was covered in art of some kind. Pencil drawings, pop art, postcards, and types of modern art that never made much sense to me, like those flowering vaginas. At least I could appreciate the intent, being a bit of an art enthusiast myself. Against the wall nearest me was a stack of board games: Carcassonne, Munchkin, Ticket to Ride, and many more.

"Wait, if no one really knows you're a huge geek, why do you have all these board games?" I asked, pointing to the stack. "Aren't those implicitly a team event?"

She turned a shade of crimson that almost matched her bandana, and replied softly, "I keep meaning to try to organize a club, like once a month. It's hard opening up to people sometimes."

It struck me as incongruous that Maximus was always the first of us to charge into battle or jump into a melee without fear, but Maxine couldn't seem to summon up the courage to invite people over to play Apples to Apples.

The bed was in the middle of the room against the remaining wall and surrounded by shelving holding paperbacks and game manuals. The headboard was strung with little purple lights and a bright white quilt on the mattress. I walked over and sat down, testing the bed's firmness. It was comfy, but I knew I'd be far more comfortable wrapped around Max in her room.

The thought struck me out of nowhere, and it took deep root. I shouldn't care one whit about Max. She'd lied to me, whatever her intentions. Not to mention she hated me. In fact, I should be on the next plane out of Knoxville back to Florida. Yet I still wanted her. And I was tired of not getting what I wanted. I'd been given the shaft by life too many times. I was carting around ten years of longing. Ten years of crappy relationships because the person I was with could never measure up to an ideal. So

Max was a liar of sorts who thought I was an asshole. I gotta say, I lived for a challenge.

"Bathroom is across the hall. Towels are in the cabinet," she said, still looking uncomfortable.

"And is the bathroom some kind of den of mystery, also?"

She had a gleam in her eyes, and for a minute I knew she was considering screwing with me, like telling me the hot and cold taps were reversed on the shower or something.

After a beat of silence, she said, "Nope, standard issue. Just don't let the cats in with you. They have this thing about playing in the water. She-Ra will jump right in the shower with you."

Something she'd said earlier, before I was distracted by her gaming room, suddenly stuck out to me. "What kind of accident did you have? I don't remember you telling the guild about anything like that."

Color drained from Max's face, and she lowered her eyes. "It was ten years ago. And it was the kind of accident where a guy wails on you with a tire iron while his buddy tries to pull him away, if you must know." She pointed to a barely visible scar along her jawline.

I was sorry I'd asked, not only because I'd possibly triggered her, but because I had never wanted to commit murder before. It wasn't a good feeling, and I hoped I never ran into the men who had committed such an awful crime against her.

"Don't pity me," she said, her voice firm. "Don't you dare."

She shot me a glare, and I recognized the pain of a wounded warrior in her eyes. I'd seen it in Norman's often enough after his discharge from the military.

"I don't think I could ever pity you, Max. But there's a difference between pity and wanting to protect you." And God, did I ever want to protect her. I hadn't felt this protective of anyone, other than the women in my family.

The longer I spent with Max, the more I realized how full of contrasts she truly was. She was prickly edges and soft curves all at once, hard but not without heart. The Maximus I knew online was definitely in there, but the surprise of this complex woman was both unnerving and delightful.

"I told you I hated you, Wrath. Why on Earth would you want to protect me?" she asked, hands on her round hips.

I raised my eyebrows. "Because I'm a knight. It's in our code to protect others," I replied, like it was obvious.

"In a game, Wrath! And you haven't exactly been a shining example of holding up the knight's code. Or is it also part of the code to give hell at every turn to certain players who have done you no wrong?" That stung, but as there was a kernel of truth in it, I didn't reply. Instead, I thanked her for the room and dug through my duffel, grabbing a new shirt and some toiletries once she left me with my thoughts.

* * *

MAX TURNED MORE than one head as we wound our way through the crowd at Genie's, the bar that wouldn't look out of place in my neck of the woods. Yup, I said woods. Max had assumed I was from Jacksonville because of the plane route, but I actually hailed from a town that felt even more remote than Green Valley. I was from the kind of place that routinely made Florida Man headlines, usually with incidents involving both alcohol and some kind of creature from the surrounding swampland.

She'd insisted upon changing, and when she emerged from her room in a vintage red dress that fell to the knee, her lips stained a dark red to match, and her hair done up in those rolls women wore during World War II, my pants suddenly felt a little tight. All of her curves were on display, and I itched to get my hands on them, to feel what this woman and I could be like together. Intuition told me that if we could get past our history, we could be dynamite. Patience. I had to have patience and somehow convince her I wasn't a total dick. I had a feeling this was going to be a difficult task to accomplish in the few days I had left.

Tick tock.

When we'd entered the bar, I instinctively placed my hand on her lower back, sending out death glares to any man that looked her way. I wasn't a possessive jerk, but I also knew she was a freakin' knockout and wouldn't be lacking for attention for long. She guided us to a booth, and for a second I considered sitting next to her. But then remembrance hit me like a gut punch. This wasn't simply a gorgeous woman I was out on the town with, this was Maximus_Damage, who despised me.

I almost hooted when I realized how pissed she must be that I'd talked my way into being her houseguest. Smiling at the thought, because it still tickled me to get her goat, I sat across from her and fiddled with the menu on the table while waiting for our waitress. We sat in a semi-awkward silence, conversation stalled since we'd left the house, listening to the music playing and watching the few folks who were dancing.

"What can I get y'all to drink?" our waitress asked. Well, here it was, the moment of truth. Or rather, untruth. No way was I going to have an intense conversation with Max about my private life while people were line dancing mere feet away. If Max asked me why I wasn't drinking, it was because my stomach was upset. Why had I suggested alcohol in the first place? I had been nervous and now—oh, the waitress was still waiting for my order.

"I'll have a coke, a water, and we're fixing to get a bite to eat when you're ready for our order," I jumped in, getting it over with as fast as possible.

"And for you, ma'am?" she asked, obviously a seasoned professional as she didn't bother writing anything down.

"Patty, it's me, Maxine Peters," Max replied, giggling a little. An actual giggle! Who knew the kick-ass warrior whose strategy had helped lead our guild to the first North American defeat of the demon Beelzebub *giggled.*

Patty clapped a hand over her mouth, then giggled a little too. "I'm so sorry, Maxine! I don't think I've ever seen you here before. You look so, so—"

"Different?" Max asked, beaming. Frickin' beaming. I knew there was a bright and brilliant person behind the vinegary wall she had up for me.

"Hot!" Patty replied with a wide grin. "Now what can I get for you, hon?"

Max blushed. "I'll take some sweet tea and some water as well, and we'd like a couple of burgers. Thanks, Patty."

"Sure thing!" She walked off with almost a tiny jig in her step, like it chirked her up to see Maxine out on the town.

I'd be lying if I said it didn't turn me on to see her take charge and order for me. Thank God I wasn't a vegetarian because I think I'd eat whatever she asked for, on principle. It just so happened that she'd ordered my favorite food. I was about to take a leap and ask Max if she wanted to dance while we waited for our order when she got up and excused herself for the restroom. I glanced around at the patrons of Genie's, wondering how all of these people had been blind to the amazeballs person in their midst, when she wasn't dressed up like a siren.

It was obvious that despite being well liked, Max didn't have many offline friends. That stack of brand spankin' new board games spoke to that. To be fair, it wasn't like I did either. It was hard to game as often as we did, work, and maintain a social life offline. Not that I minded. My guildies were my friends, and I was lucky to have them. At least I had always thought so. But what about Max? I had counted her among those friends. Who else might hate me? God, I wish I could have a drink.

Max hadn't been out of her seat for thirty seconds when a pair of women butted up against the table, the tall redhead acting like she was in heat by the way she ran her hand down my tattoo sleeve on my left arm. I loathed the way people thought having tats meant they could touch you, like it was open season. It was the same with my long hair. I'd had it touched by a fair number of women before, while at the grocery store, while out with Norman, whenever. That's why I'd taken to tying it back. I also braided it, but I drew the line at a man-bun. No way was I cutting it, but I also wanted to limit the amount of strangers who put their hands in it.

"What's a fine man like you doing in here with Maxine Peters?" the redhead purred. She pouted as I firmly removed her hand.

"Why wouldn't I be with her?" I asked back, my hackles rising. I didn't like the way she said Max's name. Like she was implying that Max shouldn't be out having fun. Or rather that there was something about our respective appearances or ages or some other intangible that meant Max shouldn't be out with *me*.

"It's only that we don't see Miss Maxine around here too often. And never out of her frumpy office garb," the brunette jumped in, evidently sensing a disturbance in the Force.

"Yeah, that woman never met a corduroy skirt she could ignore." The redhead snorted. "Or a doughnut. The only place I've ever seen her besides the Piggly Wiggly is at Daisy's—alone—stuffing doughnuts down her trap. It's no wonder she's so ... jiggly. Hey, jiggly rhymes with Piggly." She burst into laughter and moved to sit down on the side of the booth Max had vacated.

"Don't even think about it," I said, leveling a stare at the redhead. "*Miss Maxine* might be a joke to you, but she means a hell of a lot to me. You should be ashamed, talking to a perfect stranger about a fine woman you would be lucky to be friends with. Scram, before you make me mad. If you were a guy, I'd have you laid out on the floor already."

"Let's go, Marnie," the sane and sober friend said as she practically yanked the redhead away from the table.

Smiling in deep satisfaction, I watched them scurry off just in time for Max to reemerge from the ladies' room. She got a couple of eager looks from men while crossing the room, and I irrationally wanted to pummel everyone who thought they had the right to undress my woman with their eyes. My woman.

Mine.

The thought hit me out of nowhere, but that really was how I saw Max. Even before arriving, I had caveman-like proprietary aspirations toward Maximus. I had come to Green Valley with every intention of declaring my love to Maximus_Damage, a dude. Now I was faced with the reality of wooing a woman who detested me. But as I looked at her, her head down a bit as those curves shimmied through the crowd, all of my doubts melted away. I would win her over, even if that meant sharing my truth, in all its ugliness.

* * *

AFTER DOWNING our drinks and most of our meal in a fairly awkward silence, I decided to hit the gas and move along Max's original plan for the evening. Speed dating sounded perfect right about now.

"So we're supposed to be finding out real stuff about each other, right?" I asked, holding onto a fry and dipping it into ketchup.

"That was the plan," she replied, blotting at her mouth with her napkin.

"Okay. So building on the theme of this fantabulous visit where I annoy the shit out of you, you were pretty pissed earlier when I called you a librarian. I'm sorry about that. I try to be funny sometimes and I miss the mark." She snorted. I ignored the sound of derision and forged ahead with Plan Seduction. "Could you tell me what it is you like about being a librarian?" I munched down the fry and waited for her.

"Do you … care?" she asked slowly, tentatively, as though testing the ground for verbal land mines.

"I wouldn't have asked if I didn't," I replied, hating that I was going to have to prove at every step of the way that I was not Max's enemy. But hell, if pulling teeth was the only way to earn a spot in Max's circle of trust, I would do it. Because I already knew she was worth it.

"Okay," she said, placing her napkin back on the table. "Well, the library was always a place of refuge for me here in Green Valley. Things weren't always rosy at home. But at the library I learned that a book is more than an object you place on a shelf. A book is *magic*. It's freaking magic, and not enough people get that. See, a book can transport someone to another place, another time. It can make them see the world through the eyes of someone else. Through a book you can commune with the dead, learn about people living completely different lives than you. Then you can join in communities of other people who have been touched by the same book and lived that special experience. That's *magic*."

I watched the excitement on her face and the shine in her eyes, and I wanted to look at it for as long as I possibly could.

"So anyway, I knew I wanted to work with books. And as a cataloger, that's what I get to do. I know the library collections of every branch in this part of the state backward and forward because I create and maintain those records. And those books, all of them, are in their own way special to me."

I considered that for a moment, then nodded, agreeing with her assessment. But something was missing. "Did you always want to do that part of it? The records, I mean. What about the people who interact with the books?"

Her cheeks reddened. She had to stop doing that. It drove me a little crazy to see the impact of my words on her. Not that I wanted to embarrass her, but I wanted her to feel something with me other than revulsion.

"I did have aspirations to work with children, but you know, sometimes we're good at something we don't expect, or life gets in the way of the dreams we chase. Me winding up in the basement cataloging was kind of a combination of those things." She bit her bottom lip and dipped her head before looking back up with a bit of mirth in her eyes. "I get to ask the next question."

"Okay, shoot." I braced myself, expecting anything and everything. This was the same person who was beyond ruthless when processing applications to our guild, interviewing people for over an hour, drilling them on every aspect of the game and their play style. She wanted to interrogate me? Bring it on.

"Why are you such an asshole?" she blurted, and then quickly raised her hand. "Okay, wait, hold up. Let me clarify. Why are you such an asshole to *me* in the game? I don't remember ever doing anything to you to deserve it, and yet you've been bloody impossible at times. Do you know how freaked I was that you'd be coming this week? Because in my mind, you're the closest thing to an archnemesis I've ever had, other than the Iron Wraiths. And yet, here you are, in my hometown, acting all normal for the most part, and I can't figure it out. You. I can't figure *you* out."

"Who or what are the Iron Wraiths? I've never heard of that guild," was my first takeaway from that speech. If there were people out there gunning for Max, I wanted to know who and where they were.

She looked annoyed and took a huge swig of her water. "They're a local biker gang," she said, waving away my question with her hand. "Less stalling, more talking." She banged the empty cup down on the table, reminding me a little of a Viking warrior who likes their drink and wants another.

"Would you even believe the truth, Maximus?" I asked, cocking my head to one side, a frown on my face. God, please let her believe the truth.

"If you tell me something is true, I will do my best to believe it, yes. Unless this is like that time I had dry scalp and you convinced me I had head lice." Well, crap. Of course she'd remember that. I'd been nineteen at the time, and yes, I had been a hormonal and petty shit for most of my teen years. But I had never meant any real harm to anyone.

I sucked in a big breath for courage. "It's not like that at all. The truth is, I've never tried to be an asshole, not once. It was never deliberate, any of the stuff I've done unintentionally—or intentionally—to wrong you. Most of the time I was trying to get your attention because I admire you and your skills as a player and a leader, and as a human being in general. You're great. I was trying to ..." I trailed off when I saw Max lift a hand to cover her mouth, trying to conceal her laughter.

"I'm sorry, but are you serious? You expect me to buy that cow patty you're calling a pie?" Her eyes danced and her shoulders moved as she tried to contain her laughing fit.

I deflated. "Okay, screw this. Let's dance." I rose from the booth and extended a hand to her, grinning at the surprise on her face, and raised an eyebrow in challenge. She slowly raised her hand and placed it in mine, as if she were waiting for me to pull my hand back and say, "psych!"

I clasped her hand and helped her rise from the booth just as a slow song came up. I thanked the stars for aligning and led her to the dance floor. I latched my arms around Max's waist, feeling the softness of her body and relishing in the tingle that ran through me from stem to stern. We started to gently sway, and as she lifted her hands to my shoulders, another jolt shot through me. Her touch was tentative at first but became firmer as the music went on.

I leaned down a bit so we could keep talking. "Okay, my turn. Why'd you order for us? How did you know I'd eat a burger?" I was genuinely curious how she knew my favorite meal.

She looked up and we locked eyes. I had to keep reminding myself that this wasn't an epic romantic moment. She still believed I had given her hell for years because we hated each other.

She smirked and replied, "Because you said, like three years ago, that they were your favorite food, and you could eat one every day of your life until you die. Probably from a heart attack. Favorite movie?"

"Wait, you remember some crap I said three years ago about burgers?" I asked incredulously.

"I happen to have a very good memory, which is useful as a cataloger," she explained, moving with me as we turned slowly on the dance floor, her hands now clasped behind my neck. My heart was thudding so loud, I swear she could hear it, and I probably was making anime heart eyes at her. She tapped me gently. "Now, favorite movie."

"Pfft, like there's any doubt. The original, unaltered *Star Wars* trilogy. *Empire* overall."

She sighed. "How typical. I see your *Star Wars* and raise you the special editions of *Lord of the Rings,*" she replied, challenging me.

"Nice try, Frodo, but I don't think so. Peter Jackson did right by those books, and the series is epic. But nothing tops freakin' *Star Wars*."

"What about the collective body of works of Tarantino?" she asked.

"Nope," I said, shaking my head adamantly. "No amount of snappy dialogue is going to make up for 'No. I am your father.'"

She laughed. "Yeah, I guess you got me there. My favorite is *Return of the Jedi*, though. I know most everyone says *Empire* is the better film, but *Jedi* is so much happier. Ewoks! Dance parties! No incest! What's not to love?"

"Fine, you can love *Jedi* more than *Empire* and I won't make fun of you. Whose turn is it?" I asked, having lost track.

"I don't know. I'll go. Do you like to read?"

Now it was my turn to laugh. "After your 'books are magic' spiel, how could I say no?"

She stuck her tongue out at me playfully, and my heart lurched. "Seriously, though?"

"Well yeah, I read. I love Stephen King. I think I have all of his books now, but I'd have to check my list. I'm always looking at used bookshops for the ones I'm missing."

"I have almost all of them too!" she exclaimed, obviously excited to be talking books again. "The only book of his I couldn't finish was *It*. Clowns creep me out. My favorite is *Misery*." I smiled down at her, beaming that we were finding common ground. At least until she screamed and jerked backward out of my arms.

CHAPTER FIVE

MAXINE

"Wrath, so the gods help me, if you're in my way, I will take you out. Move!"

— *Maximus_Damage*

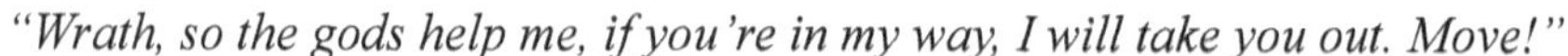

I screeched as cold beer hit me, pouring down the front of my dress and freezing my breasts. I pulled my arms free of Wrath to wrap them around my chest amidst the scuffle of footsteps around me. The impressively tall beer-spiller was drunkenly trying to apologize as his date tried to wipe me down with napkins. Patty made her way over quick as lightning and offered to let me into the staff bathroom to clean up, and I shook my head, feeling overwhelmed. I was the center of attention and I hated it—offline, anyway.

I caught Wrath's eyes with mine and silently pleaded with him to get me out of there. Reading my signal correctly, he grabbed our jackets and threw some cash on the table. He then laid my jacket around my shoulders. My eyes bulged at his next move, which was to carefully put one arm around my waist, extending his other arm to fend off the crowd, and lead me out through the doors. When the cold fall air hit me, my nipples practically cried out in pain, and he hurried us over to my Jeep. Wrath fished the keys out of my pocket and opened the passenger door, guiding me up into the seat. He then ran around to the driver side and turned on the engine, revving the heat up.

"My god, why was everyone gawking and getting in the way?" he asked, almost angrily for some reason.

My teeth chattered. "This is the S-South, Wrath. I thought you lived down here too. They were trying to help."

"But surely those *peasants* could see that a lady needed room to exit the premises!" he said, sounding like the knight he purported to be in-game. It made me snort-laugh, both his concern and his anger, but I quickly smothered it because all of his concern was centered around getting me to warmth and comfort as quickly as possible.

We drove for a few moments in silence, me shivering and holding my arms as tightly around my sodden bosom as I could. Wrath had surprised me a bit tonight, both with his quick action on my behalf and his earlier speech. I hadn't been able to contain my laughter because, as I'd asked him, was he serious? According to him, he had never been an asshole on purpose. He'd never tried to deliberately wrong me. And he admired me as a "human being in general." If he had said this stuff to me in-game yesterday, I would have told him to screw off and go back to griefing low-level players. But what if Wrath really thought I was awesome and never tried to intentionally hurt me? I wondered if that negated the fact that the hurt had actually happened, intentional or not.

I thought back to the way his hands had felt around my waist before the flying beer incident, and the way he had curved his perfect mouth into a smile, just for me. I searched for hidden motives. What could Wrath gain by being nice to me? I could up his rank in the guild, I guess, giving him access to more supplies and privileges with our guild bank. It could be a plan to disarm me into humiliating myself. Acting like he wanted to be friends so that I would reveal information I would never normally let out, and then, as he left for his plane, turning around and yelling, "Punked!"

I turned on the radio and stopped looking for conspiracy theories. I had to take Wrath with at least a little grain of salt based on everything I knew about him, but I also had to give him the chance to grow and evolve, like I was trying to do in my own life. I didn't want to be Mousy Maxine anymore. I liked the way peoples' eyes had followed me at Genie's before the situation became embarrassing and out of my control. Maybe Wrath wanted to be someone different too, even if only for this weekend. He certainly seemed to be trying to not be the same jerk I knew. I suppose I had to ask myself: Was Wrath, of all people, redeemable?

I was so lost in thought that we almost missed our turn. "Turn here," I said, pointing to the right.

"It's a one-horse town, Max. I'm not about to get us lost." He chuckled.

"No, but if you'd gone the other way by mistake, we'd be navigating some switchbacks in the dark, and if you're from Jacksonville, you probably aren't used to driving in the mountains. Even the hairpin turns that aren't so bad require some skill at night."

"Fair point. But I'm not from Jacksonville. I'm from more of a blink-and-you'll-miss-it type of town, dirt roads and all."

"Really?" I asked, intrigued. "We didn't get very far in our offline life questions. Tell me about where you're from. You're seeing my hometown, it only seems fair." I was surprised at my own interest in Wrath's private life, but there it was.

Wrath shifted in his seat, like he was uncomfortable. "There's not much to tell," he began, his voice tight. "It's swampland, pretty much. Some little spit of land in the middle of nowhere. I grew up in a trailer with two sisters and a mean drunk of a Daddy who liked to use me and Mom as punching bags. He died of heart failure when I was sixteen. Now my mother spends half her time praying and the other half lost in a pill bottle. So I started gaming, to escape it all. We were able to buy me a computer with some of his life insurance money, and I joined *Guilds of the Ages* at seventeen. Where I met you." He paused for a moment. "Anything else I should be sharing about offline life?"

"That's enough for now," I answered, a bit shaken by his revelations. I never knew Wrath to be vulnerable, and tonight he'd shown me vulnerability, consideration, and chivalry. In the past Wrath had called me—Maximus, that is—a dickbag, stolen my kills, and told the rest of the guild when I had the flu that I'd contracted gonorrhea from a prostitute.

I felt like I had Wrath whiplash. Online, he'd been awful, but face-to-face … not bad. It made me want to reevaluate my opinion of him overall. Maybe he wasn't as awful as I thought? Perhaps I was hanging onto baggage from when he was a teenager, baggage I could forgive because teenagers and common sense didn't go hand in hand often enough.

When we got home, Wrath told me to take the first crack at the bathroom, which was another kindness considering he was the guest here. I showered the beer off me and sponged at my dress, hoping it wasn't ruined. I changed into my favorite flannel penguin-printed pj's and stuck my hair up in a messy bun. I was ready for the dash from the bathroom to my room, during which I hoped to evade Wrath's gaze.

I unlocked the bathroom door and bolted across the hall, slamming the door shut behind me. Score! Wrath hadn't seen me in my pajamas. Unfortunately (or fortunately for me), standing right at the foot of the bed, naked except for a pair of black boxer briefs, stood Wrath. And holy hell, his hair was down, flowing over his shoulders and looking as silky as ever. My jaw practically unhinged when I realized I had made a dash for the gaming room, not my bedroom. I mean, it made sense when you considered all the time I spent in the gaming room, and how many times I fell asleep in there. But this—this was an epic screwup.

We stared at each other, my mouth opening and closing, all capacity for verbal communication having fled. I was now as mute as the guild rumors purported me to be.

"Stopping in to give me tomorrow's itinerary, I presume?" he asked dryly, eyeing me up and down. "Nice set of penguins you've got there."

That got the vocal cords moving. "How can you make something so innocent sound so … so … ugh!" I made a noise of frustration that sounded like a velociraptor. "And because you mentioned it, why yes, tomorrow's itinerary is why I'm here. Without knocking because that's how I roll in my house." I could hear my mom gasp from across town. "Set an alarm and be up by seven thirty. Dress code is casual outdoors, something that you can move comfortably in but don't mind getting a bit dirty. As described in the welcome email, I might add, so I hope you've brought clothing like that." I crossed my arms over my … *penguins* and held his stare.

"Work jeans, boots, and a flannel for under my jacket. Does that suit you? Or do you prefer what I'm wearing now?" Wrath put a hand on his hip and cocked it outward, making a parody of a modeling pose. All of his ink was on display, and I saw that the tattoos went across his upper chest, linking up the design on each arm. I was fascinated with the subtle touches of blue and orange mingled with the black and gray design. I wondered what it would be like to touch that skin, feel those muscles under my hands, and trail my fingers down his chest to those V-cut abs.

I shook my head and clumsily backed out of the room, harnessing every bit of willpower I possessed and putting it into not blushing. "Be up at seven thirty," I mumbled, closing the door behind me.

* * *

"AND THEN, I just stood there, gaping and staring like an idiot while he was in his skivvies!" I moaned to Lois over Skype. I had started out by texting her, but by the time I got to the beer bath and the weirdly almost-romantic dance scene, she insisted we take this shit to video chat. So I hauled out my laptop, sat cross-legged on my bed, and spilled out the depths of my embarrassment to the one person who I knew wouldn't judge me for being so stupid as to run into the wrong room in her own house.

"Oh my god, Maxine, you are either dumber than a sack of hair or luckier than a Powerball winner. And I know you're not dumb. So, what did tall, dark, and handsome look like in those skivvies?" she teased.

"I don't know!" I cried. "Hot? I was so cringed up over the whole thing, I didn't know where to look. And then he made a comment about my penguins and I—"

"Penguins? You mean your rack?" She cackled.

"Yes!"

"Well, it is a great one. So he copped an eyeful of your flannel, you saw him almost naked, then probably blushed and stammered your way through something stupid, and then ran and hid." God, this woman knew me too well. I buried my face in the nearest pillow.

"Pretty much," I said, the sound muffled by the cushion.

"Girl, this calls for wine. I know you've got a box lurking somewhere in that place. Get yourself a glass and chill," came Lois's sage advice.

I decided Lois was right. I needed wine, stat. I signed off with her, blowing kisses at the screen and promising to give her updates as often as I could and to stealthily take a picture of Wrath to send her. Hell, I'd probably ask him for one. He was arrogant enough that he would probably think it his duty to share his good looks with the world. I rolled off my bed and crept to the kitchen, where I poured myself a glass of

Tania white from the box, and then set about the task of preparing a picnic lunch for tomorrow's activities.

* * *

I WOKE PROMPTLY at 7:00 a.m., cranky and still tired. I was one of those people who tended to remember their dreams, and mine had left me feeling deeply unsettled. Because there it was, in IMAX 3D—Wrath, in my bed, in nothing but those little boxer briefs. Wrath taking his hair out of the ponytail and it spreading all over my pillow. Wrath holding me with those strong arms and gazing down at me with those piercing brown eyes. The feel of his beard on my thighs. One glass of wine and a beer dousing and my subconscious was all over that man. I shuddered as I rose out of bed, and not from the cold, but from distaste. Or so I told myself.

I had made sure to get up a half hour before Wrath so I could get ready first, in relative peace. I headed into my bathroom and got my second shock of the morning. There, innocuous on the vanity, were the little telltale signs of male occupation. A razor, shaving cream, a toothbrush, and a jar of … Noxzema? What in hell was Wrath keeping in a Noxzema jar? Unable to contain my curiosity, and slightly concerned it might hold drugs of some kind, I lifted the jar and unscrewed the lid. Inside was the odorous white face cream advertised on the jar. I stood still for a moment, dumbly looking into the cream, feeling as though the cream were looking back at me.

"Yo, Max, you better not be ninja-ing my Noxzema. That shit isn't cheap, and you've got some Pond's right over there." Wrath stood leaning in the bathroom doorway, arms crossed in front of his chest, amusement in his eyes. At least he was dressed, thank the gods.

I clapped the lid back on the jar immediately, mortified at being caught. As I scrambled to explain my behavior and apologize, what popped out of my mouth was "I'm not a *ninja,* Wrath. I don't grief others."

Now, don't get me wrong, to be called a ninja is usually awesomeness. However, to be called a ninja in-game is an insult of the highest order. Ninjas are thieves who profit off the work of others, stealing valuables for various motives, sometimes just because they can. I looked down at the jar still in my hand and considered that maybe he wasn't too far off the mark. I put it down and said, "I was wondering why you have it. You don't seem like the type of guy who bothers with a skincare regimen."

"And that's where you'd be wrong, oh mighty one. You think my skin is this kissable naturally?" He ran a hand down one smooth-looking cheek above his beard. "Besides, I'm playing the long game."

"The long … what on earth are you talking about?" I asked, genuinely confused.

"Noxzema. My great-grandmother lived to a hundred and five. She used Noxzema face cream every single damn day. For decades. Probably since the stuff was invented. Seriously, when she was a hundred, she didn't look a day over seventy. That stuff has like some kind of elixir of life in it, and I intend to harness it for a long and youthful existence."

"So, hold up. You're telling me that the fountain of youth is in a jar of Noxzema," I managed to say with a straight face.

"Exactly. So, what's for breakfast?"

CHAPTER SIX
MAXINE

"Who in the bloody hell TP'd the guild hall?"

— *Maximus_Damage*

I blamed the shock of freezing nipples and my brain taking a vacation for allowing Wrath to drive Stiles last night. Today, I was staying in the driver's seat, despite his whining about wanting to try his hand at navigating the switchbacks and seeing how fast he could take one. This morning we were headed to Cades Cove, a gorgeous spot in the Great Smoky Mountains National Park. It was popular with tourists, especially when the leaves were turning, so I focused on my driving and let Wrath fiddle with the stereo. He hooked up his phone and before I knew it, Jimi Hendrix's "All Along the Watchtower" was blasting as we weaved our way toward what I hoped would be a relaxing and fun day, not the exercise in torture I had feared all my plans with Wrath would turn out to be.

I was feeling renewed this morning, which I attributed to the gorgeous weather. I decided to grab the bull by the horns and ask Wrath head-on what I had been avoiding since he arrived. I raised my voice over Jimi's singing and said, "Wrath, how are we going to get through this visit? We keep stepping on each other's toes, and with our history … Look, I want to be able to fully relax and uncoil this spring of tension in me."

He turned the stereo down a little and twisted in his seat to face me. "I think we need to try to put some of the past behind us," he said. "Or, if that's too difficult, we can use the time-tested and true advice—fake it till you make it. We act like friends, and maybe we will be. At the very least, I won't be driving you up the wall."

"That sounds like a good idea," I murmured. But Wrath did have a point. Things would go a lot easier if we made up our minds to play nice. At least offline, he couldn't piss off half a dozen goblins and then lead them directly to my character, leaving me to fight them all or die. (See: griefing.)

I pulled up to the Cades Cove Chariot Company—a name which made little sense due to a distinct lack of chariots—and parked near the stables. I turned to Wrath with a smile and a little jazz hands wave. "Ta-da!'

"What the hell is this?" he asked, his voice oddly high-pitched and almost squeaky.

"It's horseback riding! We're going to do the two-hour guided loop through the woods Surprise!"

I was so proud of myself and my event planning skills that I didn't notice Wrath's distinct lack of enthusiasm until I saw that he had that pale look again. "Horses. Why'd it have to be horses?" I heard him mutter.

"Hey, slow your roll there, Indy. A horse isn't going to hurt you as long as you follow the guide's directions, take charge of the horse, and don't act like a dick to it. I've done this before, and trust me, it's always a good time. You won't regret giving it a try." I passed him a bottle of water, and he chugged down half of it at once. He looked damn nervous. Who knew horses were Wrath's Achilles heel? "Are you okay?" I asked cautiously, not wanting to wound his pride.

"I'm peachy," he replied dryly. Good enough for me. I jumped out of Stiles and made my way toward the stables to meet Rick, our guide and all-around horse guru. Wrath caught up with me, and I made introductions, calling Wrath "Jonathan" for the first time. It was his name, after all, and I felt weird introducing him to random people using his character name because, honestly, who names their kid Wrath? It felt almost stranger saying Jonathan as it suddenly made Wrath more than a random guildie. He was sort of my friend, and I was introducing him as such.

Rick inspected our clothing for suitability and handed us each a helmet. I had gone back and forth on what to wear today but decided to go with an older, comfy pair of jeans, hiking boots, and a Jar Jar Binks T-shirt I'd bought in college on a dare but secretly liked wearing for the reactions it elicited from others. Since it was cool outside, I'd covered it with a loose, light sweater that bore the motto *Je suis prest.* I snapped my helmet in place and thought that we couldn't have asked for a better day to spend outside. It was cool but not cold, the sun was shining, and there was hardly a cloud in the sky. We might see all kinds of wildlife, and I only regretted that I wasn't confident enough of a rider to take pictures while seated.

The idyllic nature of the day was broken when, out of the corner of my eye, I saw Wrath take something from his pocket and pop it in his mouth. He closed his eyes for a moment, and then looked at the ground. What in the world … Did I just see Wrath take drugs? No way, not happening. Not on my watch. I marched over to him and said quietly, "I don't suppose you're going to tell me that was a breath mint."

"No, but it's definitely none of your business," he clapped back.

"We're about to go into the woods on horseback for almost two hours. If you're doing something to endanger yourself, the horses, or me and the guide, it is most definitely my business. I'm going to ask you once, and I hope out of respect for me you'll tell me the truth: What did you take?"

Wrath kneaded at his forehead with his left hand, then shot me a glare that could double as a death ray. "When I said it was none of your business, I meant it. But you're not going to let this drop, plus, you are determined to think the worst of me. You think I'm out here dropping acid or something before getting on a freaking horse, of all things. How stupid do you think I am?"

"That depends on what it was you took," I replied.

"Lorazepam, okay? It was lorazepam. It's for anxiety."

"I know. My mother takes it now and then, ever since my father died." I subconsciously stuck my tongue out of the corner of my mouth and bit it. "Well, I feel like an asshole now. You were right, Wrath, it was none of my business. Other than that, you're going to be a bit groggy, but you wouldn't have taken it without knowing your own body and what it can handle. I'm sorry I cornered you into revealing something you didn't want to. Is this because of the horses? We don't have to do this. You know, there's no shame in—"

"It doesn't feel good being the jerk, does it," he cut me off, and then, without any superiority in his tone, eviscerated me. "Or having someone resent you for something you thought was the right thing to do at the time. Chew on that for a bit, Max. Maybe you'll view me a little differently."

I knew he was right. I knew it, but I couldn't stand to lose the moral high ground to Wrath, of all people. "How was it doing the right thing at the time when you opposed me becoming a guild officer? I know you talked to all the other officers behind my back, telling them I was a second-rate player with too much hype and few of the skills to back it up. We'd been playing together for years at that point, and you tried to sabotage me. Why? Why, Wrath?" My voice had steadily risen in volume, and Rick backed off and headed toward the stables.

I could see the tension in his jaw and in the set of his shoulders. "I wasn't myself when I did it, okay."

"No, not okay!" I countered. "You can't set the world on fire and say, 'Oops, I wasn't myself when I lit the match'!"

"Yes, it was a dick move. I was scared that you wouldn't have any time for me anymore, or that you'd get me kicked out of the guild. I didn't want things to change. And I was going through some shit that year that I would rather not talk about right now, but it influenced my behavior, especially toward you."

I advanced on him slowly. "At some point before this weekend is over, I am going to crack your code. No more talking in riddles about why you've been a jerk, and no blaming your behavior on mysterious things. We're going to have it out, you and me, I swear. Because I won't go back to how things were in the game between us." With that, I stalked off to the stable, leaving Wrath to eat my dust.

Finding Rick inside with Prancer, my favorite of the horses, I felt the tension drain from my body. Being around animals was grounding for me and soothed something in me. I only wished Wrath felt the same way. I was confident that if he gave it a try, he'd be as enamored with horseback riding as I was.

* * *

"Now, son," Rick began. "You saw how Miss Maxine got up on Prancer there? Slick as shit. That's what you're going to do with Buttercup. You put that foot in this here stirrup, hang onto the horn, and swing your other leg over. And bingo, you're on top of the horse. Should be simple for a tall guy like you."

Wrath stood looking at Buttercup, a beautiful, jaunty mare with a coat the color of honey, like he was Atreyu staring at the Southern Oracle and with one misstep, she'd blast him to smithereens.

"You've got this!" I called out, watching as Wrath lifted his foot. The moment Wrath's weight was in the stirrup, the saddle slipped off Buttercup, and Wrath went sailing to the ground, flat on his back, in the dirt.

"Oh my god, Wrath!" I shouted from the back of Prancer. Buttercup whinnied, like she thought we were all idiots, and made off for the stable, leaving Wrath where he fell.

CHAPTER SEVEN
JONATHAN

"Did everyone check out my boomstick?"

— *Wrath*

I coughed after I got my wind back, and slowly sat up with Rick's help. Of all the activities, why had Max chosen *horses*? I was man enough to admit when I was afraid. There was something about their beady eyes and swishy tails that made me never want to get on one's back, ever. And now, after my little trip into the dirt, I knew I was right.

"I'm so sorry the saddle wasn't cinched tight. My boy did up yours, and he normally can do it perfectly with his eyes closed. I don't know what got into him today." Rick shook his head and clapped me on the shoulder. A puff of dust rose from where he hit me, and I coughed again. My back was aching, particularly between my shoulders, and I was torn between wanting to get back on Buttercup to prove I could and heading to Knoxville or wherever for X-rays. If Dr. Google was correct, there was nothing they could do for a broken rib and I didn't have the searing pain that would indicate a disc had been dislodged.

"It's okay, sir," I replied. Max had hopped off Prancer and handed the reins to Rick's boy.

"May I?" she asked, then started rubbing my back, and suddenly all I wanted to do was kiss wayward Buttercup and the slippery saddle because the fall had gotten Max's hands on me. And God, her hands felt good, rubbing over my flannel shirt, digging into my shoulders, massaging the area around my neck and then down the center of my back. I let out an involuntary groan, and she froze.

I made to apologize when she said, "You feel a little tight, but not too bad. Do you want to go home, and I can put some anti-inflammatory gel on it? You could rest up, maybe read a book before the jam at the community center tonight."

The thought of lying on the bed, shirtless, while Max rubbed gel into my back was almost enough to override all sense of decency. But Max had planned these events hoping to show us a good time. I couldn't take that away from her, just because I was an idiot and hadn't tested my weight in the stirrup before going all in.

"Nope, as soon as Rick here can retrieve my lady Buttercup and saddle her properly, I'll be ready for the trail ride. I really want to go, Max. Honest." It was a total lie of course, but I wanted to make Max happy and not be a killjoy in the face of all the plans she had made.

Rick materialized when I said his name and had apparently caught our conversation. "Son, I hate to break it to you, but I can't let you go out there after kissin' the dirt like that. Your shoulders are going to be awfully sore as it is. You don't need upwards of two hours of bouncing around on horseback to make them feel better. I'll tell you what, how about I hitch up the wagon for a hayride, just the two of you. You can even bring your picnic with you, and I can stop near the falls if you're up for that. Would still be a nice day."

"Picnic?" I asked.

"Uh yeah, something I made up for us last night after the peep show," Max explained. "Rick, I think that sounds like a lovely solution to our problem. I appreciate it. I'm sorry the original group couldn't make it here. I sure was eager to show off our gorgeous countryside with your even more beautiful horses."

"Heck, Maxine, you know there's an extra fee for renting out the whole hay wagon, don't you?" Max smiled broadly and shrugged. "Well, that obviously won't apply today. I'm just glad you're not big city folks with talk of suing us because of your friend's tumble."

"Why, Rick! What kind of hostess would that make me? Not one my mother would be proud of, I'm sure." Ah, we were coming around to an understanding. There was a strange rhythm to small town negotiations. It was impolite to come right out and ask about money, but in their roundabout way, the result was oddly efficient. No one was getting sued, and we'd get a ride on the hay wagon.

It turned out that Rick owned a comfortable wagon for hayrides. And Max had indeed packed a picnic in her backpack; it materialized as though conjured once the wagon was hitched up. We were going to a place called the Loop Road and, if I felt up to it, we would walk for an hour and a half to a waterfall, where we would eat.

I had already been impressed by the beauty of the Great Smoky Mountains, but riding in a bed of hay underneath the multicolored glory of the trees, Max mere feet away from me and as excited as a kid over the ride and the animals we might see, made me view the area differently. It was as though a bubble of magic had been placed over the farmland and forest we rode through, the constant smile on Max's face contagious. I felt myself smile too, even if we were being hauled around by a horse.

I only regretted that I was seated so damn far away from her in the back of the wagon. Not wanting to shout to Rick to stop and potentially scare away any of the animals Max was scouting for, I got on my hands and knees and crawled over the hay toward her. Just then, we hit a dip in the road, and I lurched forward, my arms giving out and my head colliding with something soft. I heard an "Oomph!" and tried to push myself up but was instantly shoved away.

"You know, it's normally considered polite to ask a girl before diving into her breasts!" Max hissed at me, obviously not wanting Rick to overhear—or maybe she was concerned about scaring the animals.

"I didn't mean to *dive into your breasts*," I hissed back calmly, even though inwardly I was so embarrassed that I didn't know where to look.

"Look, bears!" Max whispered, grabbing my leg.

Well, that would do. Rick pulled the wagon over as we watched three young bears playing in the trees right by the side of the road. I was enchanted by their climbing partway up the trees or turning over rocks on the ground, but noticed that Max, fiddling with her phone, was missing the show. I took the phone from her, indicating that she should watch the bears, and figured out how to get her camera to work. I took a few shots of the fuzzy bears and of her as well. Before she could protest, I moved right beside her and took a selfie of us. Realizing what I was doing, I expected her to put up a fuss, but she flashed the peace sign and smiled, so I took a few more. We could always share these on the guild forums, and all those other scrubs could see what a good time they'd missed. If Max ever came out as a girl, that is.

I wondered what I should do with that information. I hadn't considered before now that I possessed info that Max didn't want the rest of the world to know. Though she had to have known that by hosting this weekend she would be outing herself. She had to be ready for all of that potential blowback coming her way. Right?

Or I could keep her secret and let her be the one to tell everyone, when she was ready. That would be the decent thing to do. And where Max was concerned, I wanted to do the decent thing. I wanted to earn her trust, her friendship, and more. If she wanted me to, I would keep her secret. I would keep any secret for her, forever.

I thought I already had her friendship, and part of me still thought that was true despite her saying that she hated me. I didn't want to overanalyze the situation, but I'd known this girl for ten years. We'd had a lot of fun together, and yes, we'd fought. Pranked each other. Yet here she was, determined to show me a good time and even host me in her inner sanctum. I saw flashes of hope for us in all that, hope that the clouds would part and Max would see what I saw—the crazy chemistry between us that's been there for years.

By the time we stopped for the waterfall hike, her hand was still on my leg.

* * *

AFTER WHAT ENDED up being a four-hour round-trip hike, during which I foolishly insisted on wearing the backpack, my shoulders and back were hurting. The payoff was the beauty of the verdant landscape leading up to Abrams Falls, and the majesty of the torrent of water coming down over the rocks. There was also the clear accomplishment Max felt for completing the hike so quickly, considering the difficulty of the trail.

"I really did it," she said, smiling huge, her sweater tied around her waist and her hair pulled up into a messy bun.

She was a bit sweaty, and I suggested she finish off our water supply since Rick was returning—with a car this time—to take us back to the stables.

"You know, I didn't want to tell anyone in town that I was thinking of planning this waterfall hike because I figured they'd tell me I was too out of shape to do it. You know, because of my size." She chewed on her bottom lip briefly, and then her tongue stuck out of the corner of her mouth for a moment.

"You're obviously not out of shape. We slayed that dragon." I smiled at her, a bit sad that she felt she had to hide things to avoid judgment. "Never let anyone dictate what you can and can't do based on your size. It's not the only factor in someone's health. You can be your size and be perfectly heart healthy, as we've seen here."

"Wow, are you a personal trainer on the side, Wrath?" she asked, wiping her brow. "That was very … motivational."

I paused for a beat, then decided to tell her about Elaine. If I wanted Max to open up to me, to trust me, then also I had to put myself out there, and nothing was more private to me than my family. I could trust Max with this. "My little sister is a curvy girl who got crapped on her whole life about her weight. I used to try to protect her from my daddy and his comments, but I couldn't take on the whole school. I tried but, well, lots of little bastards. She didn't deserve it. Anyway, she got out of there, went to college, then moved to Chicago. And she's beautiful, Max, so damn beautiful. Like you." Elaine had never seen herself as beautiful growing up, and there was no way I was letting Max have the same notion about herself now.

CHAPTER EIGHT
MAXINE

"What do you think this is, a square dance? Get it together before you get us all killed."

— *Maximus_Damage*

What did he mean, beautiful like me? Wrath didn't think I was beautiful, Wrath thought I was a pompous bag of dicks, as he so colorfully put it on a guild raid two weeks ago. We'd been all lined up, thirty of us, ready to take on the demon god Kt'hala, and Deathdrop had been refusing to turn off his music on the guild voice chat. I'd typed in that if he didn't can it in two point four seconds, he would be booted from the raid party and blacklisted from joining any guild events for two weeks. Well. Guess who had to leap to his bestie's defense? I almost booted them both, but cooler heads prevailed after a brief scrap in which I had called Wrath an irresponsible man-child whose disrespectful behavior was wearing my patience beyond thin.

And now, here he was, telling me about his little sister and calling me beautiful. And staring at me like he was waiting to gauge my reaction. All I could do was stare back as I felt sweat bead on my forehead and run down my cleavage. My brain came back online after the shock of Wrath's words, and I ended the staring contest by gesturing with my chin toward Rick in his pickup, thanking the gods for his impeccable timing.

By the time we got home, I would have given up my legendary sword to have a shower, but I knew Wrath's shoulders had to be aching, and the warmth from the water would help him. Then I could apply the anti-inflammatory gel to his back.

"Okay, first shower is yours," I said as I reached out to take my bag from him.

"You sure?" he asked, taking in my messy hair and what I'm sure were pit stains on my shirt.

"Yup. I can get you settled in bed with some gel on your back before I take my shower."

"That's probably not necessary," Wrath protested.

I shook my head.

"Hey, who's the patient and who's the nurse?" I said firmly, watching a tic form in Wrath's jaw and his mouth twitch. He was trying not to laugh at me! I rewound what I'd said in my mind, and my cheeks bloomed red as a half dozen naughty role-play scenarios marched through my brain.

"Er, you know what I mean!" I said, pointing toward the bathroom door. "Now grab some fresh clothes and march."

When I heard the shower start up, I flopped onto my sofa and let out a huge breath. Struck by inspiration, I grabbed my phone from my pocket and pulled up the photos from this morning. After about a dozen shots of Abrams Falls, I found the ones of Wrath and me in the hay wagon. We looked good together, our faces beaming, our expressions relaxed. We certainly didn't look like two people who hated each other. At least I'd never seen mortal enemies cozied up in a pile of hay before. Hmm. For the first time in ages, I allowed myself to entertain the idea that perhaps we weren't enemies. Rivals, sure, but enemies? I didn't know anymore. I texted the best photo to Lois and waited, feeling adrift. She texted me back immediately.

Lois: Climb him like a tree!

Me: Ew, no.

I wrote back smiling, then heard the bathroom door give. I swallowed hard when he emerged shirtless, all that ink and his muscled body on display. I would, however, not stare. I wouldn't stare, I *wouldn't*, I told myself as I stared—and stared and stared—literally incapable of looking in any other direction. When had I last seen a man as handsome as this? I racked my brain, thinking back to my experimental college days and shook my head. Even the time I dated a pair of guys from the swim team, I had never seen anything as breathtaking as Wrath.

He laughed but disguised it as a cough. The sexy spell now broken, I pointed to the game room. "Go in and lie down on your tummy. I need to get the gel and a glove from the bathroom, and I'll be right there. This will help you feel better, I promise. At least it never fails with me."

"You fall off horses often?" he asked, grinning.

"Only on Tuesdays."

Wrath followed my instructions, and I headed into the steamy bathroom to gather supplies. The air was full of that sandalwood, grass, and sunshine smell, it must be his body wash and shampoo that smelled so divine.

I had a well-stocked first aid cabinet based on my own clumsiness and the way I was raised. My mother was convinced that disaster was always around the bend, and it was our job to be prepared to meet it. I grabbed a latex glove and the tube of gel and made my way to Wrath.

He was lying down, arms crossed under his head and eyes closed. Holy hell, he looked like every naughty thought I'd ever had. I made my way to the bed and gingerly sat beside him, putting on the glove and squirting a dollop of the cool gel into my palm.

As soon as my palm made contact with his warm skin, he shrieked. "Yikes, warn a guy next time!"

I smiled, then caught myself, wondering what it was about screwing around with Wrath that I enjoyed so much. Maybe there was some nugget of truth to his claim that I gave as good as I got. Or that he never intended to hurt me by being a jackass, that he was just having fun, under the mistaken belief that I was too. Could it be possible?

"Wrath," I began, as I moved the gel around, rubbing it in well. "What did you mean when you said you weren't yourself all those years ago when you said that shit about me to the other officers?"

"Different topic? I'd rather not go there right now. Ooh, that feels good. Can you rub a little harder?"

Sighing, I acquiesced, digging my gloved fingers deeper into his muscles. "Okay, were you serious when you called me beautiful?"

Silence. Then, softly, he replied, "Yes."

I huffed. "Well, you're not too bad yourself. I love your hair, other than the fact that it keeps getting in my way here." I used my un-gooped up hand to move some errant strands off his back and continued to make circles on his shoulder blades, reveling in the warm feeling of his skin under my hands.

"I hate to say this, because that feels good, but I'm getting a crick in my neck."

"Oh, I'm sorry. Yeah, I'm finished." I took my hand off him and immediately missed the contact. There's a thing about being introverted and not dating or having a lot of family—you become touch-deprived. I know I have my cats, but it's not the same thing as real human contact. "I'm going to have my shower now. Let that seep in and rest in a comfortable position until I get back. Then we can decide what to do until the jam session at the community center tonight."

"I'll admit, I've had my eye on your tubs of Lego."

"I don't know how I feel about you eyeing up my tubs," I teased. Or at least I thought I was teasing. I wasn't flirting, was I? Oh, hell. Clearing my throat, I continued, "I haven't made anything new in a while. We can build when I'm out of the shower," I offered, hoping he'd say yes. I was surprised to find I had something else in common with Wrath. I loved playing with Lego. Though when I was feeling super serious, I didn't call it "playing," I called it "constructing."

"Sounds like a plan, Max," he replied in an odd tone. Please gods, tell me that wasn't his sexy voice. I didn't know if I could handle being the focus of Wrath's sexual attention.

I rose off the bed, almost falling in the process, and headed to my room to grab some fresh clothes and then off to the bathroom to breathe in more of that delicious scent.

* * *

WRATH and I sat cross-legged on the carpet in the game room, bins and bins of Lego open around us. I had a system where I sorted them according to shape and function rather than color, and I was proud of my organizational skills. Wrath, however, was fixated on one piece out of the thousands and, as it happened, so was I.

"For the last time, no. I only have two Rebel pilot helmets, and I need them both!" I snapped, holding the tiny Lego pieces like they were made of solid gold.

"You're hogging them, and you know it! You don't want to admit that my spaceship puts yours to shame," Wrath boasted, holding aloft his ship and making it do circles in the air.

"Maybe so, but it'll never be part of the Rebel Fleet," I said smugly, plunking the helmets onto the copilots in my own spacefaring ship.

"Max," he practically whined, "can't you share? I am your guest."

I recognized this for the devious ploy it was, and staunchly replied, "All's fair in love and Lego. I grabbed them first. Why don't you use the Stormtrooper heads and accept your fate?"

"Because they're lame. They're the worst shots in the galaxy. And besides, you were only able to get those Rebel helmets so quickly because you knew where they were stored."

"Oh, boohoo," I said, smiling as I took the helmet off one of my pilots and plunked it in his hand. "There, happy?"

"Ecstatic. This is awesome. Thanks." He affixed the helmet to his own pilot and looked at me. "You know, I never had this kind of stuff when I was a kid. This is my first time getting a chance to build something with Lego."

Each time Wrath brought up his childhood, it sounded like something out of a Southern version of Dickens, and I wasn't quite sure how to respond. But it occurred to me that maybe he wasn't looking for a response. Maybe he just wanted someone to listen and give a damn.

I grabbed a smaller tub and pulled out scissors and some fishing line. "Okay, time to have these bad boys on duty defending my Lego city." I gestured to the branches of my potted trees that extended over the Lego bench. "Up there will do, you think?"

"Wait, you want to save mine too?" he asked incredulously, looking down at the ship in his hands.

"Don't be an idiot. Of course I do. Unless you'd like to take it home with you," I offered.

"No, no! I want it here, patrolling alongside yours." He grinned.

And with that, we set about affixing the little spaceships to my tree, our truce holding.

* * *

BY THAT EVENING, not only had Wrath proven he was a very quick study of the art of Lego but his shoulders and back no longer bothered him, so jam night at the community center was a go. I decided to wear something a bit casual-dressy, which meant nice jeans and a tightish mint green knit sweater that showed off all my curves. I put on a full face of makeup—a rarity for me—and double-checked to make sure there was no lipstick on my teeth, also a rarity. I curled my hair a bit, and satisfied with my appearance, left my room to meet up with Wrath.

Wrath was waiting in the living room, perusing my bookshelves. When he turned, I gulped a little. He was wearing dark jeans, boots, and a black button down rolled up at the sleeves, showing off his forearm tats. His beautiful long hair was loose, hanging low to his mid back, and gleaming. He wore leather bracelets on each arm, and a silver ring on his right hand. He was, in a word, hot, and that tingly feeling came back over my body.

After the stare fest, I snapped out of it and recalled the time I was riding my trusty brown-striped zebreh through the Plains of Despair, in *Magecraft*, stalking the mighty blue buffalo. This was something few dared, as the blue buffalo were not only vicious, they were shy and expert hiders. It was almost impossible to sneak up on one undetected, but the rewards were plentiful for the victorious few. I had been giddy with excitement when one finally appeared in my sights. I climbed off the zebreh and stealthily moved through the high grass, weapon raised, when suddenly from the sky came the roar and thunder of some idiot in a helicopter, making the grasses blow and scaring the crap out of my kill. I stood there, ready to give G.I. Joe a piece of my mind. And who had climbed out? Wrath. All to show off his new pauldrons. Like I gave a damn about his shoulder armor! My blue buffalo had bounded away across the plain as Wrath strutted in front of me.

Adequately reminded of why I found him rude and obnoxious rather than sexy as hell, I gave his outfit a nod of approval and headed to the door to put on my shoes and grab my coat. He followed me to the door. "You look very nice tonight, Maxine," he said softly.

I would be lying to myself if I ignored that damn tingling that followed his use of my full name. However, I replied, "It's Max. Or Maximus. Unless you want me to start calling you Jonathan."

"I wouldn't mind," he replied, also grabbing his well-worn brown leather coat.

"Well, you've been Wrath to me for ten years. I don't know how easy the switch would be," I said, meaning it. I locked up my cottage and we climbed into Stiles, Wrath taking control of the stereo. His music choices were on point, and as we headed through the streets of Green Valley, we sang together.

I brought Stiles to a stop with his signature lurch at the community center and turned in my seat toward Wrath, determination on my face. "Okay, here are the rules," I began sternly. Stern, because I felt myself being pulled toward Wrath, and it disturbed me. I didn't trust easily since the attack, especially men.

"Rules? Our fun night out at the community center has rules?" He cocked an eyebrow comically high.

"Yes, rules," I replied. "So listen up. First, there will be lots of people here who will assume we're together-together. Every chance you get, please dissuade them of that notion. You're an old family friend from out of town, that's it. Keep the story simple." I reached into my bag to find my red lip stain and pulled down the mirror in the Jeep. It was definitely touch-up time. I was just applying it to the center of my upper lip when Wrath spoke and my application took a disastrous turn.

"You know, for someone who doesn't ever lie, you sure are good at hatching plots where lies are involved," he commented, that eyebrow staying cocked.

I felt my gut sink like a stone. He was right. I was fixing to tell the whole town more lies. And this time I was asking someone else to lie for me as well. From hiding who I was from everyone in Green Valley for a decade , to lying about not seeing the faces of those who assaulted me, to lurking behind a male avatar online instead of accepting invitations to go out in town and socialize—when those invitations used to come. Turns out, if you say no often enough, people stop asking.

I looked down, bit my tongue, and then looked back up at Wrath's beautiful and disappointed eyes. "Okay. You're my friend from an online game. But not my boyfriend. Can we stick to that?"

Wrath smiled.

"I'm proud of you, Maxine," he said, using my full name for the second time in a row. I wasn't sure what I thought of that.

"Thank you, Jonathan," I returned. Now, to wipe down my lip stain and start from scratch. My hand vibrated a little, and I thought about his real name falling from my lips. It was the first time we'd used each other's names like that, back and forth, and it felt significant. I shook off the strange feeling and got back to business.

"Where were we? Oh right, the rules. Okay, second and most importantly, do not, I repeat, do not take the last helping of coleslaw. I don't want my guest to be the one to finish it off and endure everyone's hostile stares for the rest of the evening."

This was no joke. There were always people who missed out on the coleslaw and then would stare at other people's coleslaw-laden plates to see who took how much.

"We're friends from an online game, we're not sharing a bed, and don't finish off the coleslaw. I think I got it. And your lips look great. Stop fiddling with them."

I was so surprised by his comment that I did stop, and when I took stock in the mirror, I realized he was right. I was ready, war paint and all. I could face the town, and tonight I would not, I repeat, not, be a wallflower.

The community center was hopping, and I put my platter of shamefully bakery-bought cupcakes on the dessert table while Wrath wandered behind me, sticking his head in each room we passed. Once my dessert was down, I poked Wrath in the arm and directed us to the bluegrass room, no doubt the most packed room in the place because of who would be singing tonight. Cletus had given me the heads-up at our last book club meeting that his brother, Billy Winston, and Billy's wife, Scarlet Claire Winston—otherwise known as country singer Claire McClure—were going to be in town this weekend. Their rich and melodic voices filled the space, with Cletus providing accompaniment on the banjo, Billy playing guitar, along with Drew Runous, brother-in-law to the Winston clan by marriage to the lone girl amongst the seven siblings, Ashley.

Years ago, I had rather unfairly given Scarlet a wide berth when she came back to town married to Ben McClure. I had gone to school with her and would never forget that hair or those eyes, so I recognized her right away—the daughter of Razor Dennings, then-president of the Iron Wraiths. After my own run-in with the Wraiths, I avoided everything and everyone that had even the slightest connection with them.

It had taken me a while, and some therapy, to see that people like Cletus—whose Daddy was Razor's vice president—and Scarlet were not responsible for the sins of their fathers or those their fathers ordered about. Avoiding them was avoiding good people that might turn out to be good friends. My therapist was right on one front. After sweet Bethany Winston—a co-worker at the library—had passed, I had shown up at the Winston place with a blueberry pie. Cletus had answered the door, wearing a smoking jacket. We sat on that porch and talked and talked, and I considered us allies and friends ever since.

"Holy hell, that's the Devil's Daughter," Wrath whispered, nodding toward Scarlet, and I elbowed him sharply.

"Do not ever, ever call her that, and don't let anyone hear you call her that, especially her family. Scarlet is not defined by, or responsible for, her scumbag serial killer father."

"No, of course not," he mumbled, looking taken down a peg. "So this is what y'all do for fun in Green Valley," he mused.

"Well, on Friday nights I'm usually in a raid with the guild," I replied, thinking back to all the times someone I bumped into around town had commented that they hadn't seen me at the community center. I often made excuses about not feeling well or visiting my mom, which I knew was wrong. But how do you explain that you're more comfortable socializing through your computer than joining the whole town in "real" life? How had I let myself become such a hermit that I was on my way to becoming my own mother? I shuddered at the realization and felt a jolt of fear run through me. As I looked at the faces around me, most smiling, some singing, almost all swaying along to the sweet music, I vowed that I would not become the next town recluse.

CHAPTER NINE
JONATHAN

"Free armor dyes, festive masks, and fireworks! PM me!"

— Wrath

After the group sang and twanged through a ton of damn fine bluegrass, the crowd began to thin a bit, and the banjo player declared the quartet was retiring for the evening. Max grabbed my arm and gracelessly hauled me through the audience toward the banjo player.

Our arms still linked, and with a megawatt smile on her face, she shouted, "Cletus! That was incredible tonight."

"It was, man. You've got a great sound," I offered.

Cletus looked from Max, to our joined arms, again at me, and then back at Max. I didn't want to engage in stereotypical jealous guy behavior, but I did want to sniff out who this Cletus was to her. What had he done to earn her smiles and respect?

"Thank you," he replied, then looked pointedly behind us. "Maxine, you seem to have misplaced the rest of your guests from your game. I suspect you noticed this, which is why you're hanging onto this one so tightly."

"Oh!" Max said in surprise and dropped my arm like it was a hot potato. I instantly disliked Cletus. "All the others couldn't make it. Just him. Cletus, meet Wrath—er, Jonathan Owen from Florida. Jonathan, this is my friend Cletus Winston."

Not one to let my manners fail me when needed, I stuck out my hand and Cletus gave it a firm shake. "Jonathan Owen, would you happen to be the same gentleman who enjoys harrying Maxine at every available turn?"

I spun to face Maxine. "You told people that about me? What else did you say, that I like to hunt people for sport?" I felt my face redden in embarrassment as I recalled the time I had also besmirched her good name to the other guild officers. I wasn't sure what to do with the information that she was talking unfavorably about me to her friends. I felt like every time we made some progress and I got to show her more of who I really was, something popped up to remind me of her animosity.

"Wrath, calm down. Of course not. I was telling Cletus about the game, that's all."

"Oh, I see. That's *all*," I said sarcastically.

"It would seem to me," Cletus said, inserting himself into our fight, "that you two need to have a tête-à-tête, but allow me to suggest not tonight. We're fixing to take things back to my brother's place up on Bandit Lake. Scarlet and Billy will be there singing, and I'll have my banjo and a dulcimer. If you can sit in your own stew for the rest of the evening, you can imbibe and listen to more fine music."

And with that, he packed up his banjo and gave Max a little salute as he left the room.

"So, feel like hitting up a party?" Max asked, almost cautiously.

I thought about it. I was mad as hell that not only did Max hate me, she had told her offline friends I was some kind of dastardly character. That being said, I didn't want to piss her off by saying no when she probably wanted to go. Plan Seduction would suggest that I be pliable to her wishes, even if I thought she was a jerk at the moment. I hoped that this wasn't some big rager we were headed to because being the only sober person at a party is about as much fun as watching paint dry, only the wall sometimes vomits and tries to get into your pants.

"Fine," I answered. "Party it is, *princess*." I couldn't help poking the bear, just a little. Her eyes flashed fire, and I smiled, gesturing with my arm that she should lead the way.

Back in the Jeep, she turned to me before starting the engine. "Wrath, I didn't mean to hurt your feelings, but you have to understand that in the past, you have hurt mine. I needed to decompress some of that with my friends. Can we forget about this?" The earnest look on her face was too much for me to resist.

"Consider it forgotten," I replied. "Whose turn is it to pick the playlist?"

* * *

IT WAS NOT A RAGER. After we finally arrived at our destination, which I'll admit took some skill for Max to navigate the twisty mountain road at night, we were welcomed by everyone like old friends, though I didn't have two clues who anyone was save the four performers I'd listened to at the jam session. A few new musicians joined as couples swayed on the makeshift dance floor. Max seemed determined to undo the harm done at the community center. She introduced me to everyone as "one of her oldest friends" which was enough to earn me some clout. I was offered places to sit, drinks, snacks, the works.

Better still, no one cared when I turned down the beer, whiskey, and tequila for Coke. Max hovered over me until I told her to track down some people she knew and have some fun, and I saw her head to another room of the house with a bottle of tequila. I would have liked to spend every moment with her, but it struck me that she probably didn't get out to too many parties, and I wanted her to have as good a time as possible. As the night wore on, I realized I was supposed to have taken my pills hours ago, so I figured there was no harm in having a beer since it looked like Maxine and I wouldn't be getting home anytime soon. Most of the women, including Maxine, headed outdoors holding bottles, complaining it was too hot inside with all the people. I joined some of the other bearded men in a game of cards—at which I lost horribly—and was eventually coaxed into giving the dulcimer a try after Cletus had noticed my keen interest in the instrument. I was able to pick up a few melodies as the main group played and was applauded loudly for my efforts. I'd played the guitar in high school, and my musical tastes were pretty eclectic, so I was no stranger to blue-grass and country.

The noise must have attracted the girl gaggle back inside because I saw them file in —without Maxine. I assumed she was still with them. They all looked plastered, so I could forgive the oversight, but that didn't mean I wasn't going to go look for her right the heck now. We were on a lake, it was pitch-black, and I didn't have a clue how Maxine held her liquor. All reasons to put down the dulcimer and go search outside.

I stopped the first woman I found and asked her where Maxine was. She giggled, and then looked alarmed when she saw the concern on my face.

"She was with us for a little while but said she needed to clear her head with some fresh air. I don't think she's normally a big tequila drinker." The woman hiccupped and looked green, making a mad dash for what I assumed was the bathroom.

Great, Max was wandering around outside, alone, and was probably smashed. I grabbed our coats and made tracks for the front door. I headed around the side of the house where the floodlights didn't shine.

"Maxine!" I called, looking out over the pitch-black of the yard. Dammit, what if she'd decided to go in the lake? She was probably too wasted. She'd drown. My heart started to race, my mouth went dry, and I was about to marshal up a posse to go looking for her when I heard, faintly, "Jonathan? I'm down here."

I peered out into the night and saw a dark lump move on the grass, and I quickly made my way down the lawn to her.

"What are you doing down there?" I asked, my racing heart beginning to slow, thankful I had found her safe.

"I'm looking at the stars. Come lie down with me and look. It's incredible tonight. The ground is cold, but you're so hot you're bound to be warm."

Rolling my eyes at her drunken logic, I sat on the grass next to her, and she pulled on my arm until I was lying beside her.

She lifted her free hand and said in an authoritative tone, "See, that's Ursa Major, just there. And there's Andromeda, see? And that's Cassiopenis." She hiccupped. "*Cassiopeia.*"

That set off a laughing fit, and while I was happy she was so relaxed, it was also jarring to deal with her intoxication. I kept thinking about my father, and how he would laugh and sing and then snap! He'd slap my mom or me for no damn reason. This was all harmless fun to Max, but to me it was on the edge of scary, and I wished to God I had one of my antianxiety pills here. Not that I could mix it with the beer I'd had, but it would make me feel better having it in my pocket. Plenty of people had been drinking inside, and I usually was okay being around it, but something about the fact that I loved Max made her drinking unsettling to me. I never wanted to be involved with a big drinker, and I hoped that this type of thing was unusual for her.

I was so caught up in my own anxious spiral that it took me a moment to realize Max had rolled toward me and fastened her soft mouth to mine. All of my anxieties disappeared with the feeling of her warm body next to mine and her lips exploring my own. I'd like to say she tasted like strawberries or summer, but honestly, it was tequila with a coleslaw chaser. I didn't care. Kissing Max was the most pivotal moment in my life, and I was going to enjoy every second of it. Her softness, her little moans, her hands in my hair. She nibbled on my lower lip and darted her tongue out to lick me, clumsily inserting it into my mouth. At this, I met her with enthusiasm because I knew I may never get the chance to kiss Max again. And oh god, she was drunk, and I was only a little buzzed. We had to stop. In a minute.

"Max," I panted, pulling back from her, my curiosity rearing its head. I didn't want to take advantage of her in any way. "How long has it been since you've been with a man? Or have you ever …?"

"Condoms are in my purse, and I'm on the pill. You still wanna talk?" she asked, grinding her pelvis against mine, creating sparks behind my eyelids and riotous joy in my nether regions. I opened my eyes and peeled her off me a little, so we could actually have a conversation.

"Yeah, I do," I replied.

She looked at me in surprise, like she thought pointing out the condoms would be enough for my morals to take a vacation. "Fine, but short version," she said, twining our feet together. "I'm not a blushing virgin. I've been sexually active since I was sixteen and went to college. I experimented a lot and enjoyed sex. Just nothing for the last ten years."

"Ten years, Max? Yeah, I'm going to need the long version too," I said, my eyes widening. It was hard to believe someone with as much confidence as Maximus_-Damage had trouble finding partners. There was something else going on here. I wanted to discover what it was, to unlock every mystery around this woman.

She untangled our feet and sat up. "Fine, but consider the mood killed," she said in a waspish tone.

"Roger that," I replied, also rising to sitting. I bumped our shoulders together in a friendly manner, hoping it would spur her to talk.

"You know, we could have skipped the tragic backstory part of the evening and jumped right to sexytimes. But no, you wanted exposition. Remember that when your balls turn cerulean."

She grabbed her jacket and hugged it to her chest, and I suddenly felt bad about wanting to hear her story, especially if she needed a freaking security blanket to tell it. I was about to stop her when she took in a big breath and began to speak.

"Remember when I showed you my scar? Well, there are more under my shirt."

I nodded.

"That was ten years ago. I was changing my tire and the one guy messed me up good, physically, but then there was all the mental crap that came from the aftermath." She twisted at her shirt with her fingers, her discomfort evident. "Mostly being scared of people, of men. I'm sure you can psychoanalyze why I play as a man online after being victimized by them, and why I haven't let a man touch me in all that time. I also started to act differently, but folks in Green Valley were understanding and supportive. I wore baggier clothes, took the cataloging job at the library instead of working with children, stuff like that. People have been kind to me and cut me a lot of slack for not actively participating in things in town. Everyone remembers 'poor Maxine Peters and those awful bruises.' I never pressed charges, you know. I was scared of the gang, and even though one of the men eventually pulled the guy who was attacking me away, I still thought about retribution. The Wraiths were no joke back then."

"You started to game after your attack," I stated, trying to repel the vision of her beautiful face covered in bruises that popped into my mind.

"Well. I gamed a little in college, but yeah, I got serious after the attack. I wanted to feel in control, like there was a place I could win. So I devoted my time to becoming the best player I could be. And playing as a guy … after everything I told you about my initial experience gaming as a girl, right on the heels of the attack, I guess I felt safer and more confident when other people thought of me as a man." She made a face. "As a feminist, I can honestly say that interpretation doesn't sit right with me, but it fits the best."

"It sounds to me like you had an incredibly traumatic physical experience involving men, and then when men started attacking you verbally online right after that, it was just too much. It doesn't make you a bad feminist, or even a bad person that you—consciously or not—hid your gender." I so wanted her to believe me, and I was in awe of her coping skills, to be honest. Some people would have crumbled altogether under the combined pressures she'd faced, but not her.

"So wait, does this mean I'm forgiven?" she asked in earnest.

"There was never anything to forgive, Max. I'm the one who assumed you were a guy. I never even thought to ask if you were anything else. Plus, you were under no obligation to share your gender with any of us." As the words came out of my mouth, I knew them to be true.

"That's a pretty big departure from what you were saying yesterday."

"Maybe I've had some time to think about what you said," I replied.

"Well, I've had a change of heart too. I don't want to be invisible anymore. No more Maxine the Mouse. I'm telling the guild that I'm a girl when we go back to playing. It's past time." She belched loudly, and I snickered, then my mood sobered.

"You scared of what will happen? Not to stroke your ego or anything, but Maximus_-Damage is a fairly well-known player. Some of that crap—the harassing messages at the very least—will probably start up again."

She nodded slowly, a sour look on her face.

"Well, that's what the block and report functions are for. I've got a thicker skin than I did back then, Wrath. I can handle it. And if people in the guild are put out, well they'll have to build a bridge and get over it." A beat of silence passed. "Man, why'd you have to kill the mood? I could have gotten laid," she whined, lying back down and picking long blades of grass.

"It's okay. This isn't exactly how I'd pictured our first time anyway." The words were out of my mouth before I could think, and I felt Max freeze next to me. Realizing the implications all at once, I froze too, then released a nervous laugh that sounded like a hyena.

"Our first time," she said slowly. "Our *first* time? You thought about our first time enough that you knew how you wanted it to go? You thought about it before you came here!"

I nodded miserably, waiting for her mind to take the next leap of logic.

"You thought about us being together when you still thought I was a guy. Oh my god, and I attacked you with my mouth without even realizing that you might be gay. I'm sorry!" she said, sitting back up and patting me on the shoulder.

"Wait, what? I'm not gay," I replied, wanting that cleared up first. "But I suppose I was open to the idea. I mean, I thought I kind of was, but just for you. That's part of what I was coming here to figure out, if I'm bi, or pansexual, or maybe even demisexual. I know I've never been attracted to another guy except for you—at least when I thought you were a guy. It's complicated, okay? You being a guy made my life complicated." Oh my god, what was I doing telling her all this? I was like the thing that couldn't shut up.

"How complicated are we talking here?" she asked, still stroking my arm, whether from sheer drunkenness or a legitimate desire to make me feel better, I didn't know or care. It just felt good to have her touching me.

"Complicated as in I've been in therapy since I was eighteen. My counselor's name is Tom. When he finds out he's been counseling me through the agony and ecstasy of being in lo—of liking a *girl*, he's going to die laughing."

Suddenly, both of her arms were around me, and we sat there, cleaved together while she snuggled her head into my shoulder and patted my hair. "Holy flying fuck, Wrath. I sent you to therapy because you had a crush on me. That's … I mean … I'm so sorry. I never would have concealed my gender if I thought it would confuse someone else. I can't imagine someone liking me like that. So much that it hurt them."

"It was a privilege to be hurt by you," I murmured into her hair, inhaling the coconut scent of her shampoo. "And I learned a lot about myself. Most of my time with Tom turned into dealing with other issues that came up anyway, so don't apologize."

"No wonder you were gaping at me when I tried to shake your hand at the airport," she snickered, which I blamed on the tequila. "You looked so shocked. You were waiting for some guy as dreamy as you are."

"I am not dreamy," I countered, feeling about ten feet tall as she told me this. I had been so worried about her reaction to the revelation about my sexuality that her compliment was like a soothing balm.

"Mmm, yes you are, Jonathan. Kiss me, Jonathan. Please. I feel so—"

She quickly turned her head and vomited on a patch of lawn perilously close to where she'd just been lying.

Okay, time for bed. To sleep, that is. No way was anything else happening when she was this wasted, and I had seen that much of her stomach contents. We sure as hell weren't going to be sleeping out here on the grass, and I heard the rumble of car engines, indicating that the party was breaking up. Time to take charge and make a plan. I only had one beer, so I felt good to drive but that meant wrangling the keys from Max. She was lying on her side, her eyes closed, her hands over her stomach. That's when I remembered that I had our coats, and I fumbled through her pockets. Bingo! The keys to her beat-up Jeep in hand, I gently shook her shoulder.

"Come on, time to get going, sweetheart," I said, smiling as the affectionate term fell from my lips as naturally as breathing.

"'M not sweet," she replied, shoving at my hand. Okay, so maybe she was more of a crankypants right now. I stood and reached down, hauling her to her feet by lifting her under her armpits. Not the most graceful move, but it was all I had. She was determined to stay curled on that patch of grass, right next to where she blew chunks. Once she was standing, she looked at me sleepily, blinking slow like a cat.

"I have a feeling this will be a slow process," I said, putting an arm around her waist and leading us clumsily through the dark. I didn't spare a glance at my watch, but I knew I was way late taking my meds. And I wasn't going to get a full night's rest at this rate, which really irked me. I also wondered if Maxine would remember any of our conversation in the morning. We shared a lot of intimacy tonight, and at least I felt relieved knowing that if I had to give her a play-by-play, she was way too chill to freak out.

CHAPTER TEN
MAXINE

"Strategy and in-game mechanics will always be my first love."

— *Maximus_Damage*

I remembered every detail of my drunken conversation with Wrath the night before, and I was freaking out. While nursing a hell of a hangover, I might add. That basically summed up my morning—trying to act as normal as possible around Wrath while avoiding all talk of last night. We chipped in to make a glorious blueberry pancake breakfast and ate and made idle conversation about the game and our fellow guildies.

Despite feeling like there were several vuvuzelas going off in my brain, I pondered the events of last night. I had introduced Wrath as one of my oldest friends that I had met online. It was almost not a lie. I felt like maybe Wrath and I could be friends for real if I let my guard down and we had some honest conversations about some of the more outrageous stunts he had performed against me in the game.

Wrath had taken control last night to get us home safely, and as we slowly drove down the twisty mountain, I had been hyperconscious of the fact that I was sitting next to a man who was willing to overlook the fact that Maximus_Damage had a penis for the sake of my glowing personality. And since he'd been here, I'd shown him the trifecta of disdain: snark, sarcasm, and derision. Well, except for when I let him feel me up last night. Or had I tried to get him to do it and he refused? I winced at the memory of throwing myself at him. Why had I done that? Was it simply because I was horny and it had been so long, and Wrath was so damn pretty? Was I that shallow?

Of course there was another interpretation, one that reared its ugly head. That I liked Wrath, enjoyed his company, and was also attracted to him. Ugh, of course I didn't like Wrath! He was a jerk. *Online he was a jerk*, I corrected myself. Offline, he was doing well at beating down my defenses and being a decent companion at the same time.

Like right now, I had expected him to make fun of me to no end for bodily throwing myself at him last night, but he was quiet. And that's when I remembered another little facet of our conversation—our first time. Wrath hadn't just *had* a crush on me. If I was right, he still had a big, raging, wild crush on me as he was still envisioning our first time together. Implying there would be more sexytimes to follow. So that's why he was quiet; he was embarrassed too.

I glanced at my Fitbit to get the time and realized that I had precious few minutes to initiate a conversation about this. Preparations were already underway out back, where my colleagues and fellow book club members, Naomi Winters and Finley Granger, along with Finley's partner, Zeke Masters, were doing final checks and setup for Medieval Day, a festival I had planned for my friends and guildies.

"So," I began, floundering for the right words. "I think we should talk about last night. About what I did."

"About what you did," Wrath said evenly.

"Yeah. None of it was cool. I dragged you to a party, then left you with strangers so I could go get smashed on tequila, and then I quite literally threw myself on top of you. I don't even know what to say. I don't normally do stuff like that. Drink to that extent, I mean. I was so determined to come out of my shell this weekend and not expose you to Maxine the Walking Yawn." I knew I sounded like I had rehearsed this speech in the mirror—which I had.

"Nice recap. I was there, as you may recall. And I was the sober one, so I remember the works. You should also add that you never said a thing about staying out so late so I could have gone back to your house first to grab my bag. *That* wasn't cool, Max."

"Your bag? What, like a man purse?"

"My medical bag, okay? You have secrets, great, well so do I, and one of them is I can't be late with my medication or go without decent sleep. And because of you, I have done both. So forgive me if I'm feeling ungenerous, but I feel like a piece of roadkill right now, and it's not from booze."

I felt like someone walked over my grave. "Oh my god, Wrath. Do I need to take you to the clinic? Are you going to be okay? Any pain?"

He let out a small noise of frustration. "You don't need to baby me because I'm on a bunch of medication. I'm not in pain, I'm just a bit messed up right now, and I need to get my meds in me ASAP now that I've eaten."

"Okay. I don't know if you'll believe me, but I really am so, so sorry. I thought you would have a good time last night, so I didn't ask you if you needed anything before we went up the mountain and …"

"Stop rambling, please," Wrath interrupted. "I get it. You're sorry, you didn't know. I think it's best if we don't talk anymore right now. Can we turn on some music and get these dishes done?"

"No, go take your pills. I'll clear everything up," I replied, shaken at his words. My breakfast suddenly felt like a huge lump of guilt in the pit of my stomach.

CHAPTER ELEVEN
JONATHAN

"You know, I bet if we hit up that line of goblins just right, we could drag them into town for some mayhem."

— Wrath

By the time we had arrived back at Chez Max last night, my legs were shaking and my heart was racing. I was dizzy, and my head felt strange. This is why I'd stayed on my medications faithfully for seven years—I felt like crap when I went off them. No matter how bad the side effects were, nothing was like missing a dose. Which was why I never did.

"I saw your legs shaking," she said as I got up from the table. "Do you need something sweet to drink? Some juice? My mom gets hypoglycemic and needs sugar when that happens."

I rolled my eyes but decided to let her coddle me a little, mostly because it would make her feel better, and I cared very deeply about her and her feelings.

"It's not my blood sugar," I replied. "I need a glass of juice or water, you can do that for me if you like. I'll take my pills, rest for an hour and be fine. Does that jive with whatever you have planned for the day?"

"Absolutely. And it's not a big swan through town today; we're staying here for the afternoon. I have something planned that I think you'll like." She chewed on her lower lip, her anxious tell.

I thought about how those lips felt against mine last night and instantly banished the image. She had been drunk. It wasn't right to fantasize about the kiss that set me on fire. Max opened the door and stepped to the side so I could go ahead of her. I hustled to my bedroom, where I sat on the bed and got my med bag from the bedside table. It contained five pill bottles and a little tray I could pour them into. Two meds for severe anxiety—Max never knew how scared I'd been yesterday when I saw those horses, and she never would—and three meds for bipolar disorder.

I'd started manifesting symptoms of the disorder when I was around eighteen, after my father died and I'd started gaming. I'd have a short temper or say something nasty I didn't mean, but couldn't seem to hold it in. I was tired and could sleep for days, and then other times it was like someone had dialed me up all the way and I couldn't sleep. I'd forget to eat or shower, forget everything but what I was focused on. And I mean laser focused. I would go from feeling despondent and angry to excited and full of energy. Carrie Fisher, one of my idols—because hello, General Organa—said that living with bipolar disorder was like having your brain "go very fast or very sad. Or both. Those are fun days." And she was right.

Luckily, I was already seeing Tom, and over time he recognized my symptoms for what they were and got me in with a psychiatrist to put me on meds. At first it was a lot of trial and error, trying to find the ones that worked and didn't make me worse than the disorder on its own. And I discovered that no medication made all of the symptoms go away all the time. Then after a few years, my meds failed, and I had to start over with new ones. Unfortunately, during one such medication trial I played *Magecraft* for twelve hours straight, during which I bashed Max to every officer in our guild. I was paranoid that I'd lose her if she became an officer. Not that I *had* her at that point, but you can't logic with bipolar when it wants you to believe something is true.

I heard a gentle knock on my door and looked up to see Max standing there, a large glass of orange juice in her hand. "I didn't know what to bring you, but considering you drank about a gallon of juice this morning, I figured it was a safe bet."

"Thanks," I replied, meaning it. My anger toward her was dissipating, and I reached out as she crossed the room and placed the glass in my hands. She noticed my stash of meds but looked away without asking me anything. "Just give me an hour, okay? I need a bit of rest, and these meds need to get into my system."

She nodded and beamed at me, a beautiful smile which made me instantly grin back. I had a feeling we were going to be okay, Max and me. After all, what was another dustup between us?

* * *

An hour later on the dot, I heard a faint knocking on my door and Max's voice. "Wrath? You awake?"

"I'm up, I'm up," I grumbled. I'm not the most gracious person when being woken. "You might as well come in. I'm decent."

The door opened and she bounded in, reminiscent of a rabbit. "I hope you are ready for a day of meat, mead, and medieval revelry. It's Medieval Day in the woods behind my house!"

Ah, so that was why I'd brought along an entire foam suit of armor and had to find the world's largest duffel for this trip. The welcome email she'd sent out had given wardrobe suggestions but had been mum on what exactly we'd be doing in each outfit.

She bounced from one foot to the other. "If you brought a preferred medieval cosplay, this is the time to get it out. Otherwise, I've got you covered. It's a good thing you're tall."

I scoffed. I had created this costume specifically for this weekend because I wanted to impress Max. I wasn't particularly vain, but I knew when I was adorned in the gold painted foam armor, my black hair trailing down the red cloak behind me, I was pretty damn smokin'.

"Thanks, but I do have my own. I laid it out when I first got here so it wouldn't get crinkled in my bag and stored it under the bed. I need some time to put it on, of course."

"Yeah, of course. I'll be getting my own costume on, so I'll meet you back in the living room when you're done."

I shut the gaming room door behind her and put on a light pair of pants and a shirt, then the costume, carefully tightening the armor straps. I was by no means an expert cosplay maker, but Norman was—he killed it at Dragon Con every year—so he had essentially guided me through this whole process. Okay, he may have made most of it, but I wanted to learn, and I think together we created a kick-ass suit of armor befitting a knight.

I wondered what Max would wear. I pictured her in a long, flowy pink dress with one of those head cones with a gauzy train that women wore in old movies and let out a laugh. Not likely. Though the image was appealing. Maybe she'd take a departure from her in-game character and do something stereotypically feminine like that. After all, she had worn a dress and done up her hair to go to Genie's, so it's not like she was allergic to the idea. I wondered who would face me in the living room: a fair maiden or a bloodthirsty warrior? I attached my cape and undid my hair, giving it a few shakes to lose the shape from the hair tie. Time to find out.

I strode through the house and in the main room was greeted with the sight of a battle-hardened warrior in a suit of distressed silver. Two impressive looking swords were strapped to her back, and her hair was done up in a tight bun.

"Maximus," I said, bowing before her.

"Sir Wrath," she replied, bowing back.

"Sorry, should I have addressed you as sir?" I asked, wanting to start out on the right foot. I was by no means an expert in live-action role-playing.

"I am no knight, Sir Wrath. I take coin in trade for my services and am bound to no lord, law, or land."

I held back a grin for as long as possible, and when she saw me struggle, she broke into one too. This should be good.

We traipsed through the backyard and then followed a loose trail through the woods until we entered a clearing containing a tall red tent suspended from a tree branch. The tent was open on one side and contained a rug, cushions, and three amused looking faces: two ladies who were dressed in a manner that would not be out of place in my idea of a Renaissance Faire, and a guy dressed as Luke Skywalker, for which he got a pass because, awesome. There was a table on either side of the tent, one laden with food, the other with what looked like costumes and props. A barbeque was set up for grilling, and there was a cooler which undoubtedly contained more food for said grill.

"Sir Wrath, Knight of the Swamp Realm, please pay your respects to our visiting nobles: Lady Naomi Winters, Lady Finley Granger, and Sir Zeke Masters. The ladies and I are colleagues at the library. The gentleman is with Lady Finley."

I bowed low and with what I knew was the world's worst English accent pushing through my Southern one said, "It is both an honor and a pleasure to make your acquaintance on this fine day. Ladies, you are a sight for sore eyes. If I were a poet or bard, I would compose odes in your honor."

Finley giggled and Naomi held out a handkerchief with a thistle iron-on that I knew from movies was actually a favor. Unsure of how to respond correctly, I stepped forward, bowed down low, and accepted it. "Lady Naomi of House Winters, I shall carry your favor into battle next to my heart. May it serve as motivation and protection in my trials to come."

"That was very kind of you, Lady Naomi," Max broke in, stepping forward. "I am not as silver-tongued as Sir Wrath. Any favor I earn will have to be due to my deeds, not my charm."

"And what deeds shall we judge you on?" Finley asked, playing along.

"First shall come the hunt for the wild stag. Next, the feast, followed by a feat of strength, concluding with a sword fighting competition." Max finished with a flourish, smiling through fake blood that she had splattered in droplets over her face, probably to lend an air of authenticity to her mercenary character.

I did, however, have one question.

"Um, a hunt? What are we going hunting with? I might be from the South, but I don't know how to shoot a gun."

My mom had flatly refused me having anything to do with my daddy's hunting trips, and though it initially confused me as a child, I understood as I grew that she was protecting me. Those trips were big drunk fests, where he and his friends would gamble, screw women who weren't their wives, and if I'd been there, they'd have beaten the tar out of me for amusement's sake. My daddy called me a sissy for not wanting to learn how to shoot in our backyard, but that was also forbidden by my mom after one lesson where I got clapped over the ear every time I missed a beer can. I was seven.

"We hunt with our wits, Sir Wrath, to uncover the hiding place of, and capture, our quarry. Presenting, the wild stag!" With that, Zeke stood up and plunked a crocheted bright orange hat with antlers on his head.

The hilarity of hunting a neon-hat-wearing Luke Skywalker was not lost on me, but if Max could hold character, then so could I.

"We made it that color in case there are any real hunters out there, though there shouldn't be. But you never know," Naomi offered by way of explanation.

"And indeed, he makes a worthy specimen for testing our stalking and grappling skills. Whoever captures the hat shall be the victor. We will allow the stag a three minute head start. I suggest you run, Zeke," Max instructed.

With a salute, Zeke took off at a run into the woods.

"That will give us enough time to tie on your tabards," Finley said, standing up and approaching the prop table. There were two tabards, one red and one blue. A tabard is a piece of cloth that goes over your armor and declares your house or team. "Now you, Sir Wrath, simply must be red. It will match your cape and look fabulous with all that gold and your black hair. The blue will look great against Maximus's silver."

Once the tabards were on, Max and I squared off.

"You have the home field advantage, you know," I said, crossing my arms.

"I have the advantage when it comes to wits too," she smugly replied.

Before I could reply to her burn, Naomi had raised a Viking-esque horn and blew, announcing the start of the hunt. I turned toward the forest and ran.

* * *

MAX AND I SAT BACK-TO-BACK, panting, and dripping sweat. Laying on the ground beside us were the tattered remains of an orange hat, yarn poking in all kinds of unintended directions. Seated against a nearby tree was Zeke, who looked at us and slowly shook his head.

"I know you warned me about your competitive streak, Maxine, but I have never witnessed anything quite like that in my lifetime, and I never hope to again. That poor hat!" Zeke exclaimed, running a hand through his sweaty hair.

"Just be glad you were only tackled and de-hatted," I said. "Had you been a real stag, she might have thrown you to the ground and ripped your throat out with her teeth."

"Oh, like you were so innocent, faking out a congratulatory handshake so you could get close to the booty! I didn't destroy that hat myself," Max groused.

"So who's the winner?" Zeke asked.

"Me," we both replied at once.

"You?" Max shouted. "I chased down and captured the quarry, I got the hat. All you did was help destroy it after the fact by pretending to be chivalrous and congratulating me. I think it's clear you're down by one round. Now we can sit here and argue like a bunch of lamewads or go back to the camp for the feast."

"She's making some good points, Wrath. Sorry, man," Zeke said, wincing as he stood up.

"You okay?" Max asked, her voice full of concern.

"Yeah, I twisted my ankle a little going down. I'll ice it at the camp, and it will be fine, but I think I'm out for the games. It'll just be you two, unless the ladies want to join in."

Max snatched the destroyed hat by what once were the antlers and rose victoriously, walking over to offer an arm to Zeke. Not to be outdone—I was a knight, after all—I got up and grabbed his other arm, and the three of us hobbled back to camp.

CHAPTER TWELVE
JONATHAN

"A knight never besmirches another's honor."

— *Wrath*

As our trio wove our way through the forest, we could smell the delicious aroma of grilling meat. Saliva filled my mouth, and I realized how hungry I was, having worked up an appetite chasing Zeke and Max all over the damn mountain. I saw a flash of red up ahead and knew it was the tent, so I called out to the Finley and Naomi. "Almost there!"

"About time too," Zeke said good-naturedly. I liked this guy. He had a good sense of fun and didn't seem phased by much, unless it was a crime against a hat, apparently.

"Anyone know what's on the grill?" I asked, the smell getting closer and more appetizing with every step I took.

"Wild boar," Max said, still helping me support Zeke.

She was breathing hard but holding her own. I was proud of her, not only for organizing all this—and with "real" friends too—but for how well she kicked butt in the hunt. If anyone looked at us, they would probably say I was fit and in shape and

Maxine wasn't. But they hadn't seen how darn fast she could run, or how determined she could be.

"No, really Max, what are we having?" I laughed, thinking it cute that she was being super serious about the medieval theme.

"Wild boar," she repeated. "When I told my book club about today, Cletus insisted that we needed to lend authenticity to the event with some of his sausage. He hunts the boars and then prepares the sausages himself. They're delicious."

"It was nice of the girls—er, ladies—to get it going while we were off terrorizing Zeke," I commented, now fully engulfed by the scent.

We came down a small hill and were back at the tent, Naomi and Finley having been working like mad while we were away. The blanket was spread outside of the tent, with cushions strewn about. Various drinks were popping up out of a cooler filled with ice, and on the food table was a fruit platter, another plate piled with cheeses, and plates, forks, and knives. On the grill, manned by Finley, were the promised boar sausages, along with veggie kabobs.

"Hail, the conquering heroes!" Finley said when she saw us.

Zeke made his way over to her, pulled her into his arms, and said just loudly enough for us all to hear, "Don't ever leave me alone with the two of them again."

Max threw her head back and laughed a deep, full belly laugh that made her look radiant, all white teeth and a sheen of sweat on her forehead, her cheeks flushed.

"And who was victorious on the hunt?" Naomi asked, looking us over, her eyes pausing on the remains of the hat in Max's hands. "Ah, Maxine. I mean, Maximus. Well, I should have known from the start you were the horse to bet on."

"You have earned my favor, Maximus," Finley said as she shut the grill off. She reached up her sleeve and pulled out a handkerchief which she presented with fanfare to Max. "Now, before this food gets cold, everyone grab a plate. And I think our sacrificial stag should go first," she said, and we all murmured and hummed in agreement.

We filled our plates and sat on the ground or on a cushion and ate and drank. Max and I told tall tales from the game to the others. And you know what? That was the best damn sausage I'd ever eaten. Cletus rose in my estimation. I could respect a man who knew how to handle his meat.

* * *

"Now," Zeke began, in a serious voice, "you each stand in opposite corners and hold the watermelon over your head for as long as you possibly can."

"This is our feat of strength?" I asked Max, trying not to laugh.

"Shush," she said. "Do not question the ways of Sir Skywalker. Grab the melon and hoist it up, okay? It's not as easy as it sounds."

Feeling ridiculous, I waited for the blast of the Viking horn and then picked up my melon, holding it high above my head. And held it, and held it, and held it. All was going well—I could see the strain on Max's face—when I felt something, some kind of pressure on my leg. And then I saw Max's eyes go wide. The sensation moved up my leg, now accompanied by little chippy noises. Oh God.

"What is that?" I screeched and stood stock-still, not wanting whatever it was to chomp through my foam and decide the family jewels were worth checking out.

"It's a squirrel!" said Naomi. "How cute."

"How cute? How full of rabies! Oh God, it's climbing higher, isn't it? This thing is going to be at my face in a minute, I know it." I closed my eyes and tried to remember to breathe.

"Hold still, Wrath," came Max's voice from about ten feet away. "It doesn't look like it has a murderous face."

"Oh, thank you, Madam Squirrel Whisperer!" I shot back, the melon over my head wavering. The pressure moved again and again, higher still.

"For the … Naomi, pass me that staff from the prop table."

Now armed, Finley made her way over to me and extended the staff. She poked at the squirrel, and instead of jumping down, the thing scurried straight up onto my shoulder, hiding behind some of my long hair.

"Well, that was unexpected," she said as my eyes went as wide as dinner plates. I may have shrieked, and the melon went flying, tumbling down the hill beside us where it landed with an explosive plop. I reached up with my thankfully gloved hands and swatted at the squirrel while simultaneously trying to extract my hair from the animal's grasp. After making several passes at the astonishingly large animal, it finally gave up the game and ran back down my chest and leg, leaving me bent over and panting hard, my hands on my knees.

"Yo, Max," I said. "I think you can put down your melon now. Mine appears to have been killed by a woodland creature."

She victoriously waved the melon around like a professional wrestler holding aloft a belt they'd just won. "And that's two to nothing heading into the sword fight! Sir Wrath, would you like to concede defeat now and save yourself the humiliation of the sword or would you like to continue for honor's sake alone?"

"I'd like to continue so I can kick your ass straight up," I said, still panting. "You got lucky with that squirrel."

I'd be lying if I said the squirrel hadn't made me panicky. I needed to breathe and get something to drink, and I would be fine. And then Max would be going down. See, what Max didn't know was that I trained in kendo—Japanese sword fighting—and I knew what I was doing with a sword in my hand. So I'd lost grabbing a hat and my melon had gotten smashed to smithereens. I was going to get Max where it hurt—her battle skills.

"Let's take ten minutes and recuperate," Max suggested, grabbing a bottle of water and tossing it to me before taking one for herself. "Naomi, Finley, would either of you be interested in joining the sword fight?"

Finley chuckled. "And get in the way of your epic rivalry? No way. This is too entertaining to watch."

Naomi nodded in agreement and smiled. "Sorry, Maximus. This is all you and Sir Wrath."

We squared off at the prop table, looking over various Nerf and foam weapons, me pretending that I was considering what to choose when I knew the katana was my weapon of choice. I was going to go full-on *Kill Bill* on Max, and she'd never see it coming. After a few moments I decisively grabbed the foam katana and gave it a few thrusts through the air. Not bad. I could do this. Max picked up a foam claymore—otherwise known as a Scottish great sword—and we met in the clearing where the feat of strength had taken place. Naomi dropped a favor, and when the handkerchief hit the ground, it was on like Donkey Kong.

We paced around each other, like a pair of great cats moving in for a throw down. I could practically hear "Eye of the Tiger"—oh wait, that's because Zeke was playing it from his cellphone, holding it up into the air on what had to be max volume.

Quick as lightning, she thrust, and just as quickly, I dodged. I returned her thrust with one of my own, which she didn't parry. I tapped her arm with the sword, and she didn't fail to sell a look of pained annoyance.

"That's one point for Sir Wrath!" Zeke called, still holding his cell aloft. "First to three wins!"

We walked around in a semicircle until I saw my opening and took it. With two fast slashes, I scored two hits on Max's breastplate before she even began to block. And just like that, it was over. I had lost the tournament, but I had regained my pride. Zeke whooped and the ladies clapped heartily while I extended a hand to Max.

She took it, then simply said, "Dude. You've been holding out on me. I expect a lesson before you leave Tennessee."

"Sure thing. And consider that retribution for all the times you've kicked my butt in-game in duels."

"Well, I don't know if that makes up for *all* the times," she said playfully, smiling. "But we can say with certainty that keyboard warrior skills don't easily translate into real warrior skills, like you seem to have. What was that, kendo?"

I nodded. "Yup, I have a thing for Japanese swords. It may have started because of *Rurouni Kenshin*, but it became real damn fast. I needed a way to both exercise and become more mindful. Kendo offered both."

"I cannot believe I'm in the woods, covered in foam armor, holding fake swords and discussing mindfulness with you, of all people." She laughed. "Just when you think, after ten years, you know someone. What kept you from bragging about doing real sword fighting in the guild chat?"

I shrugged. "It wasn't an omission by design. It felt … private. Like how I wouldn't share stuff about my mom, or my sisters, or what I do for a living."

"But you've shared all those things with me," she interjected, cocking her head to one side.

"You know you're different," I said softly, and reached out to tuck a bunch of errant strands of hair behind her ear.

"That crush you had on me," she started, then seemed to change her mind. "Never mind. Topic for another time. Let's get stuff cleaned up so we can head home. I don't know about you, but I'm still tired and sore from chasing Zeke all over the Appalachian mountain chain."

"Right?" I said, snickering. "That man can run."

"It wasn't even running at times, I swear he was galloping."

We both laughed. Sharing a laugh with Max was quickly becoming one of my favorite things in the entire universe, along with building things, my family, and *Grey's Anatomy.*

CHAPTER THIRTEEN
MAXINE

"I hate sounding like a drill sergeant, but you call that a line? Beelzebub will eat us
for breakfast if you don't get in formation, stat."

— *Maximus_Damage*

After flipping a coin to see who went first, Wrath and I had showered and were about to dig into amazing smelling fried chicken that Naomi had graciously picked up from Genie's. We ate in relative silence, but this time it was comfortable, both of us so tired, and the food too good. It was after we'd loaded up the dishwasher and I put on the coffee pot that we started making more than errant small talk.

"So, I have a theory," I began. "Everyone who games as much as we do—the hard-core gamers—is running away or hiding from something. Otherwise, they wouldn't be living in the game, they'd be out living." I poured the coffee, loaded the cups on a tray, and headed toward the sofa. It wasn't cold enough to start up the fireplace, but I did have the electric heat up, and it was warm and cozy in my little cottage.

Wrath grabbed a seat and replied, "Hey, I take offense to that. I think that memories and relationships we forge in-game can be as important and real as those we make offline. Remember that time I was trailing you in the Misty Forest and we found the

Wild Hunt? We joined forces to prove that we were worthy of leading it, and we won! We flew through the night sky on horses made of blood and stardust and it was amazing." His eyes were lit up like a kid's, and I couldn't help but be caught up in his enthusiasm.

"It really was an epic night," I agreed, grinning.

"And we didn't argue once. You kept raving about how much fun you were having. That was a good memory, and there are dozens more. When we defeated Meglathor and you won the Helmet of Healing? What about when we had the last guild party and I gave away all the armor dyes from my special reserve? People were stoked to get those, like they got a genuine gift. Remember the fun? Why does it have to be all bad with us, Max?"

"I don't remember you doing that at the party," I said quietly, picking up my coffee mug. "I think I might have a bit of a blind spot when it comes to you, Wrath."

He threw his arms up in the air. "As I've been trying to tell you! You know, I was having a tough time when I first met you, and I think you're still holding a lot of that against me."

"And what about more recent transgressions? Five years ago, when I went up for officer. You said you weren't yourself when you tried to sabotage me and then refused to explain further. Why? Who were you?" I turned to face him on the couch, as though he would have trouble speaking loud enough to be heard.

"Let's say this crazy theory of yours is correct, and we're all running from something. Then, at the time, I was running from myself, hiding in the game. Hiding from my diagnosis. I'm … fuck, Max. I can't—"

He started gulping for air. I was alarmed until I saw him close his eyes and slow down his breathing.

I reached out and clasped his arm. "Hey, I'm here. It's okay."

"No, it's not okay, because it's you, and I don't want to look weak in front of you!" he almost shouted.

I shook my head. "Wrath, I don't care about things like that. You're not weak for being sick. Please, tell me what's going on. I'm freaking out here. Is it cancer?"

He laughed rather morbidly. "No, it's not cancer. I have bipolar disorder, Max."

I chewed on that for a minute and then squeezed his arm. "You thought I would see you as weak because of a disorder in your brain that you have absolutely no control over? What kind of person would that make me?"

"It's not something I'm exactly proud of. I don't like being out of control, saying and doing things that I later on regret. Before I was diagnosed, it got bad. And then, over the years as I've had to try new medications, there've been times I've felt plain crazy."

I thought about what this must feel like, to not be in full control of one's thoughts or actions, and to be burdened with the knowledge that this was a lifelong condition. I remembered things Wrath had done in-game that had hurt or irritated me and felt I had to view them in a different light.

"You don't need to use that word," I said. "Crazy, I mean. You have a complex disorder, you're not the—"

"Complex disorder? What do you know about it? I mean, how are you cool with this and not freaking out?" His hands moved erratically as he spoke, and he put one hand in his hair, giving it a pull.

I paused and pursed my lips, then rubbed my temple with my free hand. "My father. He died in a car accident when I was a teenager. He was a sheriff's deputy out on patrol in bad weather and his car went off the road. My mother, she never got over it, convinced it was her fault that she let him go out in the storm. Never mind that it was his job. She's become agoraphobic, you know, a shut-in?" He nodded. "I do her chores for her outside the house, like running to the grocery once a week, and I spend time with her when I'm not working or gaming. I've suggested she play *Magecraft* as a way to meet new people. My point is, she's suffering with this condition, but it is in no way her fault. I see how she tries, and I'm so proud of her for that. Though most times, I miss the woman she was, the family we were. But listen to me, making this about me when we ought to be focusing on you."

I shook my head as if I could shake off the feelings bubbling up about my parents. I couldn't quite believe I was sharing all this with Wrath. I supposed fair was fair. He'd been open with me, so I could be open with him and let him into the small circle of people I talked about this with.

"No, no. It's fine, trust me," Wrath said. "It helps to know you have a bit of knowledge or history with this stuff, but I wish it weren't so … sad. I'm sorry, Max. It sounds like we both have some difficulties when it comes to our parents." He picked up his coffee mug and took a long drink before placing it down on the table again.

"My mom always relied on Jesus, but after Dad was gone, she filled the gap he left with hypochondria. She's tried therapy, and swears she'll go back to it one day, but for the past few years her anxiety about illness just drives her up the wall and into finding relief out of pill bottles. Not that I'm one to talk. I live out of enough of them myself." He looked down and fiddled with a throw pillow seemingly unable to keep his hands still while we were having a heavy conversation.

My heart was beating faster in my chest. To avoid panicking, I took a deep breath in through my nose and let it out slowly through my mouth—a technique my old therapist had taught me. The depth of this exchange was unexpected on the heels of what had been an amazing day. I did have more questions though, so I steamed ahead.

"Are you ashamed of that? You know that if you were diabetic, you'd take your insulin as prescribed with no shame. No fear of telling others. So what's the difference with taking medication for bipolar disorder? It's a mental illness, yes, but it's still an illness. It's still something wrong with your physiology. And medications can help that, right?"

Wrath leaned back, his hands folded on his lap, and let out a huge puff of air, tension radiating from him. "You sound like my therapist, Tom. And yes, they can and do help. Some days they seem to help more than others. I still experience symptoms, they just aren't as strong. Some days I'm completely 'normal,' whatever that means. And some days I'm not myself at all, and that's when my meds might be failing, I might need a new dose or a new drug altogether. Those times are always a bit chaotic and my behavior reflects that. I say tons of shit I don't mean during those flare-ups."

I considered that. I know I easily got emotional when I played *Magecraft*, and there were times I said tons of things I didn't mean without having the reason of an illness driving me to it. Wrath turned toward me and leaned forward, reaching out and touching my arm. "Look, I'm not blaming being an asshole on my condition, but I am saying that there are times when I've regretted so hard what I did, but haven't had the guts to say why I did it to begin with, so I've said nothing. Going behind your back when you were up for guild officer and trash-talking you was one of those times. I'm sorry I did that."

"I accept your apology. Though, given the explanation, the apology is unnecessary. I know I come off as tough in the game, Wrath, but I'm not actually heartless."

"I see that," he answered softly. The air felt thick between us. I wasn't sure what was going on, just that I needed to stop it. We were having a pretty intense moment, sharing all of that, and I had reached my peak. Anything more, and it would be too much.

"So, who's ready for movie night?" I asked, forcing myself to sound upbeat as I got up off the couch. "I need more coffee before we start. Do you?"

I was babbling, and I knew it. Why was I so nervous? *It's because Wrath was acting like he was going to kiss you*, a voice in my head murmured.

"You know, when you said movie night, I kind of pictured a theatre, not your cottage," Wrath teased.

"A theatre?" I mock-gasped. "Where do you think you are, Nashville? One-horse town, remember," I teased back.

I had arranged a viewing of the just-released Blu-ray of *League of Magecraft: The Movie*. By arranging a viewing, I meant that I bought the movie from Amazon and picked up some microwavable popcorn, but it was the thought that counted, not the glamour.

"Drink your coffee, I'm going to make popcorn. Be back in two minutes, thirty seconds."

I controlled my speed as I made my way to the kitchen, not wanting to appear too eager to get away from Wrath. As I made the popcorn, I kept my back to the living room and thought about the moment that could have been a kiss. Did I want Wrath to kiss me now that I was sober? I'd certainly wanted it badly enough on a tequila binge. Wrath was gorgeous, yes, and that would have been good enough for me while I was a teenager or in my early twenties. But that wasn't really a factor in my decision-making now. It was his mind and heart I had to be attracted to, to want that kind of contact.

I thought about Wrath's heart and mind. What did I really know about him? I knew he liked me romantically. I also knew his chivalrous streak wasn't entirely put-on for the game. He had a good sense of fun, and I could appreciate his humor, when I wasn't bearing the brunt of it. Okay, even sometimes when I was.

As an entrepreneur, he had to be a self-starter and hard worker, which I respected. And Wrath had a point about us having good memories together in *Magecraft*; it wasn't all squabbling and snarky comments. Kindness to my cats had also endeared him to me, and to top it all off, he trusted me with his medical condition even though there is so much stigma attached to mental illness. Explanations for his erratic behavior made sense in light of what he had been going through, and though Wrath had said he wasn't going to blame being an asshole entirely on bipolar disorder, I knew that a lot of his more dickish actions were probably the illness at work. And he made me feel beautiful, like I never wanted to put on an ankle-length skirt and cardigan two sizes too big again. All in all, there was a lot of good in there. Was it enough to reform someone who had been akin to a Sith in my eyes?

The answer was as clear as it was disturbing. Yes. Absolutely. Wrath was right. Fake It Till You Make It: Friendship Edition had clearly worked because I would call Wrath my friend now. The microwave beeped, and I poured the popcorn into two bowls, bringing the saltshaker with me into the living room and popping both bowls down on the coffee table. I went back to get some Cokes and turned down the lights.

"I don't mean to be a downer here, Max, but don't you generally need a television to watch a movie?" Wrath asked, swiveling his head around the room.

I grinned and picked up one of the remote controls from the basket on the coffee table. A push of a button later, a ceiling panel retracted, and down came a projection screen. With another remote, I pointed up at the projector, and we were in business.

"I splurged last year on Black Friday," I offered by way of explanation. "Librarians aren't exactly rolling in it, but getting a local handyman to do the install in exchange for a few home-cooked meals, and having a super deal on the parts meant it wasn't as expensive as I thought it would be. And I love movies so much, I figured why not have my own cozy home theatre right here?"

"It's cool, Max, honest. And I'm so excited to finally see this movie. It only took them an age to get it made. The trailers looked awesome. I'm gonna love it, I know it."

* * *

"HOLY SHIT, this is the worst movie I have ever seen." Wrath's voice came muffled from behind a cushion where he was currently hiding his eyes after hitting himself on the head with it a few times. "Who is this guy talking again?"

"I think we agreed to call him white dude number four with longish brown hair and a beard. He's talking to incredibly poorly rendered CGI troll number two." I crammed some more popcorn down my mouth and tried to follow the obtuse dialogue and plot with holes you could drive a monster truck through.

"Nope, that's troll number three. Remember, two doesn't have the ears hanging around his neck."

"Hey, you're right. Wait, so where are generic white dudes one through three again?" I asked, confused.

"I don't know! Argh, this movie is awful, Max. Do you have anything else we could put on?"

I did, but I was a little bit nervous about bringing it out. It had been out for quite a while now, but I only ordered it along with my new coaster-slash-*Magecraft* movie, and I wanted to see it so freakin' bad. Okay, time to put on my big girl panties, take charge, and show him what I wanted. I turned off the film, which we had only seen all of thirty minutes of, and then opened a drawer on my bookcase where I stored my Blu-rays. I pulled out the one I wanted and turned, holding it out to face the judgment of Wrath.

"*Detective Pikachu*?! Are you serious? Why aren't we watching this right the hell *now*? You honestly made me suffer through a half hour of that rubbish when you had this probable masterpiece sitting in a drawer?" he exclaimed.

"Oh, come on, Wrath. I know you've made fun of Pokémon in guild chat in the past. Why would I think you'd want to watch this with me?" I asked.

"I only made fun of it to throw people off the scent. The scent of my love for Pokémon."

"Well, lucky for us, it is a passion we share. And now it's a secret we share because *no one* is going to know about how much I love it either, right? Now shush, I'm going to start the movie." I grinned as I popped the disc into the player and settled back into the sofa, sitting a touch closer to Wrath than I had been before.

CHAPTER FOURTEEN
MAXINE

"Being a team means we pull together, not apart."

— *Maximus_Damage*

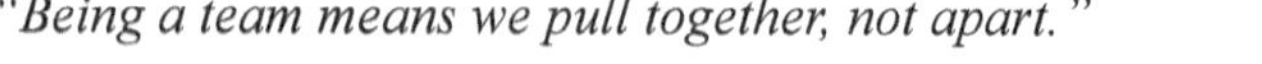

By the time the credits rolled, my feet were in Wrath's lap, and he had begun firmly rubbing the right, after finishing the left. I had been wincing and trying to rub my own feet while sitting through the last half of the movie, and Wrath had just leaned over, picked up my feet, and started rubbing away. I'd never had a foot massage, so nothing could have prepared me for how good it felt. And how strangely erotic. Strange because I wouldn't have thought my swollen, sore feet from yesterday's hike and today's run could be sexy in any capacity.

I shut the projector and Blu-ray player down and put the screen back up with the remotes while Wrath lifted my feet and put them back on the floor. Wrath then did the strangest thing. He scooted over on the couch until he was right next to me and brought his hand up to cup my cheek, his other hand tucking my hair behind my ear, like he'd done earlier.

"Would it unnerve you if I told you that seeing the excited expressions on your face while you watched Pokémon turned me on? That you looked so beautiful, it was all I could do to wait until the end to kiss you?"

His eyes shone in earnest, and I saw a deep longing in them.

"Unnerve me? No," I replied, my heart beating faster and my pulse pounding in my ears.

Did I want this? He stroked my cheek for another moment, then leaned in, pressing his lips to mine. Our mouths fused together, and it was so good, so much better than last time when I must have tasted of tequila and desperation. Now nothing was fogging my brain, and I could appreciate the strength of his hands, one on my back and the other in my hair; the soft groans he made as he took control and kissed the hell out of me.

He held onto me, and after a bit of jostling where he almost fell off the couch—it wasn't the widest sofa—he changed our positions so I was underneath him, his one hand still in my hair, the other supporting the bulk of his weight. His incredible scent was all around me, and he tasted like popcorn and salt. I supposed I did too. I followed his lead and got my hand into his hair. I carefully undid the ponytail tie so his hair fell down around me like a shiny black curtain. It was silky and smooth in my hand, and I reciprocated the little tugs he was giving to my hair, increasing the pleasure by adding a tiny bit of pain.

I realized about thirty seconds into this position that he was purposefully holding his lower body up from mine, and honestly? Screw that noise. I reached down with my free hand and pushed on his lower back at the same time I thrust my hips upward. Our pelvic regions met in a delightful explosion of sensation, his hardness only a few layers of clothing away from meeting my wetness.

"Max, wait," he said, gasping for air. "How far do you want to take this? I want to know while you are still clearheaded and not blinded by your insane lust for me."

I laughed, and then hit him in the shoulder. "If anyone is lust-crazed around here, it's you. I don't know how those pants haven't split a seam yet."

"I'm serious, Max, how far? What do you want from me?" His voice shook, and he leaned back down and nibbled on my neck for a second before getting a hold of himself and backing off again.

I considered him and our situation. This was his last night here; he flew to Florida tomorrow late afternoon. If I wanted to be with Wrath, to see what we could be like, then this was my perfect opportunity.

"Everything," I whispered into his ear. "I want everything from you." I found myself meaning it more than I'd meant anything in a long time.

I gently pushed his shoulders backward, and he got up off me enough for me to sit up. I leaned in and kissed him, then stood and extended a hand, hoping like hell he would take it.

He reached up and put his hand in mine, and it felt like fate. And sweat. He was all clammy, probably from nerves. Well, I wasn't going to be nervous. I was going to enjoy this to the fullest possible extent. It had been ten years, and it suddenly felt like ten years too long. I led him to my bedroom, sparing a moment to be thankful I'd picked up the laundry and made the bed fresh that morning. As we crossed the threshold to the room, it hit me like a frying pan to the head—sex and Wrath. I was going to have sex with *Wrath*. My enemy for a decade, my most loathed opponent, had wormed his way into my affections and was about to get into my panties. Oh gods, did I choose a nice pair today, or did I toss on granny panties? My thoughts swiftly changed direction to relief when I remembered putting on the cute blue pair with the lace edging.

"Max? You still okay?" Wrath asked. I stopped on our way to the bed and turned, shaking my head slightly.

"It's just, I don't know if I can think of you as Wrath anymore. You've been Wrath to me for ten years, and in that time, I've hated you, I've been *mean* to you. And trust me, you were no prince to me all the time either. But looking back, I see you differently now. I see all the times you wanted my attention and had to fight for scraps of it. I see how we fell into patterns of you getting my attention when you did something to annoy me, so you annoyed me a lot. I can see how I stopped giving you chances to explain yourself back when you were still a teenager and never let you grow into a man in my eyes. And I never once asked you what was going on in your personal life when you behaved erratically. Instead I assumed you were being extra-jerky that day. So I don't want to be Maximus_Damage and Wrath anymore. Not out of game. Not even in-game, between us. I want to be Max and Jonathan. Maxine, if you prefer."

He chuckled. "In case you haven't noticed, I've been calling you Max since I arrived here. And yeah, it wound up being a shortened version of both your names, but I was prepared to call you by anything you wanted. You've never been just *the* Maximus_-Damage to me. You've always been Max, the person I've been crazy about."

I leaned up and kissed his cheek, and he was right—it was kissably smooth. I made a mental note to buy some Noxzema.

"Thank you, Jonathan," I whispered, and resumed our walk to my bed.

When we reached the king-sized monstrosity, Jonathan stopped and stared. The bed took up almost the entire room, and I laughed at what he must be thinking.

"I like to roll around," I said defensively. "Trust me, if you decide you want to stay in here tonight, you'll be glad you can get far away from me. I'm also a kicker in my sleep."

"Duly noted," Jonathan said dryly. "Though, if I have my way, we won't be doing much sleeping tonight."

I burst out laughing. "Dude, that was so cheesy. You're a closet soap opera fan, admit it."

"Is *Grey's Anatomy* close enough?" he asked, also laughing. "Look, my moves might be lame, but they're what I've got to work with. I don't think I have as much experience as you, to be honest, and I'm a little nervous."

"Trust me, you have nothing to be nervous about," I said, looking him over from head to toe.

I looked down at my own body, and a bloom rose to my cheeks. Why was I suddenly feeling anxious about my body? That wasn't sexy. Jonathan may be the most perfect male I have ever seen outside of an underwear ad, but I was usually confident in my curves and swerves, at least in my own head. I know I hid them in frumpy clothes, but that had been an attempt to hide me as a whole, not my size. And there were the scars on my side. No one outside of a medical professional or my mom had seen those. Only momentarily thrown, I decided to screw anxious. I dropped his hand and grabbed the bottom of my top, pulling it up over my head and tossing it to the floor. He made a noise of appreciation as I went for my pants and undid the top button.

"What are you staring at? Get busy, strip!" I said to him as I took one leg out of my pants, almost fell over, then recovered by catching myself on the bed. I gracelessly got both legs out of the pants and sat on the bed in my bra and panties, crossing my legs and waiting for him to join me.

He stared at me, mouth slightly agape, and I saw his chest rise and fall quickly. Oh my god, was he having a heart attack? I leapt to my feet.

"Jonathan, hey," I said, taking his head in my hands. "Look at me. Everything is fine, okay? I'm going to take your pulse and check your blood pressure if that's alright with you. I have a home monitor. Can you sit on the bed for me?"

He nodded, sat down, and then said, "I'm not having a heart attack. You don't have to give me a medical exam, though I can see the appeal under a role-playing scenario. I was just … thrown. By seeing how gorgeous you are, and that you were sitting there, waiting for *me*, after all of these years. Max, I finally got you, and so far it's been better than my wildest—okay, maybe not my wildest—dreams. I think I started to have a bit of an anxiety attack. But I'm … I'm feeling much better. You have magic hands." He lifted my right hand to his mouth and kissed my palm.

"Let's get you undressed, and we can see how magic they are," I teased, knowing the cheese factor would make him laugh.

It did. I peeled his shirt off him and ran my hands over his tattoos, having been itching to get my hands on them since I first saw them. I then traced my fingers down his chest and over his abs, settling on the hard front of his pants.

"Pants off. Now," I said almost breathlessly. I scooted up the bed to the pillows so I could lie down, and he quickly followed, undoing his pants as he shimmied up the bed.

"Oh god, Max. You're so beautiful like this, sweetheart. May I touch you? Taste you?"

He reached out to stroke my face, and I felt tears pricking at my eyes. I hadn't felt like this in a very long time, cherished, like I was something precious.

"Yes," I whispered. "Please, Jonathan. I'm so ready."

That smirk could not stay off his face as he reached down and yanked on my underwear, pulling them to one side so he could touch me. His finger found its way to my slick folds and he moved his finger up and down over my slit, making me dig my ankles into the mattress. He pushed one finger, then two, inside me, and I moved against the sensation, encouraging him with soft moans and the steady rocking of my hips. With his other hand, he pushed my bra up, freeing my breasts, and latched his mouth onto my nipple, sucking and biting until I was rocking my hips aggressively, impaling myself on his fingers and crying out at the sensation in my breast. It was too much, it was perfection, it was everything. It was us. And as I climaxed, I breathed out "Kiss me," and he complied. I moaned my pleasure into his mouth and felt so free of my inhibitions that I never wanted this thing between us to stop.

He gently pulled his fingers from me, and I gasped when he put them in his mouth to suck off my juices. He then helped me take off my bra, slipped me out of my panties, and pulled down his boxer briefs.

"Were you serious last night about having condoms? Because I don't have any." He sounded like he was hoping to the gods themselves my answer would be yes.

"Yeah, I have a few in my purse, but there are more in there, in the bedside table drawer. They're not expired, I keep them up to date. I guess hope springs eternal and all that."

I closed my eyes to collect myself. I felt him move around and heard the opening of the drawer, then the crinkle of the foil packet. By the time he rolled back over to me and I felt his hardness poking into my hip, I was ready for round two. He leaned in and kissed me on the mouth gently at first, then with a possessive passion that had me panting hard again. I pulled on his shoulders and, getting the message, he climbed on top of me and reached his hand down, positioning himself at my center. We locked eyes and he pushed forward, his girth hurting a bit but definitely in a good way. When he was sheathed all the way inside, I let out a sigh of contentment, and he nuzzled into my neck.

"God, it's never felt like this, Max. You feel so damn good. I never want to be anywhere else."

I hummed in agreement, encouraging him to move with a slight push of my hips. He started thrusting in earnest. We moved together like we'd been doing this for years, with only a few missteps along the way. My breathing went ragged as he pushed me to higher states of sensation, and I hoped I was making it as good for him. I let out a cry as my second orgasm ripped through me, and he quickly followed, emptying into the condom, and sucking my breast.

I was breathing heavily and felt like a limp rag. Jonathan collapsed on top of me, then rolled off as I groaned under his weight. He put his arms around me from the side and mouthed at my neck, his breath coming in short pants.

"Max, that was …"

"I know," I said, snuggling into his side.

"Before we get too comfortable, I'll be right back," he said and rose up off the bed, heading to the bathroom. I heard the taps run. He came back with a facecloth and wiped at my core where the lubrication from both myself and the condom had made a bit of a mess. I was touched by his consideration, and a scant minute later, he was back in bed with me, and wrapping me up in his arms.

"If we don't get under these covers, we're going to get cold, fast," I said sleepily. He peeled back the blankets on the other half of the bed and scooted me over, tucking me in. He then climbed in and resumed holding me. All cuddled up in his warmth, I forgot how much I liked to roll in my sleep; I forgot I was a kicker. All I wanted was to fall asleep like this. So I did.

CHAPTER FIFTEEN
JONATHAN

"E*verything,*" she'd whispered in my ear. "*I want everything from you.*"

I woke with the sweet memory of those words echoing in my brain, making me so happy I wanted to burst into spontaneous interpretive dance. Now, I know those words could have a broad meaning. She could have meant she wanted sex. However, in my mind, I was already picturing Lego-building super babies with excellent hand-eye coordination with my black hair and her greenish eyes. It wasn't impossible, right? That we sleep together and she has an epiphany that we belong together, and romantic music swells in the background as we kiss in front of a water fountain as strangers break into song?

Maybe I was getting ahead of myself, just a little bit.

But what if I wasn't? This could be a whole new beginning for Max and me. I moved as stealthily as I could so as not to wake her. The time on her alarm clock read 7:05 a.m. Perfect. I'd have time to get breakfast made before she woke. I hoped she liked

French toast because it was one of the few breakfast foods I could manage on my own that looked and tasted awesome.

I decided to skip a shower for now, hoping she might invite me for one with her later. After putting on the coffee. I started the bacon I found in her fridge, and mixed up the eggs with nutmeg, cinnamon, and a teeny splash of vanilla. Then the fun part, dipping the bread and frying it up. The house was smelling heavenly when I heard footsteps, and an appreciative noise, behind me. I turned, and there stood Max, wearing my T-shirt, little red panties, and nothing else. My fears that she was going to freak the hell out this morning in light of what we'd done evaporated as she made her way over to me in what I can honestly call an unsexy zombie-esque sleepy lurch, wrapped her arms around my torso, and put her head on my shoulder.

"Mmm, this all looks and smells fantastic. And you even put on the coffee pot. I think I love you right now," she said, pulling back and kissing me quickly on the lips.

She opened the cupboard where she kept the mugs and asked me if I wanted a cup. I nodded, unable to speak. How could she be so cavalier with those words? I know she was just using an expression, she didn't mean she was in love with me, but I was in love with her, dammit. Though she didn't know that, did she? Because I'd been too much of a wimp to tell her. She knew about my "crush," but that was it. I think I had a new mission today—tell Max the rest of the truth, whether it would freak her out or not.

I finished preparing breakfast while she drank her coffee and viewed me appreciatively, distracting me now and then by kissing my back, my shoulder blades, my side. And that tickled too, darn it. But she was so playful, so sweet, how could I be mad? I was used to dealing with her while she was practically a harpy in-game.

"Did they hurt? Your tats, I mean," she asked out of nowhere as I plated up our food.

"Of course they hurt. It's a needle on a gun that shoots ink into your skin. It's not fun, unless you've got a pain kink." I carried our plates to the small table, and she carried our mugs. "Why do you ask?"

"Because I feel like doing something I've always wanted to do but never had the courage for," she replied. "I've wanted a tattoo since I was a teenager, but I was always scared of the needle. But now I see your ink and how beautiful and badass it is, and I want that. I've wanted a sleeve on my left arm forever. And holy shit, this is delicious." The last line was spoken around a mouthful of French toast.

I grinned at her and replied, "It better be. That's my mother's recipe."

We ate in a comfortable silence for a few moments.

"Are you sure about a whole sleeve? That's a lot to commit to. Why not start somewhere like high up on your arm and get one part of the sleeve, one image, that means a lot to you. And if you can handle the pain and like that end result, keep going. But don't, and I mean don't, pick your artist on a whim. You've got to get someone who knows what they are doing. Most artists will have an online portfolio for you to check out. Do your homework."

"Aye, aye, captain," she said with a salute. "I wouldn't feel entirely comfortable getting it done without you seeing the person's portfolio anyway. You'd be able to judge better than me if they have what it takes to make something that looks as nice as yours. So, what's something you've always wanted to do but never got around to or had the courage to do?"

Tell you I love you, I thought. But another answer slipped out of my mouth. "Get a dog," I replied.

"A dog? What's so hard about that? I can see you with a golden retriever puppy or a German shepherd puppy, and in my mind it's adorable."

"My living situation wouldn't allow for it," I answered. It felt natural to be open about my personal life now. "I know I already told you I live with my mom. She's not well, mentally. She has hypochondria, remember? That causes her issues like exhaustion, irritability, anxiety. She wouldn't handle having a dog in the trailer too well. That's the other part—the trailer. It's smallish, and a puppy would tear through that place and get into everything. And I don't want to leave the dog chained up outside all the time. So it wouldn't be fair to the dog for me to adopt it. I'd be taking it into a home where it wasn't wanted by everyone living there, and also possibly condemning it to a lonely life outside."

She seemed to think on that and nodded. "Yeah, I get all that. I think I might have a dog, if I didn't game so much. I work five days a week, and I either read or game pretty hardcore when I'm not working. And I have to take care of my mom too, to an extent. Getting her whatever she needs from the grocery or pharmacy, and spending time with her. Did I tell you she's got agoraphobia?" I nodded, and she continued, "I think it's a matter of priorities for me. Do I want to spend my time walking a dog and playing with it, or sitting in front of my computer talking with my friends and getting grouched at by my cats?"

"Do you think they're really our friends, though? I've been struggling with that question for the last few days. I mean, I thought *we* were friends, ever since *Guilds of the Ages*. And it turns out you hated me all that time. Who else might secretly hate either of us?"

She lowered her fork and reached out, taking my hand in hers. "You can't think like that, Jonathan. People in the guild love you. You're funny, you're a leader, you suck at duels, but you are generous with your time and materials. You give a lot to the guild, and people appreciate that. There was talk last year of making you an officer."

I reeled. "I call bullshit," I blurted out, tact having fled me. "Why would the top guild in North America want me for an officer?"

"You know how much you piss me off when you try to tweak my strategies during the actual fights or prefight planning, in front of everyone in the damn raid party?"

I flushed. "Yes," I mumbled.

"Well, the truth is, your ideas are always, or almost always, good ones. Sometimes they're brilliant. If we had you planning the strategy with me beforehand in private, we could present a united front to the guild and not confuse the members with last-minute changes, or piss everyone off by having yet another public argument. The only thing holding you back in joining the leadership of the guild is your attitude. You change up your behavior a bit, and I guarantee you'll be called up to join us. Think on it, okay?"

I nodded. "Now, whatever are we going to do until my plane leaves?" I asked, trying to sound seductive and sexy. I'm sure my words came across as creepy and lame because she grinned wide and put her hand over her mouth.

"The original itinerary for today was gaming—tabletop games, I mean—at the gaming shop in town. I was going to host it here, but since there's only two of us, I suggest we head down there, grab a table, and see if anyone wants to join us."

"That does sound like a possibility," I returned. "But I have a better idea of who could use our company today."

* * *

After a glorious shower where she had gotten down on her knees for me underneath the hot water and I'd made love to her standing up against the shower stall, it was a wonder I could even think, let alone execute a plan. We tumbled into the bed together, still partly wet, to kiss and roll around, touching every inch of each other. We spent about a half hour like that, until I said only partly in jest that if we didn't get up both of our hair would be ruined, and I wanted to look my best for where we were going. Max reluctantly agreed, and let me have first crack at the hair dryer, while she picked out some appropriate games.

When I emerged from the bathroom and made it into the gaming room to get dressed, I saw Scrabble, Yahtzee, Cribbage, and Trivial Pursuit laid out on the bed. Perfect. I put on my nicest clothes that I had brought with me and gathered up the games, meeting Max in the main room. Her hair was up in an attractive bun today, and she was wearing a black skirt with lots of that poofy ballerina stuff. She had on a tight red cardigan and bright red lipstick to match. The overall effect was one that made me want to put down the games, throw her over my shoulder and drag her back to the bedroom, but we had a plan, and I was determined we made it happen.

"Did you call her?" I asked, leaning down to give Max a peck on the cheek so as not to ruin her lipstick.

"And trigger her anxiety? No way. If I give her a heads-up that we're coming, she'll start cleaning the house like mad, try to bake, and will fuss forever about her wardrobe. Trust me, a straight-up ambush is best for her."

"Well, she's your mother, you would know." I smiled.

This was it, my grand plan. I wanted to meet Max's mom. I wanted to win her over, show her the type of man I was, and that I was very serious about her daughter and had every intention of doing something about it. And if we stopped at the Donner Bakery to pick up what Max assured me was the best banana cake in the state, well, I knew sweetening my suit couldn't hurt.

* * *

STILES LURCHED to a halt in front of a nice-looking two-story house on the other side of town. I was momentarily shaken by the size of the house Maxine had grown up in, wondering what had compelled her to leave. She could probably save a bundle on mortgage payments and other bills if she had stayed home with her mother. But everyone wasn't like me and my big sister. Some people, like some flowers, needed room to grow and blossom. You plant them too close, and they withered and died.

We climbed up the front steps. Max knocked, then rang the bell and went ahead and used a key on her chain. "Momma? It's me, Max."

"Maxie!" A voice came shouting back. "I wasn't expecting you until Tuesday! Let me get my robe and—"

"Momma, I brought a friend with me, a man. Is that okay?"

Silence.

"Maxie, you brought a gentleman caller? I ought to have expected this. Mrs. Howser stopped by with a casserole and said she saw a young man staying at your house, and Mrs. Potter has been telling anyone who would listen about your new *suitor*." Then I heard a familiar giggle. "Bring him in. I'll get dressed."

Max smiled wide at me and managed to give me a thumbs-up while holding the banana cake. I had the stack of board games in my arms. We set down our things to remove our coats and shoes, and then headed down a long hall to the kitchen. Max unboxed the banana cake and put on the teakettle while I put the board games down in the middle of the kitchen table and looked around. On one wall in the hallway, visible from the kitchen, there was a large cross-stitch sampler that read, *In this home, we believe magic is real, the answer is 42, Frodo lives, the Doctor is in their T.A.R.D.I.S., the cake is a lie, and the Force will be with us, always.* I grinned wide and was about to ask Max about it when her mom entered the room. She looked me up and down, then turned to Max.

"Momma," she began, "this is one of my oldest friends. His name is Jonathan, and he lives in Florida. Jonathan, this is my mother, Rose."

I extended a hand toward the short, dark haired woman and she took it. I slowly made to kiss the back of her hand, giving her plenty of time to yank her hand away or smack me if she didn't want me to. Instead, she smiled wide and giggled a little, that exact same giggle Max had given our waitress the other night.

"It's nice to meet you, ma'am," I said, tipping my head.

"Oh boy, here we go," Max said, smacking me on the arm.

"Maxie! What on earth?" her mother asked, sounding scandalized.

"This is where he oozes charm and magically wins you over, and that's before I even tell you he bought the banana cake."

"There's banana cake?" she asked with interest.

"Yes, Momma," Max replied, smiling a bit.

"You may call me Rose," Max's mom said to me, smiling wide. "But don't think you've bought your way into my affections! I'm very particular over who I like, but I get feelings about some people. You, I like."

I wanted to do a victory lap around the room. "Thank you, Rose. I like you too. And I hope you're prepared to get a bit competitive because we've brought games as well."

"So let me get this straight, Maxie. You brought home my favorite cake, a handsome man, and games. Is it my birthday?"

"Nope, we wanted to include you in our weekend," Max said. "It was Jonathan's idea. He's heading back to Florida today, and he wanted to meet you before he left Green Valley."

"Max!" I exclaimed, playing along. "That is confidential information you are handing out like free samples."

"Ah, he wanted to meet the mother. So how long have y'all been sleeping together?" She poured some tea into a cup and spooned in some sugar, then made eyes at the banana cake. "Will that be three plates for cake?"

Max hid her face behind a hand and mouthed "sorry" in my direction. I wasn't sorry. Rose was a hoot.

"Rose, now you know it's not polite for a man to talk about a woman he wants to court. And I am serious about your daughter. Very serious. So yes, I wanted to meet you. I've known Max for ten years, and I can honestly say that I think we are well-suited to each other. And yes, three for cake."

Rose plated up the cake while Max finished up the tea, and we took our places around the table.

"That may be all well and good, but how suited are you and Florida? You know my Maxie has an excellent job at our local library."

"Whoa, everyone take it down a notch! Momma, we just slept together last night, if you *must* know. We haven't talked about Florida, or *being suited*, or anything. And I don't want to have that talk for the first time in front of my mother, no offense."

Max was breathing especially hard by the end of her speech, and I had to respect her for speaking up when she did. My mouth tended to have a mind of its own when strong feelings were involved.

"Oh my," Rose said. "I had assumed things were far more advanced than that. I apologize for being nosy."

Max snorted. I'm guessing this wasn't Rose's first time crossing a line.

Speaking of lines. "I'm sorry too. I let my emotions take over where I should have let my brain stay in charge. Forgive me, Max?"

Max looked me over, and smirked. "Yeah, yeah. Forgiven. You too, Momma. Now are we going to eat this cake and get to some Trivial Pursuit or what?"

We spent three hours with Rose, and in that time she bloomed, like her name suggested. I saw so much of Max in her, and my heart ached that she had experienced the loss of her husband in such a traumatic way. She was so vivacious, it was hard to believe she lived almost entirely in this house all alone. I wondered if there was something I could do for her to help, but I knew I would be hard-pressed to do it from several states away.

When we made ready to leave, Rose gave us each a tight hug and a kiss on the cheek. Then, just loud enough for Max to overhear, she said to me, "Take care of my Maxie. She acts tough, but she needs someone to lean on."

Once we were belted in to Stiles again, Max turned to me and said with all seriousness, "You won't say it because you're not even allowed to think it." I wracked my brain for a minute, then realized what she meant.

"Oh, come on, Maxi-Pad, there's no shame in having an embarrassing nickname from your parents."

I should have anticipated the thwap that came at my arm, but for some reason it didn't seem playful to me today. Maybe visiting Rose had made me think of my own parents. I turned to Max and said quietly, "You're never going to hit me again, whether it's as a joke or not, okay? I spent too many years getting my ass beat to think that it's funny anymore." She held my eyes and nodded, then gently rubbed the spot she whacked. I appreciated the gesture.

* * *

BY THE TIME we arrived back at Max's place, a weird, charged tension cracked in the air between us. We had less than two hours before we had to leave for the airport, and my lizard brain knew exactly what it wanted to do for as long as possible. As soon as we lurched to a stop, Max surprised me by leaning across the console, giving me a kiss on the mouth, then jumping out of the Jeep and running as fast as she could toward the front door. I scrambled to get my seat belt off, which appeared to have gained sentience and wasn't about to let go of my body, then fought with the tricky door handle before leaping from the vehicle and running to the cottage, just as Max was about to slam the door in my face.

"Ye shall never take me alive, ye scurvy knave!" she shouted, laughing.

"And why should I want you, you shrieking shrew!" I hollered back, my foot now wedged firmly in the doorframe.

"Because you love it when I shriek for you," she retorted, still pushing on the door for all its worth.

I grinned. She was right, I did love it.

"Maxine Peters, is that man trying to break into your house?" The cry came from behind me. I turned and saw an elderly lady on the sidewalk armed with a cane and a cell phone.

Well, damn. I moved my foot out as quickly as I could considering it was being squashed, and then Max got with the program. She stopped pushing on the door, opened it gently, and shouted, "No, no, Mrs. Howser. It's my houseguest. We were playing a game."

I snickered. Well, I suppose foreplay is a kind of game, when it comes down to it.

"You young people are so strange these days. Too young and full of vigor to come to the church socials, too old to be playing games on the front porch that terrorize your neighbors!"

"We're sorry for the disturbance, Mrs. Howser. Enjoy your day!" Max grabbed me by the front of my shirt and hauled me inside, slamming the door behind me.

CHAPTER SIXTEEN
MAXINE

"Look, if you want patience, talk to your mother. If you want to get shit done, come to me."

— *Maximus_Damage*

After slamming the door metaphorically in Mrs. Howser's face, I pushed Jonathan back against it, kissing the hell out of him while She-Ra and Catra buzzed around our feet and rubbed their heads against our legs. And okay, while the cats were cute as anything, I couldn't make out in front of them. It felt … wrong somehow. Like they were silently passing judgment.

I unlatched my mouth from his, and panting, managed to say, "Bedroom, now. Cats watching. Icky."

"Agreed," he said, kissing and holding me as we made our way awkwardly toward my bedroom, me walking backward.

He gave me a gentle push when we reached the end of the ginormous bed, and I flopped down, opening my arms wide to accept him on top of me. Only, he surprised me. He knelt on the floor beside my legs, and starting with the left foot, he took off my stocking. Then the right. Next, he reached up and undid the zipper on the side of my skirt, slid it and my panties off, and tossed them in a pile of black tulle. I had never felt so exposed since my sexual escapades as a teenager, and that was a long time ago—before cellulite. My legs involuntarily quivered with anticipation and nerves as he spread them slowly, then settled between them, bringing his mouth to my core.

Let me say this: if I thought Jonathan was a good kisser, I knew nothing. Because what he was doing now with his mouth and tongue was like a man possessed, with one goal—to bring me to climax. I bucked my hips up and dug my hands into my quilt, fisting the fabric as the pleasure rolled over me, giving me one of the best orgasms of my life. Possibly the best. Oh, who was I kidding, it was definitely the best because it was Jonathan and because I had never wanted anyone so much in my life.

I reached down to grab his hand and pull him up on the bed beside me, and I could see his erection tenting his pants.

I grinned. "Reciprocation is a vocation any lover should indulge with exultation," I said dreamily. "I'll get to you as soon as I can catch my breath and my arms stop being limp noodles."

"I'm in no hurry, as long as I can play with your breasts while I wait," he said cheekily.

I groaned, wondering how his hands would feel on me—on top of the endorphins running through my body—but started pulling at my cardigan anyway. I let him unfasten my bra, and he sent that sailing in the same direction as my skirt and underwear. There was something decadent about being completely naked while he was clothed, as though I were laid out for him to worship.

He kissed me hungrily, then wrapped both arms around me and urged me up to the pillows where we could stretch out without hanging halfway off the bed. I accidentally bit his tongue in the move, which turned his little moans of pleasure into a loud grunt of pain.

"Okay, love, no more kissing for a few, at least until my tongue returns to its original size," he said. I covered my face in my hands in embarrassment.

"I'm so sorry!" I cried, unable to believe I had klutzed up a kiss.

Actually, I could completely believe it. If it wasn't lipstick on my teeth, it was almost biting off my lover's tongue.

He managed a chuckle, and gently peeled my hands from my face.

"Hey, it's okay. It'll be a funny story one day."

I stiffened a bit. Would there be a "one day" for Jonathan and me? We'd been having such a good time, but could that hold up in the real world, outside this bubble of a charmed weekend with no real responsibilities and no one else getting in the way? My thoughts were interrupted by him promptly rolling me over from where I was on my side to flat on my back and climbing on top of me.

"I can't wait anymore. You're too damn appealing all laid out for me like this." He started to tear at his clothes like a man possessed, and once he had his pants and boxers down, he stopped and said, "Condom. Damn, I almost forgot."

"Me too," I confessed. I'd never been irresponsible in that way before, but this explosive chemistry between us made me as dumb as a rock.

He reached into the bedside table, fished around for the strip of condoms, and rolled one on. Next thing I knew, he was lifting my left leg and bending it at the knee, thrusting inside me so fast and hard, I gasped. And it was so, so good. As we joined our bodies, I had this sense of something bigger happening, something I had never felt before. Like I had been asleep, and now was awakening.

* * *

As WE LAY TANGLED TOGETHER in my sheets, the quilt long having gone the same route as our clothes, we felt each other everywhere, with fingers, lips, and—very carefully—with tongues. I felt warm and safe, and wanted to stay snuggled together for as long as humanly possible.

Which, sadly, ended now. I knew it, and so did he because my cell's alarm had gone off, scaring the crap out of both of us. Tears pricked at the corners of my eyes as I thought about driving Jonathan back to the airport. How strange, that he had arrived as Wrath, my archnemesis, and was leaving as Jonathan, my lover. *Leaving* being the operative word.

I made to rise from the bed, but he pulled me back down into his arms. "No one is going to know you're a girl until you say so," he said quietly. "I won't tell anyone, not even Deathdrop."

And with that, I started to cry. Big, fat, embarrassing tears rolled down my face out of nowhere. I wiped them quickly on the edge of my sheet as I nodded.

"Hey, I was trying to reassure you, not make you break out the waterworks," he said.

"That means so much to me. When you first arrived, I knew I would be outed, and now I can do it when I want. It means you respect me. It's just … a lot. Thank you." I took a large, steadying breath and focused on the task at hand. "We should get rolling. I don't even know if you're packed, and we definitely need showers. Like regular, no hanky-panky showers. There's no time for anything else."

"As my lady wills it," Jonathan replied, kissing the back of my hand. "Now, no more tears. I'm packed, so we only need to shower, and I don't see any reason why we can't save water and share, as long as you can manage to keep your hands to yourself."

"Me? You're ten times worse," I retorted, wiping my eyes.

"We'll have to wait and see. Last one there has to wash the other's hair!"

He had a good head start on me with those ridiculously long legs, but I made it to the bathroom door first. We laughed as we shut the door on two very invasive cats.

The trip back to the airport was quiet, whereas all our other trips had been punctuated by bouts of car karaoke. I thought back to Thursday when I first made this trip, and the dread that had coiled inside me at the thought of meeting and being stuck with Wrath. How life could change so quickly!

Four days later, and I was anxious about never seeing Jonathan again. We hadn't discussed keeping in touch, though we've normally been in daily contact via *Magecraft*. But would he want more? Would he want to see me again, to try whatever this was long distance? That was a big commitment, and not the easiest one to keep. And considering I didn't even have his phone number, it wasn't looking great.

As if reading my mind, Jonathan asked if he could borrow my phone. I said yes, and a moment later I heard a beep going off from his pants pocket.

"There, now we have each other's phone numbers," he said, grinning. He reached across the console and rested his hand on top of mine. "Look, I get that this sucks, and we haven't had time to talk about how this will work or anything. I want you to know that what happened between you and me, that kind of thing never happens to me. And I wouldn't want it to, not with just anyone. You're special to me, Max. I don't think I'm ready to say more than that, not when we are about to say goodbye, but you have to believe that you are important to me in ways I didn't even know existed."

As I pulled into the airport parking, a lump formed in my throat. "That means a lot to me, Jonathan. Or should I go back to calling you Wrath, since we'll be seeing each other in-game from now on?"

"Hey, who says we won't talk outside of *Magecraft*? I gave you my digits, woman. I expect texts, calls, Skype, email, faxes, telegrams, courier pigeons, the works. Though you might as well stick to Wrath in-game because I don't want to be the only freak with a real name in there, but it's Jonathan anywhere else, okay? And you, Maximus in-game and Max out?"

"Just Max. Maxine when you're feeling frisky," I joked.

"Okay, Maxine, let's get this duffel of mine onto a luggage cart and get inside. I think we overdid it with that shower, and I don't want to miss my flight."

"I told you we didn't have time for hanky-panky but did you believe me? No, of course not. Typical man."

"Me?! You were all over me."

"You loved it."

"You know it."

Jonathan insisted on pushing his own duffel, and we made it to departures with enough time to say a short goodbye. A very public goodbye. There were tears again this time, only they weren't mine, they were his, welling up in his eyes but not spilling over.

I reached up and held his face gently in my hands and said, "Sir Wrath of the Swamp Realm. My Jonathan. May the road rise up to meet you. May the wind be always at your back. May the sun shine warm upon your face; the rains fall soft upon your fields, and until we meet again may the gods hold you in the palms of their hands."

"Well, that really was a goodbye, wasn't it? Better than anything I've got," he managed to say.

"It's an Irish blessing, though I messed it up a bit since I don't believe in just one god. But, as they say, the show must go on and so must your flight. Whether you're there or not, so you better get going."

He leaned down and embraced me, squeezing the air out of me.

"I won't forget you, Maxine Peters. Never. Not as long as I draw breath."

I gulped down a lump in my throat and replied, "Now what more could a girl ask for than that?"

He nodded, and with one last kiss, he broke apart from me and headed through the security barricade. I watched him go, until he rounded a corner and was out of sight.

* * *

"AND THEN HE WAS JUST *GONE*," I said to Lois over Skype, trying not to weep and wail like it was the end of the world.

"That's generally what happens when you drop someone off at the airport, Max," she replied.

It was only 5:00 p.m., and I was in the flannel penguin pajamas, the box of wine having migrated from the fridge to my bedside table. I had remade the bed, and for a crazed minute considered saving the soiled sheets from earlier, the way new brides in centuries past would. After a second of indecision at the washing machine, I threw in the sheets, realizing I was not the star of a historical romance novel.

"Max, normally I wouldn't ask this, but how much wine have you had?"

"Like, three or four glasses," I replied, and then burped.

"Okay, Mama Lois is officially cutting you off. I know you. You can't hold your booze worth a damn, and three glasses for you is like six for me. Enough wine and misery."

I nodded numbly and leaned over to scritch She-Ra behind her ears and rub Catra's tummy. With Jonathan gone, they had formally reclaimed their positions in my bed, one of them on either side of me.

"So what did he say to you as a goodbye? Was it like an awkward kind of 'see ya' or what?" she asked, sipping her iced tea.

"He said he would never forget me as long as he drew breath," I replied, sighing.

Lois's iced tea came flying out of her mouth. "He said *that*? That's like some next-level shit, Max. Have you reconsidered my theory that that boy is stark raving mad about you, and you let him leave?" She frantically wiped at her laptop with a cloth while I rolled my eyes.

"Let him leave? Lo, how could I have gotten him to stay? For the love of the gods, his life is in Florida."

"In some backwoods swamp in Florida that he might consider leaving if he knew how you feel about him!"

"*I* don't know how I feel about him!"

I leaned over and buried my face in my pillow. My pillow that smelled like him, all sandalwood and sunshine. I hadn't gotten to play with that hair nearly long enough.

"Ack, gotta run, Elsa is screaming her head off," Lois said, turning to the monitor one last time. "Look, I think you owe it to both of you to find out how you feel. And that's only going to happen with a lot of soul-searching. Maybe getting to know him a bit more outside of the context of the game. And keep the wine to one or two glasses a night in case of emergency, you lush."

"G'night, Peily."

"Night, Maximus."

CHAPTER SEVENTEEN
JONATHAN

*"Yo Max, remember that time you fell off a cliff in the Floating Isles? Epic fall, man.
Seriously epic."*

— *Wrath*

Not even the clouds matched Max's beauty, I thought glumly as I sat on my flight back to Jacksonville. I wondered what on earth I had done leaving her. I mean, I knew we had separate lives, separate jobs, our own families. But I *loved* Max. Everything that had happened between us last night and today cemented that fact, it didn't change it. Even if we hadn't slept together, I would still love her. The problem was, I wasn't exactly forthcoming with my feelings for her because she hadn't expressed any feelings for me. I didn't want to put myself out there and be made a fool of.

I suppose there were worse things than feeling like a fool, such as flying away from the love of your life. Yes, Norman's words from Thursday were bang on. Max was the only one I wanted, and the only one I think I would ever want. But what to do about it? My job was here, with Norman, running our business. My big sister depended on me to help out with taking care of our mom, especially since she was popping more pills than she should. It didn't matter that the love I found was only a few states away. Tennessee might as well be Mars for all the freedom I had to be with and build a life with Max.

We landed in Jacksonville, and I wove my way through the airport to find Norman waiting for me, an excited puppy expression on his face. "How did it go? Did you get laid? Oh my god, you got laid. I know that look. I was so right to ruin the weekend for everyone else! Up high!" He put his hand up in the air looking for a high five. I shook my head.

"Idiot. Get your hand down," I said, annoyed but happy to see my best friend.

Norman lowered his hand but didn't give up on the interrogation as we walked through the airport to his car.

"Tell me that you did at least get into Maximus's pants. That was my primary goal in staying home."

"I'm not going to comment on anything that happened between us," I said firmly, giving him a death glare.

"That means something happened for there to be something to theoretically comment on," he replied with glee.

"Norman, you need to keep your mind on your own dick and off mine." Jesus, this duffel was heavy. Why I hadn't grabbed a luggage cart, I'd never know. "Look, I'm exhausted, and I'm pissed and sad and I feel like an asshole and I want my best friend to be supportive, not pick at all the places that make me want to punch something."

Norman was quiet for a minute, then reached out and grabbed my bag, heaving it over his shoulder. "Come on, Jonathan. I'll get you home as soon as I can, or you can come to my place if you don't want to deal with your mother and sister on top of everything else. I won't be a dick, okay?"

"Deal. I'll come to your place for a bit. Can I use your computer when we get there?"

"Lucille? Man, you are whipping out the big sympathy guns if you think you'll get some face time on her."

"Ugh, I don't even want to know about the special relationship you have with your machine. Just let me log in to *Magecraft* and check my email and shit, okay?"

"Done."

* * *

I SAT down at Norman's gaming desktop when we finally got to his place and shuddered when I saw the Kleenex box and lotion beside the monitor. I didn't want to know. Really. I found the *League of Magecraft* icon and clicked on like it was second nature, which it was. The login screen loaded, then *Loading ... Downloading Patch ... Buffering ... Playable.* I hit the Play button as soon as it was available and typed */who is Maximus_Damage.* A scant moment later, I got back, *Maximus_Damage, Level 100 Dwarf Warrior, Mountains of Mystery.*

She was online! Okay, now what to say, what to say. I wracked my brain for a moment and then typed a message.

Wrath: Yo yo yo

Maximus_Damage: Jonathan?

Wrath: Yeah, I panicked. Don't ask me where the "yo yo yo" came from.

Maximus_Damage: Oh, I know where it came from. 1993. How was your flight?

Wrath: Depressing because I was flying away from you.

Maximus_Damage: Shit, hold on, meglatharion on my tail. Running like hell down the mountain.

Wrath: Mistake. Turn to stone and ride out the attack. You'll survive.

Maximus_Damage: Oh hell no!

Wrath: Do it, or you're lunch.

Maximus_Damage: Ha! I used a bubble of protection to give me time to summon my wing rider. I flew away from its jerky butt. Speaking of flying away, I'm sorry your flight sucked. I missed you too, driving home. My car karaoke partner was gone :(

Wrath: I'll share my playlist with you. And you give me yours. At least we can listen to the same music.

Maximus_Damage: Okay, I'm logging off. I have to prep for going back to work in the morning. I'll have a bit of a backlog from taking Thursday and Friday off. See you.

Wrath: Yeah, see you.

I couldn't place the feeling of disappointment I had as I logged off. No, I could. I was in love with this girl and all I got was a "see you" as a goodbye? Of course, I hadn't told her I loved her, but we'd had sex several times, and that meant a lot to me. What did it mean to her?

"Yo yo yo, my man, you done in there?" Ah, so that's where the "yo yo yo" had originated. Figures. "Lucille's been acting up lately, so she might disconnect on you. I gotta rip her apart and figure out what's going on. Pretty sure it's the motherboard." Norman stood beside me and watched me close out the game. "Ah, talking with your man. Good stuff?"

"Yeah, great," I said distantly.

How was I going to handle this distance from Max without the support of my best friend? The only other person I could talk to would be my sister Elaine. The more I thought about it, the more I realized she was the perfect person to confide in. I checked my watch and confirmed this was a good time to catch her.

"Norman, can you drive me home after all? I should check in with my mom after four days. Olivia might be going out of her mind."

I wondered how horrible a person it made me to be deceptive over my big sister's and mother's mental states when all I wanted to do was sit and Skype with my other sister in Chicago.

Norman navigated his truck from his trailer park to mine as if he'd done it hundreds of times before, which he probably has considering this was where we worked every weekday. I kept the trailer and garage as repaired and clean as possible, and despite every negative stereotype in the world about trailer parks, we lived somewhere where people took pride in their homes. Mom was out on the porch, so I grabbed my duffel from the back seat, gave Norman a friendly shoulder bump, and thanked him for the drive. He sped off with a honk of his horn and a wave. It may have been a little impolite under some circumstances not to come and greet Mom, but we learned over the years that a quick and clean exit strategy was important when you didn't have all day to spend with her.

I climbed the stairs to the porch and leaned down to kiss her cheek. Her eyes were hidden behind sunglasses, so I wasn't sure if she was asleep or awake until she lifted a hand and patted my beard playfully.

"I prayed for you while you were gone, darling boy," she said dreamily, and I wondered how many benzodiazepines she had taken today.

"Then your prayers and my prayers must have joined forces because I had the best time. Mom, you have to brace yourself. I have to tell you, do you remember how for the last ten years or so I've been in love with someone in Tennessee? Well, that's where I went when I was away," I reminded her, speaking clearly and hoping this was getting through. "Mom, I finally met Max, and she's a girl. A beautiful, kind, strong woman."

"A girl? But how … how did you not know for almost a decade?! You know I would love you no matter who you fell in love with, man or woman. But now I don't have to worry about the Sutton boys beating you up with a crowbar like they did that poor Osbourne lad."

I vaguely recalled hearing about the vicious hate crime she mentioned, one that had happened in the 1970s. She must be in one of her confused states, where the past and the present blended together. "A woman, imagine that."

I laughed. "Come on, I have dated girls, you know."

"Ah, but son, this is different. Because this is the one. Ever since you started talking about him—her—and cried yourself sick in my arms that evening, I knew I would have three sons-in-law one day, not two, and I immediately made my peace with it."

"I don't want to argue with you, but you tell me all the time you're praying to Jesus that I choose the 'right path' for my soul." I knelt down next to her.

"And you thought I was talking about choosing a man or a woman? No, no, no! I was praying that you would have the courage to go after the path your heart set out for you. That's the only 'right' one."

I realized that she was far more lucid than I had given her credit for, and tears pooled in my eyes as I also realized that I hadn't given her the benefit of the doubt all these years. I assumed the worst of my own mother, and why? Because she was prone to having spells or got a little lost in her head sometimes? Because she talked out loud to Jesus randomly? She had found my therapist, Tom, after all. I should have trusted in her, always.

"Thank you, Mom," I said. "Now, you'll be fine out here while I go use the computer for a bit? How about I bring you a glass of lemonade first?"

"No thank you, dear. Go ahead and call Elaine. I know you want to."

I grinned at her almost psychic-level knowledge of her children and headed inside. My other sister, Olivia, was evidently out, probably doing the shopping. She never left Mom for too long. Neither of us did.

In short order, I was looking at Elaine, and something in me shook loose. Those tears that had been threatening to flow all day came back. I wiped them with the back of my hand and started at the beginning, pouring out the entire story to my little sister.

* * *

"OH, Jonathan, you big, stupid, drooling male. Of course you got a 'see you' from her. What did you expect? You left her without defining the relationship. Now she's probably scared of being too clingy and making you squirrely and driving you off. You didn't have to declare your undying love, but you should have said something to let her know you feel seriously about her. For all she knows, she was a weekend booty call."

"Elaine!" I said sharply. "Considering I'm in love with this girl, and she may be your future sister-in-law, never refer to her as a booty call again, okay?"

"Fair. But I'm serious, Jonathan. You need to lock that down, in the non-psycho way. And if you don't know how, start by being a friend to her. Be there for her. Listen to her. Look, these rules are as old as the freaking wheel, dude. Show her you care by stepping up when she needs someone." Elaine sipped at her perpetual mug of green tea, and I let out a loud sigh and scrubbed one hand through my hair. She was right, these were obvious things to do, under normal circumstances anyway.

"And the fact that she said she hated me?"

"That was before the weekend and the sex fest. Her feelings might have changed. Maybe she was confused over how she felt about you. You said it yourself, you've been a fixture in her life for ten years. If she genuinely hated you, she would have found a way to cut you out before this. No one puts up with their archnemesis that long. I'm freaking serious. Think about it. If you hated someone, would you put up with them for ten damn years? Would you invite them to your hometown? Not a chance on earth. I think it's possible, Jonathan, that you've found a woman who knows herself even less than you know yourself."

And there she goes, spouting off truths mixed in with sweeping philosophical statements designed to make her sound smart. And they worked, dammit.

"What do you mean, I don't know myself?" I asked, annoyance creeping over me. There was always a lemon to suck on with Elaine, despite her being an excellent person to talk over problems with.

"Jonathan, you have had a question mark over your head about your sexuality since you were seventeen. I get the 'no labels' approach, I do. But I know you. You need a label so you can understand it now that you're Team Maxine. Personally, I think you're pansexual. The way you described it to me once, that you think a person's heart and mind and soul are more important than what body they're in? That's it. And there is no shame in it, you hear me? None." She pointed her finger at the screen, like she was going to shake it at me.

"Okay, you don't need to read me the riot act. I got it. I'm pansexual, and not ashamed. I also feel that it's irrelevant now because of Maxine. I'm not looking for anyone else. But thank you. What else you got to throw at me?"

"You've had a fair bit of trouble managing your bipolar disorder in the past few years. Hell, ever since your diagnosis. There's always some kind of mess that happens, usually with your meds. And you have to move from crisis to crisis, and it makes you a real jerk sometimes. I'm not blaming you for that. But you've lacked the peace and stability that you could find if you would do things like meditate more, increase your mindfulness practice, and avoid situations that will set you off. Obviously, this game is one of them because she thought you were an asshole, and you are anything but. Now, I know you're not going to stop gaming, especially since it's where you get to hang out with Maxine, but please talk to Tom about the other stuff. This shit gets results."

I knew this was important to her because she was using the puppy eyes she whipped out whenever she wanted something very badly. And this time, what she wanted was for me to be healthy. Well, so did I. I was sick of being sick with a manageable disorder. I also had to come clean with Maxine. I'd painted too rosy a picture of my condition with her on Medieval Day. I had wanted to share with her, but without scaring her off. No more secrets, and no more lies—there had been enough of those between us.

"Mindfulness. Meditation. Medication. Truth. Got it."

"I hope you do and aren't just humoring me."

"Elaine! You know me. I'm not going to dick around when it's something this serious. If these are the barriers between Max and me, you better damn well believe I'm going to break them down, one by one."

We chatted about Elaine for a bit, her telling me about her eccentric friends and workplace. She was happy in Chicago, and I wouldn't wish any other life for her. I begged off the call, saying it was getting late and that I needed to call Tom as soon as possible, which was true. I had no sooner called Tom and left a message on his phone to schedule an appointment when I heard a familiar truck pull into the driveway. Norman, back again. What the heck did he want?

CHAPTER EIGHTEEN
MAXINE

"This may be a game, but these are my people. This guild is my tribe."

— *Maximus_Damage*

The first thing I did when I woke up was grab my tablet, as usual, to check for any pressing email from work or issues with the guild I needed to deal with. I was surprised to get an email from Jonathan at my public guild address, until I remembered that we'd never exchanged private emails. Clever.

From: Jonathan Owen <jonowen@supernaturalcomputers.com>
To: Maximus_Damage <maxattack@dragonlegion.com>
Subject: animal wrangling

Max:
Last night, Norman dragged me to one of those two-bit honky-tonks out in the sticks that you are aware I'm so fond of. Here's a photo of me on the mechanical bull. I stayed on for six seconds, which I felt left my manhood intact. (Literally, I had to feel around afterward to make sure my manhood

was intact). Norman kept throwing single women at me, presumably to lift my spirits, when he doesn't know that you're the one I'm crazy about.

I was thinking about your position with the guild and your big reveal. I'm so proud of you that you made that choice. Think about how proud of yourself you will feel once it's done. Think of all the girls you can be a role model for, after you've explained why you've been silent until now. You have a chance to use Maximus_Damage's reputation to do some good in the world. And if people hate it, screw them. You've never had a problem riding the moral high road, have you?

Hugs,
Jonathan

THERE WAS INDEED a photo of him on the mechanical bull attached, and I burst out laughing at the expression on his face. After attending to some guild business, I logged into my personal email and fired back a reply.

From: Max Peters <maxine@mpeters.com>
To: Jonathan Owen <jonowen@supernaturalcomputers.com>
Subject: Penguins

Jonathan:
I've given a lot of thought to what you said about my revelation to the guild and the example I could set with Maximus, as well as the light I could shine on in-game harassment, if that becomes an issue. I'm going to do it on Wednesday night—I've asked to be the raid leader for the first few fights using voice chat. We'll see how it goes, and your butt had better be there, so sign up for the raid now, okay? I wouldn't want you to miss my debut.
Now, I'm going to cuddle some more in bed wearing your favorite pair of my pajamas, the flannel penguins. Am I a fashion icon or what? By the way, nice pic. I especially liked how it looked like you were about to piss your pants.

Cheers,
Maxi-Pad

From: Jonathan Owen <jonowen@supernaturalcomputers.com>
To: Max Peters <maxine@mpeters.com>
Subject: pride

Max:
That's fantastic news! I signed up for the raid—just a couple of more days
now. I'm proud of you, you know. I know you're doing all the work, but I will
be your cheering section, always.

Cheers (literally),
Jonathan

I CLOSED out my email and lay there with a big, wide smile on my face. My alarm
wasn't due to go off for another twenty minutes, so I had the luxury of lying in bed
and stretching, which felt so good after the last few days of intense physical activity.
Not that I was complaining, given the nature of most of the activity. I felt like part of
me was rejuvenated, and my spirit felt lighter.

I ran through the day in my head. Work from nine to four, a quick stop at the liquor
store to buy some wine—in a bottle, no less—then book club tonight at seven.

Now that several of my colleagues knew I was a total geek after Medieval Day, there
would be no more holding back. No more hiding behind ankle-length corduroy skirts
and cardigans that swallowed me whole. Part of me thought my wardrobe wasn't that
big of a deal, but I knew that hiding every possible aspect of who I am was all tied to
the attack. I needed to make real peace with what happened at long last and not be
Mousy Maxine anymore—and not just for one magical weekend. I decided to toss off
my duvet and climb out of bed early, turning off my alarm and yawning wide.

First, I grabbed my cell phone and dialed my boss, our head librarian, Thuy Nguyen.
I told her I needed to take a mental health day, despite having taken Thursday and
Friday off. I assured her it was important, and she honored my request. I then texted
the book club group chat and asked everyone if they could reschedule for tomorrow
night. My next call was to my old therapist to schedule an appointment. Last, I dialed
the sheriff's department.

* * *

Jackson James, a sheriff's deputy I'd gone to high school with, sat across from me in a conference room. I blew on some truly atrocious coffee and waited for him to finish perusing my file. Not that there was much to peruse. Other than photographs of my injuries and an original fudged incident report, that was it. I took in the sights and smell of the building my father had spent so much time in. In that moment, I missed him so much I had to fight down my tears, and my throat tightened.

"So Maxine—er, Miss Peters, sorry—why don't you walk me through it one more time, now that we're sitting down and I'm all caught up."

I took in a deep breath and clasped my hands around the disposable coffee cup, the warmth giving me comfort.

"I lied, ten years ago. When I said I didn't see their faces, I mean. Everything else I said was the truth. I was stuck out in the sticks near the old Samuelson place struggling to change my tire, and these two guys on bikes pulled in behind me. They were wearing the patch of the Iron Wraiths. The first guy offers to help me, and I was in a jam, so I said yes. I should have sent them away and called for a tow, but I didn't know … Anyway, it was going okay. We were even cracking jokes. Then the second guy starts freaking out while he's got the iron in his hand and charges me. The first guy tried to pull him off. He kept cursing and yelling at the other guy to stop, but it was like the guy with the tire iron was possessed. I think he was on something. I mean, why else would he act that way?" I shuddered and pulled my hoodie tighter around me and zipped it up as if it were a suit of armor. I wasn't enjoying this trip down memory lane by any stretch of the imagination, but it was long past necessary.

"I have to say, Miss Peters, I'm surprised to see you here after all this time. Do you think your attacker recognized you in connection to your father? He was a well-known and damn good cop. Maybe there was bad blood between him and the Wraiths, even beyond the obvious of him being in law enforcement."

I thought about that possibility and dismissed it, as I had a decade ago. "No, there was no recognition on his face, just rage. He was like, tweaked out or something, I'm sure of it. I don't know how he had the coordination to ride his bike on these roads. Anyway, after the first guy pulled him off me, they both got on their bikes and took off, and I was found by another passerby not too much later." I sighed and drank a gulp of sludge in my coffee cup, making a face. "At the time, I was too scared to identify the men. I justified it to myself by thinking that the one guy had tried to save me and that if they wanted me dead, or raped, they would have done it, and that a bit of a beating wasn't so bad. But if I'd pressed charges, maybe the Wraiths would have come back to finish the job or hurt my mother. They weren't known for being kind to their enemies."

Jackson pulled a frown. "It looks like you got more than a bit of a beating, Miss Peters. What happened to you was a serious assault. Now, I know you didn't come here without doing some research first, and I'm sure you're aware that the statute of limitations on assault has passed I could talk to the district attorney, but honestly—"

"No, Jackson—Deputy James—thank you, but no. I wanted to correct the record of what happened to me and put my attacker's description on file. Maybe it can help build a case against him for something else if he's found, I don't know. I don't know much about this process at all, which I know you'll find hard to believe, my daddy having been a sheriff's deputy. But Mom wanted that part of him, his job, to not impact us as a family, so he left that at the door every night."

Jackson let out a puff of breath and nodded his head. "Okay then, I'll take down their descriptions, if you are comfortable giving them to me."

Pen poised above the page, Jackson waited for me to recall the faces which so often haunted my dreams. Describing them was like a time warp, except instead of a jump to the left, it was a jump ten years back. To feeling alone and vulnerable and useless as I had curled into myself, hoping to block the worst of the blows.

I remembered my manners enough to shake Jackson's hand when we were done, with Jackson reminding me that Mom and I were welcome to come by the station anytime to socialize. We hadn't been forgotten by the department, and the receptionist wanted a full breakdown of how Mom and I were doing. As the receptionist excitedly chattered, I had a sudden memory of being four and coming with my dad to work one day because Mom had an appointment. I drew pictures with pencil on lined paper, one for everyone in the department, and my father's eyes shone with pride as we handed them out.

The next thing I knew, I was sitting in my Jeep crying my eyes out, wishing Jonathan were here to wrap his arms around me, and for me to breathe in his delicious smell. I tried to remember what my therapist had told me about managing my anxiety with regard to the attack, and I calmed my breathing, glad that I had booked a new appointment with her. I blew my nose into a tissue, then carefully made my way home in silence. I swear my ribs ached where I'd taken the worst swing of the tire iron all those years ago. There was something cathartic about talking to Jackson and then having a good cry, and I decided to share what I'd done with Jonathan as soon as I got inside.

From: Max Peters <maxine@mpeters.com>
To: Jonathan Owen <jonowen@supernaturalcomputers.com>
Subject: The Fuzz

Jonathan:
Today I played hooky from work and took one small step for Max, one giant leap for Max-kind. I went to the sheriff's station and gave a description of the scuzzbag who attacked me, and of his friend. The statute of limitations is over, but I at least feel like I did something that had been weighing on me for a long time. You ever feel that way? Like there are things in the world that are just hankering for you to finally acknowledge them or accomplish them? And when you do, you hear in your mind a soft little, "Oh, *there* you are!" like something is telling you that you did right, you did good?
Anyway, the faces of those men are in my file, and maybe someday that can help someone else. I don't know. I do know it's done, and I want to put it behind me. Perhaps with a ritualistic burning of every corduroy skirt I own.

Cheers,
Max

As I HIT SEND, I felt a sense of accomplishment and peace settle over me. Catra jumped up on my computer desk and meowed loudly, reminding me it was feeding time at the zoo. I got up and smiled as I moved to the laundry room to feed the beasts.

From: Jonathan Owen <jonowen@supernaturalcomputers.com>
To: Max Peters <maxine@mpeters.com>
Subject: wow

Max:

That's amazing news! I mean, I know it won't result in those guys paying for their crime against you, but you never know where your actions today might lead. At the very least, you know that you've done everything you can, and screw it that it was on your timeline and not someone else's. You did what you needed to do for you, back then and today. I'm so damn proud of you. Hey, I saw on the guild forums that there's a senior officer's meeting tonight. Are you going? As yourself, I mean? I'll be online if you need support or someone to rage at ;) Now, on the subject of these atrocious skirts I have heard so much about but never saw in person: don't you dare try to light up a bonfire on your own. Flame on with friends.

Jonathan

I GRINNED and closed out my email and decided to kill the next few hours until the officer's meeting on my PS4 with some *Kingdom Hearts III*. Technically, I could have still held book club, but I wasn't feeling too social after my day at the station. I think I needed some time to let what happened seep in, to accept that it was over, before I leapt right into entertaining.

At ten o'clock, I was in my gaming room, and for the first time I was wearing my headset and had the microphone plugged in. I felt like I was about to make calls offering people lower rates on their car insurance. With a slightly shaky hand, I logged on to the guild voice chat room, and mentally prepared for anything. I heard a series of dings letting me know everyone else was arriving.

"Hey, noobs. Sound off in Mouseketeer fashion for the minutes," Iskander, our guild leader said. "Then we can have Maximus talk about the epic fail of the gathering, and what we're going to do about Deathdrop apparently telling people it was canceled? Man, I swear it's always some scheme with him."

"Agreed. And Mirage here," came the deep voice of our guild banker.

"PwnyUp here," came the equally deep voice of the player versus player leader. Why was I suddenly so conscious of how … male … everyone sounded? Oh, right, because I was the only female officer, much to my sudden anger. We were the best guild in North America, and we could only scrounge up six guys to represent all of us on the senior council? I suddenly wanted to hurry this revelation along.

"Burninator here," barked our raid leader.

"Phantasman here," said the player versus environment officer.

I took in a breath. I was so damn ready. "Maximus here," I said, representing the member at large position-slash-tactics. "And the gathering wasn't a total wash—okay, so maybe it was—but Wrath still showed up, and he explained that Deathdrop went behind his back too and told Nedris that it was canceled. Carebear lost her childcare. So instead of five of us, it was just me and Wrath. We didn't expense a hotel room to the guild because he was able to stay at my place. So, silver lining for you, Mirage."

Silence. Deathly silence.

Then came Iskander's voice. "Well, shit on a stick. I wouldn't have said half the dumb crap I've said over the years if I'd known we had a girl in here. I bet you were having a laugh over how stupid we all were."

"Yeah, what gives, Max? Didn't you trust us?" Mirage said, sounding hurt.

"At the very least we could have told the girl gamers that they do have a voice on this council," Burninator chimed in. "Don't think that we won't be doing that now. Some players have been clamoring for more fairness amongst the officers. We wanted the next officer to be Wrath, which would have added to the claims we're nothing but a sausage fest. At least now we can say we've had a girl on board for years."

"What the fuck, guys?" PwnyUp said angrily. "Maximus has been lying to us for literally years and everyone is okay with it? And what, relieved we don't have to recruit from the honest players in the guild?"

"I haven't been lying," I said, defending myself. "I never confirmed to anyone at any time that I was a guy. I play a male character, I'm a tad aggressive when I play, and people assumed things about me. I wasn't ready to open up and let people get close to my offline life, but that doesn't make me a bad person or a bad player. I respect all of you, and I hope you can say the same about me, after you've had time to think on it."

"I don't need time to think on it," said Iskander. "Whatever your reasons were, your gender isn't the most important thing about you as a player in this game or as an officer in this guild. Your skills and dedication have spoken for themselves over the years, again and again. Anyone who doesn't like it can go piss up a rope as far as I'm concerned."

"Yeah, we got your back, Max," Mirage concurred.

"Agreed," said Burninator.

"We're not doing this," PwnyUp said. "I'm pulling a Rocket and telling you all we're not doing the thing where we stand up one at a time and pledge ourselves to truth, equality, and all that. The rest of you have no problem with it? Fine. Personally, I feel misled. I said crap in this game to Maximus I'd never say in front of a girl. It's like she stuck a sock in her jeans and waltzed into the guy's locker room or something. Does no one else honestly see no problem with this?"

Goddammit. PwnyUp was one of my closest friends in the game. I wasn't having my name dragged through the dirt, especially by someone who I had respected and had fun with, even though he was being a dick now. I cleared my throat. Fine. If I had to go there, I was going there.

"He broke my jaw, Pwny. He broke my jaw and a bunch of ribs with a tire iron. A man. And I wanted to play to escape all that, and not get hit on by random dudes in a video game. I just wanted to hang out, have fun, and not be creeped on online when I'd just been busted up offline. And the longer I was Maximus, the harder it was to bring up my gender, so I didn't. I've valued you as a friend. I hope you can think about it and then still say the same about me."

"Who. Hurt. You," came Pwny's voice, slow and deadly sounding. I resisted the urge to either cry or laugh. Apparently, friendship could overcome my vagina after all.

"It was some asshole from a local biker gang. He's moved on, though, so it's not like I have to see him or worry about the gang anymore. It's okay. I'm okay, I mean."

"Jesus," muttered Phantasman. "You knew when you agreed to host the gathering that you would be revealed as a girl. So we can't say you were actively hiding from us, or intended to hide for much longer. I'm sorry you went through that."

A message popped up in the chat box, and for the first time in-game, I was happy to see Wrath's name.

Wrath: How's it going?

Maximus_Damage: We're about to sing around a fertility sigil I painted on the floor.

Wrath: Seriously?

Maximus_Damage: No, you fool. We're talking it out and getting back to guild business, namely your bestie. I was accused of being a liar, like with you, but I defended myself, and it's going okay, I think.

"Wait, hold up! You said it was just you and Wrath all weekend. And he stayed at your house! So what's going on there?" Mirage asked in a voice that was either serious or teasing, I could never tell with him.

Maximus_Damage: Yikes, gotta go. They are trying to ferret out if we slept together or not.

"Y'all realize you are as gossipy as a group of old women," I teased, not wanting Jonathan and I to become speculation fodder for the entire guild. "Can we move on to the next item on the agenda? I think we were supposed to discuss what to do with Deathdrop."

CHAPTER NINETEEN
JONATHAN

"A week-long suspension?! You can't prove I had anything to do with that parrotling!"

— *Wrath*

My cell pinged at 11:30 p.m. I snatched it up eagerly, hoping it was Max. Instead, I saw it was Norman.

Norm: I got suspended from the guild for a month. A MONTH, man. I hope whatever you got up to last weekend, you will eventually tell me because this stings. No raids, no good loot, nada.

Jonathan: You'll survive. I'm sorry that happened, though. I know you were doing me a solid. Max and I would never have gotten together without you interfering.

Norm: Wait, hold up ...

The phone rang in my hand. Sighing, I picked up. "Yes?"

"What do you mean, you would never have gotten together? So you totally hit that. Or that hit you? I don't know which and don't want the deets, but that's awesome, Jonathan. You've waited so long for him."

I decided I needed to talk to Max now, about fixing Norman's assumptions. Elaine was right, I needed to be able to talk about all this with the people closest to me.

"Norman, I gotta call you back, okay? I know this sucks for you right now, and I appreciate it and all. Maybe take this time to step back from the game and rebuild Lucille."

"Yeah, yeah, go call your man," he said, hanging up.

I sighed, and dialed Max.

"Hello?" she answered, a bit sleepily.

"Hey. I'm sorry for calling so late. If it's okay with you, I want to tell Norman about you being a girl. I know your debut is Wednesday, but now he won't be there to hear it, and he keeps referring to you as a guy, and I feel like dirt not correcting him. I'm not trying to pressure you, it's—"

"Jonathan, I get it. You don't need to lie by omission to your best friend just because I essentially did. Tell him, but please ask him not to out me until I can do it myself, okay?"

"Absolutely." I heard her yawn. "So who do I have to thank for Deathdrop's stay of execution?"

"Iskander. He pointed out that we don't want to come off as being assholes for kicking out one of the top players in the guild over a prank. I mean, the only person who lost out on anything was Nedris, and apparently Ned didn't care either way about the weekend. He had a refundable plane ticket, thank goodness. But we obviously had to do something kind of harsh so Deathdrop learns his lesson."

I hummed in agreement.

"I'm going to let you go so I can call Norman back. I kind of bailed mid call so I could ask your permission."

Shit, now that I thought about it, should I have cleared it with her before talking about her with Mom and my sisters? I hoped not. They didn't know her or play the game like Norman did, so I assumed it was okay.

"Thanks, it's appreciated. Goodnight, Jonathan."

"'Night, Maxine." I smiled and disconnected, then dialed Norman back.

"Yo, what was that?" he asked.

"You can't tell anyone until Max tells the guild Wednesday night, man. I gotta have your word on that first."

"Yeah, whatever you need. What's going on?" He sounded somewhat serious, which was a departure from his class clown persona. Norman had some real substance to him, once you got past the bullshit that he used to cover up his wounded warrior status.

"Max. We did hook up. It was amazing, and I'm so in love. I had to tell you thank you for setting us up, thanks for being my friend through all this. Here's the kicker, though, why I had to get Max's blessing to tell you, so I didn't screw anything up. Max's real name is Maxine."

A beat of silence, then, "Whoa. Dude. I think it's great you're so cool about that. So, he needs to dress like a girl, or he had surgery, or what? Actually, that part is none of my business. And oh, should I be saying she? Sorry, I'm not the most informed person in this area. Just give me a pronoun and it's all good."

Okay, so he might be awesome, but he was also a little thick at times, despite shocking me by knowing what a pronoun is.

"Maxine isn't transgender, Maxine was born a girl. I'm telling you that Maximus_-Damage is a woman. I've been in love with a woman for ten years. A woman who, four days ago, hated me."

A burst of laughter came over the line so loud I had to pull the phone away from my ear.

* * *

TUESDAY ARRIVED with heat and a pile of work for Norman and me to catch up on. Our business, Supernatural Computers, was doing damn well, some of our builds having gone viral online. We'd been best friends since elementary school, growing up in adjacent trailer parks and tinkering with whatever electronics we could get our hands on. Norman had gone into the military out of high school, whereas I stayed home to help Olivia with Mom and pay toward the bills by working at a local hard-ware store.

When Norman came home from the military, he was changed. He was quiet, distant, and would have nightmares that left him texting me at two or three in the morning for a talk, or a beer. Too much beer. I knew something had to give, so I suggested we pool our resources and start doing what we loved, which was building things. I also introduced him to *Magecraft* as a way of letting out some of his frustrations and anger, and hopefully build some other friendships along the way. Our trailer parks weren't hopping with a lot of people our age; many had left to go to school, the mili-tary, or find jobs.

As we sketched out the design for our next custom build, my thoughts strayed to Max and Green Valley. I tried to envision her wearing a hideous corduroy skirt and stuck in the basement cataloging. She had spoken about how sometimes in life we don't get the dreams we chase, when I asked her about working with the library patrons. Was she really happy with her current situation? Would she continue to come out of her shell, like she did during our four days together?

Prior to the weekend, I would have called Max one of the most confident people I knew. But seeing her vulnerable side and learning about her past had changed my perception of her. I now thought she was the strongest person I knew. A survivor, a real-life warrior offline who was taking tentative steps to spread her wings and fly. Feeling inspired, I sketched out the design of a bird's wing for the custom desk the computer build would go with, and decided I liked it.

"Hey, good idea, man. What inspired that?" Norman asked, pointing down at my sketch.

I was the artist between the two of us as Norman couldn't draw for beans, though I suppose building computers in itself can be described as an art.

"Eh, half daydreaming," I replied, smiling softly.

I made some adjustments to the drawing to accommodate where the tower would go, then sketched out the design for the legs and some shelving. Satisfied, I nodded at Norman and we discussed which pieces of lumber in our inventory would suit, and how long the build of the desk would take. In cases like this, where we were constructing both a custom desk and a machine, Norman would take point on the computer, and I would whip out my carpentry skills and hopefully not lose any fingers while working on the desk.

As we broke for lunch, I got a ping from my cell in my pants pocket. I grinned wide when I saw it was a text from Max.

Max: Yo, what's up?

Me: The usual. Fast cars and frisky women.

Max: Oh, same. I was just felt up in a Corvette by a very handsy redhead.

Me: Was she impressed by your lumpy cardigan?

Max: I'll have you know that I am wearing an open cardigan over a band T-shirt, black pants, and strappy sandals. I even kept my hair down and curled it a bit.

Me: Please tell me you didn't have that ritualistic skirt burning.

Max: I may have considered floating the idea at my book club tonight. But honestly, I'd rather donate the clothes. I wasn't brought up to be wasteful.

Me: I can see that about Momma Rose.

Max: I can't believe she had you calling her that by the end of the visit.

Me: I thought it was cute.

"Jonathan! Are you done with that sandwich yet? We're backed up, remember?" Norman called from inside the garage.

Me: Okay, getting the call from the drill sergeant over here. Gotta book it. Talk tonight? Maybe Skype?

Max: I'll email you. I have book club, remember?

My heart sunk. I knew she wasn't giving me the brush-off. This was a planned event, and it was important for her to socialize with friends offline. I wished I could capture that magic we had from the weekend, bottle it, and then drink it in whenever I needed to. I was still love-drunk on Maxine, but what nagged at the back of my brain was the thought that she might already be over me. That maybe I was a convenient stepping-stone on her path to a better life. Because her life was in Green Valley, whether I liked it or lumped it.

I thought of her, all dressed up and parading into Genie's with the cocky confidence of Maximus, without my arm around her. I wonder how many men—or women— would ask her to dance, and if she'd say yes. Goddammit, I had to stop thinking about this. Norman was right, we had work to do, and I would drive myself bonkers if I let myself obsess over Max like that. She said she would email me. That had to be good enough for me, for now.

Me: Email is great. Have fun!

* * *

IT WAS AROUND eleven o'clock that night when I heard the little ping from the phone by my bedside table. I'd climbed in bed, tired after pulling a few extra hours with Norman in our workshop, and then hopping into *Magecraft* for a while. I opened up my email and an instant grin hit my face when I saw that it was from her.

From: Max Peters <maxine@mpeters.com>
To: Jonathan Owen <jonowen@supernaturalcomputers.com>
Subject: Book Club and Lego

Yo yo yo! (I'm never going to let you live that down, you know). So tonight was my book club, and I asked if anyone would be interested in playing a board game now and then on club nights, after we've discussed the book. They said yes! Then, after we were through discussing *The Testaments*—no, not part of the Bible, the book by Margaret Atwood—I asked if anyone wanted to stay a bit later and build some Lego. I pulled a few tubs out of the gaming room, and we drank wine and built little additions for my Lego city. Cletus had to get home, but Finley and Naomi worked together on a mobile library. It was seriously so much fun. I don't know why I was afraid to let my friends in more a long time ago. No, I do know why. I know you helped me embrace my confidence offline, and boosted my spirit. You made good points about coming out, as it were, and it turned out to be fan-flipping-tastic.

Good night!
Max

I PUT my phone back on the bedside table, rolled over onto my stomach and crossed my arms under my head, grin still in place. I was glad she had taken my advice and had a fun time showing her friends more of who she really was. Then I felt the smile slip off my face, and I wasn't above admitting I felt slightly jealous that I didn't have a wider group of offline friends like Max did. Who would I invite over, other than Norman? I guess somewhere along the way, I had let my own social circle shrink to my immediate family and him. Of course, I had my guildies. Didn't I?

CHAPTER TWENTY
MAXINE

"Sometimes I feel like all I do is bark at people."

— *Maximus_Damage*

Wrath and I stealthily made our way across the Burning Isle, wary of fire lords and dragonkin.

The haunting music of the desolate zone filled my headset as crackling flames burst randomly from the ground. Our mounts whinnied and growled as we picked our way across the rocky ground, gently leading them. Mine was my trusty zebreh, Lilith, and Wrath was leading a maned lion he called Goldie.

"Let's mount up, Max," came Wrath's voice over the in-game voice chat feature. "We need to get out of here. I don't like the firestorm headed this way."

"Agreed," I replied, clicking the button to make my avatar leap atop Lilith.

"The treasure under the lava waterfall is going to have to wait for another day if you want to make it to the raid on time, oh mighty leader," he teased. "The next jump point is right around the corner from here."

It was so bizarre—yet also familiar—playing with Wrath as an ally. If I gave it real thought, I realized we had played together plenty over the years, but there was always an undercurrent of tension even when we were both on our best behavior. Even that epic night with the Wild Hunt, I had been sending pointed glares at his avatar now and then.

After a quick run to the jump point, we portaled back to the guild hall. I was set to get ready for whatever was coming my way with my guildies. Then, right on time:

Iskander: Maximus, Burninator and I need you to go over the tweaks you made to the strategy.

I nodded, even though no one could see me, and said into the private voice chat, "Jonathan, I need to ungroup with you and join up with the bigwigs. Have fun tonight in the raid and message me if you have any problems. But please don't feel the need to leap to my defense, okay? I can handle whatever comes."

"Sure thing." His voice came through my headset, full of confidence. "You've got this. Screw any noise you get."

"Thanks, pookie bear," I teased.

"You're welcome, schnookums. Now go tell them what's what, and lead your raid," he said and then disconnected from our private chat. I smiled as I clicked on Iskander's icon and joined him and Burninator, the usual raid leader, on voice chat.

I took a long sip of the sweet tea that always accompanied my raid nights, and said confidently, "Evening, boys. What can I do for you? Everything not clear about fighting I'shaka? Phase two can get tricky so ..."

THREE HOURS LATER, I tossed my headset onto my desk in frustration. I had expected that some people might be butthurt over my "lying" to them, but I didn't expect people to act so juvenile. You had to be at least eighteen to join our guild, so I thought I was dealing with a community of adults that would act like, well, *adults.*

Maybe it wasn't as terrible as I was making it out to be. Of the assembled players who heard my voice for the first time tonight—a grand total of forty—three were vocally upset with me. Three others who weren't there messaged me saying that I was a lying bitch. Two asked if I had a boyfriend. But I had also received about a dozen private messages of support, as well as public support in the guild chat from the leaders, and from many whom I considered friends.

I grabbed my glass and headed to the kitchen to get a refill, reminding myself that it went well. I was out. No more hiding online, and gradually, no more hiding offline either. I hope Jonathan didn't mind that I left without saying goodnight, but after the third "bitch" came through the chat messages, I'd had it. The raid boss was dead, the loot was distributed; there was no need to stick around and get the brunt of people's emotions. I decided to let things chill for a day and then log in on Friday to join that night's raid.

I paused mid-pour. Friday was *always* raid night, but Friday was also the jam night at the community center. I felt myself being tugged in different directions. Did I want to spend my time gaming as usual—only now, enjoying my time with Jonathan rather than wanting to throttle him—or did I want to join in the fun with the town? Last week's session had been amazing, and I remembered how folks commented on how lovely it was to see me out and about. Most folks probably thought I was on my way to becoming another town recluse. I finished pouring, took my sweet tea, and headed to the sofa, unsure where my priorities should lie.

No, that wasn't it. I knew what I wanted to do, it's just, change would be hard. I wanted to go to the community center, having baked my own cupcakes for the dessert table for once, enjoy Julianne MacIntyre's coleslaw, and listen to some toe-tapping music while talking to folks I haven't connected with in a long damn time. I could feel it, I was ready to try that much.

I'd settled into the sofa and thought about putting on something soapy and light on Netflix to de-stress when I felt a buzzing in my pants pocket. Smiling, I pulled it out to see a new message from Jonathan.

Jonathan: Do you want to know what was said after you left? People don't know we are whatever we are, so they were openly talking in front of me.

Me: That's sweet, you going all undercover for me, but sorry 007, your recon was for naught. I would rather not know. To quote the fabulous RuPaul, "What other people think of you is none of your business." I know that's a departure from what my anxiety told me, but after getting called a bitch a few times in a row, I'm quickly realizing that I don't need extra toxicity.

Jonathan: I can respect that. I'll keep it to myself, then. Now, I know you don't want me to go all knight-in-shining-armor on you, even though that's exactly what Wrath is (lol) but may I at least defend you if I see something I don't like?

Me: You are free to say whatever you want, I won't stop you. I didn't want a fight tonight in the raid. The last thing the guild needs is people arguing over something stupid like this.

Jonathan: It wasn't all bad. Many were happy for you that you weren't really a mute.

Me: I saw some of that!

I had no sooner hit send when the phone vibrated in my hand, indicating a call was coming through. Grinning at the caller ID, I answered with a "You can't resist me, can you?"

Jonathan chuckled, his voice deep and rich and giving me goose bumps. "My fingers were getting sore from texting after gaming all evening and working in the shop today," he explained.

"Ah, yes. When I deal damage instead of tank, my fingers get so sore from typing all day at work and then gaming too. So, um … what should we talk about?"

I bit my lower lip, hoping I didn't sound as awkward as I felt.

"Well how about how awesome that raid went? Your tweaks to the fight with the

healers and the mages really made a huge difference. I don't know anyone who knows this game like you do. It's like you have some weird sixth sense for what needs to be done to take down each new fight." He sounded like an excited puppy, and I had to laugh. "You were on freakin' point, Max. I was so proud of you. I can't wait until Friday's raid when we can kick Me'kthala's ass."

Oh.

"Um, yeah, about Friday. I'm not going to be there. I want to go back to the community center, Jonathan." I sighed, unsure of how to best break this news except to simply say it. "I'm thinking of stepping back from the game for a while. There's going to be online fallout about Maximus_Damage that I honestly would rather not deal with, despite how prepared I felt for it. I felt so good spending time in town with you on the weekend. Maybe I do need to unplug more and reconnect with the folks here in Green Valley, including my mom, rather than hang out online with the people in *Magecraft* so often."

There was a short pause on his end, and I knew I had surprised him.

"I can't say I was expecting this, but watching you open up last weekend was a beautiful thing to see. What are you going to do about your spot on the council?"

"I was going to offer it to you, if you wanted it. You know as much about tactics as I do. And I can hook you up with all the mods I use, share my data with you. The other officers like you, even if you've been a jerk sometimes. I mean, let's face it, I'm not always a peach myself. I'm sure it will fly with them, even as a temporary solution." I swallowed the rest of my sweet tea and waited for his response.

"I would be honored, Max. Really," he said, but something sounded off in his voice. Was he … insecure? Or had I hurt him by deciding to stay away from the game? My heart ached at the thought that he was upset, and I had to say something more.

"You know, me wanting to leave the game behind for now doesn't mean I want to leave you behind too," I said quietly but firmly.

"Well good, because I don't plan on going anywhere," he replied.

* * *

Ping! Ping! My cell phone had turned notifications back on for the morning after being muted overnight, and the pings indicating I had new email just kept coming. I lay in bed and continued to stretch, undecided if I wanted to look or not. Considering that I had a public guild email, my private email, and a work email, in theory the pings could be for any of them. I groaned and reached across to the bedside table, checking my notifications. Forty-two emails for Maximus_Damage, none of which were from the guild leaders, and zero for Maxine Peters. Okay, so it was nothing I needed to dive into right away, but my curiosity got the better of me. I checked that my virus protection was up to date and then opened the first one, from someone whose name I didn't recognize.

From: Kaylee <kaylee@dragonlegion.com>
To: Maximus_Damage <maxattack@dragonlegion.com>
Subject: thanks!

Hi! My name is Kaylee and I'm eighteen and newer to the guild. I started playing the game last year, and I follow your posts on the game forums because you always have something useful to say about strategy, or knowing your class inside out, or even sexism in the game. I saw tonight that the forums were aflutter that you "fooled" everyone for like a decade, and I gotta say, props to you! You've played this game and kicked its ass on your own terms, and now everyone knows, if they didn't before, that a top player can definitely be of any gender. Keep on being awesome.

Hugs,
Kaylee

WELL THAT WASN'T SO bad! That was freaking fabulous. I couldn't wait to dive into the rest of the email pile. But first, I opened the game's general forums to see if there was anything there in the wider community about last night. I didn't flatter myself to think there would be, but I scrolled down, and my mouth hung open in surprise to find a dozen posts with a few hundred responses between them all. Holy shit! I clicked on a few of the posts, despite knowing that reading the comments on the internet was like wading through piranha-infested waters.

My gut was spot on. There were quite a few comments calling me names, a liar, an underskilled and overhyped player. All crap I'd heard before but now with overtly misogynistic tones. The good part? These comments were loudly shouted down by the swarm of people who had my back and shared messages of support or their own stories of in-game harassment for being a girl gamer. I decided to stay out of things for now, and let people work their feelings out without me tossing gasoline on any fires.

I put the phone down and did a few more arm stretches before sitting up and running through the day in my mind. Work, then going to the Piggly Wiggly for Mom, home, and then what? On any other day I'd say hop into *Magecraft*. Now, I wasn't so sure. I did know I'd have to at least glance at the rest of those emails to see if there were more like Kaylee's which were worthy of a reply. I could tackle that tonight. And of course, I wanted to talk to Jonathan. How weird was it that we'd only shared this bed for one night, but it felt so vast and empty now without him in it? Maybe I'd sleep in the gaming room for a while.

Feeling ridiculous for mooning over Jonathan when he was several states away and not a viable option for a relationship, I got up and hopped in the shower. While I washed my thick, long hair, I remembered some of what he'd said to me. *This isn't exactly how I pictured our first time*, and whispered when he must have thought I was asleep, *God, you are so damn beautiful and perfect.*

Despite every instinct I had going into last weekend, I missed Jonathan, whether that made me ridiculous or not. I missed the way he didn't let me get away with things, and the way his eyes lit up when he was excited about something. And that tender look on his face when we made love turned my insides to goo. That look like I was something precious.

I paused with my hands in midair, my hair in a mohawk, and the thought hit me like a ton of bricks: *Why* wasn't Jonathan a viable option for a relationship? Because of the distance? I wasn't exactly hot stuff in the Green Valley dating scene. It's not like I would be missing out on something if I did have a long-distance relationship with him, but how would that feel, to be together and yet apart? Could I handle not seeing him often while I was still trying to get to know who he was offline? Would we meet every few months for bouts of crazy monkey sex? Closing my eyes and sticking my head back under the showerhead, I decided that the next time I spoke with him—which was in all likelihood this evening—I would put out some feelers about where he was at with the whole "us" concept. As for me, I wouldn't say I was all in yet, but I definitely was interested in what might be there. We had some kind of connection, that was undeniable.

Satisfied, I rinsed off, then as I dried my hair, I methodically ran through my workday, mentally grouping tasks and assigning labels to each group. Lois calls my daily mental gymnastics my "librarian brain." I have to admit, being able to organize information in my head in such strict patterns did come in handy with cataloging. Hair finished and waiting to be braided, I selected an outfit that I would call geeky business casual from my newly mixed wardrobe of college era clothes and the last decade's work garb. Just as I was getting ready to leave my cottage, I had a light bulb moment. I needed to talk to my boss, stat.

CHAPTER TWENTY-ONE
JONATHAN

"Do you ever think we play this game too much? No? Same!"

— Wrath

Thursday morning, I woke to a persistent shaking of my right shoulder, annoying me into consciousness. Through bleary eyes I could see that it was Norman, and if the smartwatch he was flashing in my face was to be believed, it was almost … ten o'clock?! What the hell was I still doing in bed? I gave him a shove to get off my mattress and I sat up, running one hand over my face and yawning while the other ran through my tangled hair.

"Rise and shine, sunshine!" Norman said with an irritating amount of cheer. "You've already missed your mom's French toast, and damn, it was good. Bacon too. Why the smell alone didn't wake you, I'll never know."

I did. I had slept horribly last night, haunted by nightmares of running away from a never-ceasing firestorm, unable to save Max and me from the oncoming flames. Not our avatars in the game, but actually us. That had me wondering through the night if there even was an "us" to worry over. She had been kind and friendly in her emails and texts, but nothing overly flirty that conveyed the affection I held for her. I mean,

I loved her, for God's sake. We'd had an incredible weekend together, and that was something that didn't happen to me, ever. I'd had relationships with women, sure, but they always fizzled out as quickly as they started because the girl never understood me. But Max did. Would she and I fizzle out like all the rest?

By the time Norman gave me another tap to the shoulder, I muttered, "Buzz off," and got up to get ready and get my ass into the shop. I'd lost two hours of work this morning, and my mood was tanking as I realized we were still backed up. The bird's wing desk was coming along very well, and I wondered if Norman had done anything this morning besides eat my breakfast.

"Norman," I called from the mini bathroom attached to my bedroom. I was brushing my teeth, and his name came out slurred. "Why'd you let me sleep so long? We've gotta book it to get the Myers order back on schedule."

I spat into the sink. Now, clothes. I pointed vaguely in the direction of my chair that held a stack of clothing.

Norman lifted a shirt from the pile, smelled it, and then tossed it to me, hitting me in the chest. I confirmed that his sniff test was spot-on, and it would do. I slipped the shirt over my head and waited for his explanation as I tried to run a brush through my tangled hair.

"I was surprised you weren't in the shop already, so I came in. Your mom told me to let you sleep because you were 'plagued by nightmares,' and she told me I was too skinny and to sit down at the table. I'm only human, man. I can't go against the orders of your mom, she's known me since I was in kindergarten."

"Fair points," I said, picking up yesterday's jeans and slipping them on.

I still wasn't feeling any less grouchy, but at least I was ready to toss on some socks, shoes, and face the day.

"Meet you out there in five?" I asked, intending to at least grab a piece of fruit to have with my morning meds.

I was about three hours late taking those, and while such a small time frame might not impact my mood, I still felt like shit this morning. The last thing I wanted to do was varnish a desk in the hot driveway while Norman got to work inside the air-conditioned space we'd made in the garage for our computer parts and builds.

"See ya in a few," he called, heading down the hall.

I got my pill case out of the bedside table where I kept it and sat down on the bed, puzzled. The Thursday through Sunday boxes were empty. I hadn't poured my meds for the full week. Why hadn't I done that? I *always* remembered to pre-pour my meds at the beginning of the week, with the exception of last weekend when I wanted to have the original bottles with me while traveling. And except when I was having memory issues, of course.

I closed my eyes and made a concentrated effort to control my breathing, in through my nose nice and slow, then out through my mouth, like blowing out a candle. In, and out, with one hand resting on my belly so I could feel the rise and fall grounding me, calming me. Because I forgot to count out my pills for the whole week didn't mean my memory was getting spotty. It didn't mean that my mood was going out of balance, dipping down into depression or swinging up into hypomania or full-on mania. *Not necessarily,* a wicked little voice in the back of my mind chimed in. *Remember last time? Remember how it all started with crap sleep and forgetfulness?*

Shut up, I firmly told my inner voice. I wasn't having any other symptoms, right? I mean, my mood had been a little low these last few days, despite how I tried to act around Max, but that was because I missed her. It didn't necessarily mean I was sinking into a mental quagmire. I picked up the bottles one by one and poured the proper amount of each pill into every empty little square in the dispenser. Satisfied, I took my Thursday morning handful and grabbed a drink in the kitchen to wash them down on my way out the door.

* * *

THE BIRD'S wing desk was almost dry, and Norman had told me to get my sweaty self inside for lemonade with Mom while he finished up for the day. We were going to get this project done and shipped on time, barring a disaster, and I felt pumped. I didn't want to go inside and chat with Mom about her soaps, I wanted to go for a run, or better yet, start sketching out the next computer on our order list. The next few builds were cool PCs only, no desks. Easy as pie.

I sat down at the desk in the corner of the air-conditioned part of the workshop and started to sketch out some ideas for a PC with a Pride theme, but I couldn't seem to settle. I felt like I needed to move, to work my legs and burn off some of the energy humming through me even after working a seven-hour day. I got up with my sketch pad and started pacing as I drew, instinctively copying Max's habit of sticking her tongue out of the corner of her mouth while thinking. My drawing may have been in shades of gray, but I could see the strips of rainbow lights inside the chassis as clear as day, and I toyed with the best way to customize the case itself. The problem wasn't that I didn't have ideas, the problem was that I had too many.

I bumped into the table Norman was working on while I was distracted, and he gave me a "Hey! Watch it" look. He must have seen the notebook in my hands because he asked quietly, "What are you up to? Your work is done for the day. You didn't even pause for lunch when Olivia brought us sandwiches, man. I think you get a pass on starting another project a half hour before dinnertime. This will keep until tomorrow."

I put down the notebook to redo my ponytail which had come loose and noticed my hands shaking. I also noticed the look on Norman's face. Calm, but almost too much so. I knew that look.

"I'm fine," I snapped, surprising myself with how salty I sounded.

But who was he to look at me that way? As if I was an animal that needed to be approached with caution or something. *He's your best friend*, I reminded myself. Leaving my hair loose, I decided to listen to Norman and head inside, not just for a cold drink but to reacquaint myself with the shower. I knew I reeked of sweat and varnish, and I suddenly wanted this whole day to be over so I could crash into bed and wake up tomorrow in a better frame of mind.

The cell in my back pocket buzzed while I was gulping down my second glass of lemonade in the empty living room, Mom in her room probably riding her meds, and my sister Olivia still not home from work at the grocery store. I tossed together a sandwich for my supper, flopped on the couch to eat, and then yanked the phone out of my pocket. It was an email from Max, and I smiled instantly.

From: Max Peters <maxine@mpeters.com>
To: Jonathan Owen <jonowen@supernaturalcomputers.com>
Subject: An Epic Day!

Jonathan:
I hope your day has gone as well as mine has! I had to tell you as soon as I
got home from the library about how freakin' epic this day was. I had an
epiphany this morning while getting ready for work, and damn if I am not
chuffed over the whole thing. My boss, Thuy Nguyen, is luckily always open

to hearing new ideas, so I approached her today. I said that I would be willing to loan the library my gaming consoles—I've got a PS4 and Switch, remember?—one evening a week so teens could have somewhere to get out of the house and have some fun.

I pointed to studies done on the benefits of gaming, such as increased hand-eye coordination, increased literacy, and the social benefits of making new friends. Plus, it will get them into the library, making them aware of what we offer. Luckily, it wasn't a hard sell with Thuy. We already have a teen night and educational games installed on the library computers for elementary age kids, and in my view, this is the next logical step.

I also went *way* out of my comfort zone and offered to supervise the program if Naomi or Sabrina weren't available, or if it would unfairly add to their workload. I don't know if that will happen or not, but at least I took a small step to what I had originally dreamed of when I became a librarian—working with and for the kids. Wow, that was a lot of librarian chatter! I'm sorry, I'm so excited. Who would have thought that life could roll along so quickly if we take steps to make it do so? I will be online later if you want to hit me up for a quest or a chat.

Cheers,
Max-attack

I LET OUT a puff of air and felt down, probably unreasonably, after reading her email. At least she was writing to me. Although she was writing to me as if I were one of her random gaming buddies, not as her lover. But then, we weren't lovers anymore, were we? I was the only one in love. For her, I was probably a weekend booty call. Or a stepping-stone on her path to making her life roll along more quickly.

I sighed and thought about what I knew about Max. I wasn't being fair. She was strong, brave, loyal, and often kind. She wouldn't deliberately use me and lose me. But I wanted more than an email.

Unable to wait another minute, I swallowed the last bite of my sandwich and clicked on the Skype button on my phone. I found her pretty easily and sent an add request. Within a minute, she had approved me, and I clicked through to place a call. I knew I probably looked like hell right now before my shower, but I didn't care.

Max picked up on the second ring, smiling at me, with one eyebrow raised in question. She had her hair in one of those side braids from *Frozen*, and her green eyes were complimented by a hint of eye shadow. Her perfect cupid's bow mouth lifted in a smile.

"Hey, Jonathan. What's up?" she asked, cocking her head to one side. I swallowed hard, and began.

CHAPTER TWENTY-TWO
MAXINE

"There's no crying in Magecraft*!"*

— Maximus_Damage

Jonathan looked at me with desperation in his eyes, and he appeared exhausted, sweat trickling down his forehead. He must have just finished working. My smile dropped, and I tipped my head to the side in my default listening pose.

"I can't keep doing this, Maxine," he croaked, closing his eyes for a long moment. Before I could ask what he meant, he continued, "We're talking to each other now like we're friends, which is a huge step up from before. But it's not enough! Don't you feel anything deeper toward me after what we did last weekend? I know it was at least ten years for you since anything like that had happened, but nothing like that has *ever* happened to me. Not the sex, but the connection between us. I was so sure you felt it too, that you were in it with me. And now I get updates like I'm anyone else you know and are friendly with. Is that how you feel? About me, about us?" His voice steadily rose, not in anger, but in something resembling panic.

Someone could have tipped me over with a feather in that moment. I swallowed hard and schooled my face into as neutral of an expression that I could make, but I could feel myself blinking rapidly. *Do not cry*, I told myself. *Don't you dare. Warrior up, already!*

"Jonathan, I felt a lot of things last weekend," I said, sitting down on my sofa, careful not to jostle the phone too much. "It shook me, hard, getting so many of my defenses beaten down at once. I had only planned on being more outgoing in my life, I hadn't planned on …" I trailed off.

"On us. You can say it, Max. You hadn't planned on *us*." His voice was firm, but I swear I saw him pleading with his eyes.

"No," I agreed softly. "I hadn't planned on anything that happened between you and me. That first time I kissed you, I know I was plastered, but I remember feeling very surprised, even though I wanted to kiss you."

Plastered was probably an understatement. I was never drinking tequila again. I swallowed hard and fumbled for my librarian brain to kick in and organize the jumble of thoughts in my head where Jonathan was concerned. But it wasn't happening; the jumble was still there.

"Please tell me I'm not alone in this, Max," he said, licking his bottom lip and still making those kicked puppy eyes.

I couldn't pretend to be ignorant of what he was talking about. He had already admitted that he had feelings for me at one time, and given his reaction to our casual contact since he went back to Florida, I had to assume he still had those feelings. So the big scary question before us now was, what did I feel?

I thought of the email I had drafted on my lunch break and then had been too afraid to send, almost shocked by the depth of my own desires I had voiced in it.

Jonathan:

I'm beginning to feel that we are doomed to a Regency era romance, if a romance is what this is. We write letters, we talk via text. The written word has replaced the spoken, and the miles have replaced the embrace. I've been thinking a lot about what happened between us while you were here, and now to be thrust into a situation where we can't touch and can't seem to talk beyond the mundane every day, makes me wonder what it all meant. Did spending time together irrevocably change us? At this point, you are essentially indistinguishable from my other friends. I don't want you to be indistinguishable. I don't want to write letters and never see your face. What I do want is a bit more difficult to define. I want to hold you again. I want to whisper secrets as we lie under the covers, and sing out every song we know together. I want to cook for you and have you tell me how terrible it is, then dance with you in the kitchen while we wait for the pizza to arrive.

Yours,
Max

WHAT HE WAS SAYING, what he was brave enough to give voice to, wasn't that far off what I wanted in that letter. But now that I was actually confronted with the feelings, I was confused. How could I feel this deeply about someone I'd only just met in person? It was all so new and scary, and I felt like I couldn't trust it.

"I'm going to be completely honest here, because I want there to be nothing but honesty between us, Jonathan," I started carefully. "I don't *know* how I feel. If I did, I would tell you right now, I promise, and I don't make promises lightly."

He closed his eyes and made a low, self-deprecating chuckle. "I know you don't. You're so damn honorable that way. Well, let me make myself crystal clear, even if you're not ready to hear it. I love you. I've been in love with you since we met, and I'll stay in love with you because I know I have no other choice. You're it for me, Maxine. You."

I felt my eyes widen, and that neutral expression fell right off my face. "You can't know all that, Jonathan. We just met last week," I said, almost whispering.

"We met when I was seventeen, and you damn well know it," he countered, that kicked puppy look gone and replaced by determination. "I can't begin to count the number of conversations we've had, the amount of hours over the years we've played together, the two of us. Think, Max. If you really hated me, would you have kept grouping with me? Questing, dueling, fighting, whatever, we've been in each other's lives. You have to acknowledge that."

Were he and Lois trading notes behind my back? And what did it mean that both my bestie and my … my … Jonathan, were saying essentially the same thing? As his words sunk in, I knew this wasn't a point I could argue with him. Jonathan believed himself to be in love with me. Lois had guessed as much, from his behavior and words. They were both right in that there was a lot of history between us, so even though we hadn't met in person until a week ago, we really had met and been *something* for a long damn time.

But what would it mean for me to acknowledge his love for me? This morning, I had thought I needed to declare myself somehow. Now that I had the perfect opening, I wasn't brave enough to commit to anything. I was scared that this was too much, too soon. Even in my rowdier college days, I had almost no experience with an actual boyfriend, and forget romantic love. I had liked the variety of playing the field too much.

What had changed since this morning, when I was so keen to put out those feelers about how he felt about the concept of us? Was I discombobulated that he had been the one to bring it up, not me? And over Skype, to boot, where I couldn't hide behind my avatar? He looked at me expectantly, but I didn't know what to say.

"The stuff you said when you were here about not deliberately hurting me over the years, about thinking I was a decent person all along; you meant that," I said, the sincerity in his earlier words only now resonating with me.

"Of course I did," he replied. "I've been in love with you the whole time. I didn't always know how to express my feelings or frustrations. I was immature, and I was attention-seeking. I know that now. And I'll apologize for how I've behaved, over and over, if you need me to."

"No, I believe you," I said, and I realized I meant it. He had no reason to lie. He really believed he loved me. Or rather, he really *did* love me.

"Well, thank God for that much," he said, looking away and scrubbing his hand over his face.

"Jonathan?" I started, his name a question on my lips. "I'm scared that I can't trust this yet." When his face fell, I added, "Honesty, remember? It's all so new, and I've thought about you in such horrible terms for so long. What if I go down this road with you, and it crashes and burns in our faces?"

He closed his eyes and exhaled loudly, then nodded. When he spoke, there was a tone of defeat in his voice. "Yeah, I get it. Look, I gotta go. I reek and have to shower, and then I should make some supper for Mom and Olivia before I crash. I won't be online tonight, I'm tired."

Suddenly afraid he was going to disconnect, I blurted, "Jonathan!" I caught him by surprise, and his eyes darted back up to the camera. "I've missed you. I don't know how I feel about you, except I've never felt like this before either. It feels like this horrible pit in my stomach, but somehow not horrible too. I don't know. I mean, give me a little time to think about all this, please?"

A grin split his face. "Yeah, you can have time, sweetheart." I smirked. I was no sweetheart!

We waved at each other, and he said, "Talk to you tomorrow, Max. I know you're heading to the jam then, so when should I call you?"

"Same Max-time, same Max-channel works for me," I replied, returning his smile. And with a click, he was gone. I looked to She-Ra and Catra, both buzzing around my legs for food, and said out loud, "*Now* what?"

"HE STRAIGHT UP SAID HE loves you, no holds barred, while you were on Skype, probably looking like a deer in the headlights?" Lois asked, sipping her iced tea, while I drank the last of my boxed wine.

I was lounging on the bed in the gaming room, that sandalwood and sunshine smell still lingering around me, facing my laptop. I was wearing my flannel pajamas with a kitten print this time, and my hair was still in its now slightly frazzled fishtail braid from earlier.

"Yes! I'd never seen him like that, Lois, but then I only ever saw him for four days. Though I've talked to him plenty, and heard his voice through the game, and he's never sounded like that. He was practically desperate."

"He was probably desperate to get through that thick skull of yours where your own self-worth is concerned, Maxine. I know you're trying to come out of your shell or tear down those walls around you—pick your metaphor—but that can't happen overnight. It has to be a sustained effort over time, or you'll fall back into bad habits and thought patterns. And one of those is thinking that you're not worthy of affection or love. I mean, why else would you have denied yourself romantic or sexual relationships for over a decade?"

I sighed. "Lo, do you always have to go right for the freaking jugular?" I asked, downing the last of my drink. I put the empty glass on the bedside table and noted that it was now past eleven o'clock. I should be in bed instead of drinking alone and getting life-coached by my bestie. "Can we talk about you for a minute, instead of rehashing the hash that is my love life?"

Lois laughed. "But your life is so much more interesting than mine! All I do is work a job I don't love to pay rent on an apartment in a city I don't love anymore, and of course I have Elsa to take care of."

That gave me pause. "Wait, what's wrong with New York? You used to be nuttier than a squirrel about the city."

"I know, but I'm getting older, Max. I'm a single mom, raising a daughter in a city with no backyard, no room for a dog, or a zillion other things I had growing up in the country. I remember chasing lightning bugs and grasshoppers, not finding a condom in the sandbox at the park. I wonder if I'm doing right by her, raising her so differently than how I was. I want her to have those same kinds of childhood memories we both have. And on top of it all, my company is downsizing. I've got the feeling I'm on the chopping block, and I don't know what to do next."

My mind whirled with this new information. Lois and I had never met in person in the ten years I've known her, but she was like a sister to me, truly. Her parents were out of the picture, having disowned her when she had gotten pregnant and married a man of color. He lived in Europe now and didn't always send back child support regularly, and I worried what would happen to her if she did lose her job. From what I understood, it barely provided enough for them to get by. I couldn't believe I was so wrapped up in my own self that I didn't know how she was feeling about the city and her tenuous situation at work. A seed of an idea formed in my brain, and then sprouted. I thought of my mom, alone in that big house, with three spare bedrooms.

"So Lois," I said, leaning closer to the laptop. "It sounds like you want to make some changes too, especially if you lose your job. Ever consider moving?"

"Where?" she asked, narrowing her eyes at me. I grinned wide and raised my eyebrows a few times suggestively. If Mom wouldn't welcome the company—which I was sure she would—then we could always convert my gaming room into a space for Lois and Elsa. It would be cramped in the cottage with a child, but all we had to do was open up the back door and she'd have all the room she could want to run and play in.

"Well, we *do* have plenty of lightning bugs," I said.

* * *

THURSDAY MELTED INTO FRIDAY, and I had another Skype video call with Jonathan after work. He seemed calmer, more focused, but something was still a little off. He was probably anxious, waiting on me to figure out my own heart. Hell, I was anxious waiting on me to figure it out. I kept waiting for some kind of signal to whack me upside the head and tell me what to do. Barring that, I was going to have to plow along with my life and wait for my heart to quietly reveal itself. I dismissed that drafted email as a flight of fancy during a lonely moment and decided not to send it, at least until I knew for sure that was how I really felt.

The cupcakes I baked after my Skype call were still a bit warm when I dropped them off at the dessert table at the jam session. A lot of folks nodded at me, or smiled, and asked about my mom; the predictable, everyday type of conversations. But what I didn't expect was the keen interest from the good citizens of Green Valley in my gentleman visitor from last week. I should have known I was wading into shark-infested waters, and the town gossips could smell blood. I made it out and back home relatively unscathed, with a few comments on how nice it was to finally see me with a man, and how much Mom would love a grandchild before I was too old to have them. I couldn't decide which irked me more, being written off as a spinster or this new and overeager interest in my theoretical love life.

The weekend dawned bright and sunny, full of the glory of autumn in the Great Smoky Mountains. Days like this were why I'd agreed to host the gathering here in the first place. The trees were like various shades of fire, and the wind blew softly but cool and crisp. I couldn't stay inside and game all day like I would on a typical weekend. It was too nice outside, and a walk across town to Mom's sounded perfect. After breakfast, I tossed on a *Doctor Who* T-shirt, a light hoodie, and faded jeans, then pulled my backpack from the closet and loaded up a few games. I laced up my running shoes and stifled a yawn, resisting the teeny part of me that longed to climb inside some cozy yoga pants and take a seat in my comfy gaming chair at the computer. As I was leaving my cottage, I caught a glance at my reflection in the mirror by the front door and realized I should go to Knoxville and visit some plus-size clothing stores. I couldn't keep wearing my old, worn out college clothes, and frumpy, oversized business casual wasn't going to cut it anymore either. I resolved to do that before going back to work on Monday.

My mind cleared in the fresh autumn air, thoughts of Jonathan bubbled up. I shook my head, almost like a wet dog, and instead thought about Lois and her situation. The

Green Valley job market wasn't exactly booming, but she could probably find something in the region. And it's not like I would charge her rent on a house that was already paid for, thanks to what was left to me by my grandparents, were she to move in with me. I was sure Mom would feel the same about her house.

This morning, mom and I would hopefully have a nice, long talk about it, and about my situation with Jonathan. I had a therapy appointment next week in light of what I had gone through at the sheriff's office, but there was something special about my mother. She always had this way of putting things into perspective for me. Her neighborhood crept up on me faster than I though. I checked my watch and realized I made some good time. Go me!

CHAPTER TWENTY-THREE
JONATHAN

"I looked down into the cavern and all I saw was chaos. I wasn't going in without backup."

— Wrath

I awoke with a start when Olivia heaved opened my door, crossed to the window, and pulled back the curtains, letting in an instant headache-inducing amount of brightness. She then flung the window open and set about picking up discarded clothing and heaping them into a laundry basket she carried.

"Ugh, what time is it?" I asked, my mouth dry and tasting like a used gym sock probably would.

"It's 3:00 p.m. On Sunday, in case you were wondering about that too." She sounded cross as she made her way around the room, loading up the basket, then setting it down to pick up discarded cans of Red Bull.

"I wasn't, but thanks," I replied, feeling almost more tired than when I fell asleep sometime around 4:00 a.m.

I had been formally welcomed onto the senior council of officers in the guild and had celebrated by raiding, talking, and gaming into the wee hours. The only problem was that we still didn't have a female officer with Max stepping back, so we decided late last night to split the tactics and member-at-large positions. That would allow me to focus on strategy and they could recruit a woman to take the newly created post. Everyone missed Max, but they got why she wanted to step away from the game for a time.

"That surprises me. You've been in this cave since after work on Friday. There's a smell emanating from this room. And have you even eaten anything lately, or just lived off the sugar in these?" She held up a can in an accusatory fashion.

"Hey, I had food," I replied, sitting up in bed and yawning wide. Shit, I'd missed my morning pills. Again. I was supposed to take them around the same time every morning, but my pill schedule was becoming erratic.

Olivia held up an empty package that once contained turkey jerky. "This," she proclaimed, "is not *food*. When Mom or I go to the trouble to cook a meal, the least you can do is drag your tail down the hallway, in some clean clothes, and sit at the table to eat it. You just have to show up and plunk yourself in a chair. How hard is that? You know you need to be careful, Jonathan."

"Olivia, please don't start with me, not when I've just woken up."

"And that's another thing! Why are you—"

"Olivia!" I interrupted her. "Do you think you're helping the situation right now by getting in my face over it? I know, I screwed up. I let my routine go. I'll be more careful, okay? I'll hop in the shower and then put on my own laundry. You're not my maid."

"Well, you're damn right about that," she said with a soft smile and affection in her voice. "I worry, you know. You've been different since you got home." She put the laundry basket down on my chair and sat down on the bed next to me. "Is there anything you need to talk about? I'm always here. And that reminds me, when is your next appointment with Tom?"

I thought for a minute before eventually grabbing my cell off the bedside table and checking my schedule. "It's next Thursday," I replied, knowing what would happen next. The pursed lips.

Olivia let out a puff of air, then turned to me, pursing her lips like they've never been pursed before. "I think that's too far away. You should call in the morning and try to get in tomorrow. Whatever work you have to do isn't as important as your mental health," she said, sounding so sensible and yet so irritating.

Everything was irritating me, from the sunlight, to the mess that was my room, to Olivia preaching to me. I closed my eyes and tried to breathe in and out for relaxation like I'd been taught, but it wasn't helping the low-level hum buzzing through my brain.

"Liv, I love you, but I think I need you to go before I say something I don't want to," I managed, noticing my hands shaking.

She must have noticed too. "I'll leave you alone after I watch you eat a sandwich."

I flopped back down on my bed. "Fine. Sandwich, shower, garbage, laundry. In that order. Will that make you happy?" I snapped at her.

"Yes," she replied simply, then rose and headed out my door, calling back to me, "And don't you dare fall back asleep!"

The sandwich and the shower did chirk me up, and I conceded that Olivia was right to pull me from the chaotic squalor my room had descended into. I picked up Red Bull cans and dirty socks, then vacuumed the room. That hum of energy was still buzzing through me, like ants were crawling under my skin. I needed to run, despite the heat. I had the presence of mind to grab a water bottle and my earbuds for my cell so I could turn up my music and drown out my brain, which was whirling, whirling. Max was still on my mind—of course she was—and I needed to burn off some of my frustration.

I laced on my bedraggled running shoes and headed out into the humidity. I stretched for a minute, then ran like hell for Norman's house.

* * *

NORMAN HANDED me a can of Coke, took a beer for himself, and we sat down in his air-conditioned living room. Unlike me, Norman lived alone, his mother having passed about five years ago. He never knew his father. The trailer looked like it did when she still lived here; in other words, it was neat as a pin. No stray beer cans, no sink heaped with dishes. I thought the discipline Norman learned in the military had a lot to do with that since he'd been a total slob before. Or maybe he didn't want to dishonor his mother's memory by trashing her house. I lifted my can of Coke to the back of my neck for a moment and closed my eyes, relishing in the coolness after the humidity outside.

"Not that I don't appreciate this unexpected visit, but what's up? You looked like you ran as if hellhounds were at your heels. It's boiling out there today. Why didn't you drive?" he asked, opening his beer and taking a long drink.

"I had to work off some of this energy," I replied, popping the tab on my can and drinking half of it in one long gulp.

"Energy?" Norman asked, sounding confused. "I hate to break it to you, but you look like something I hauled out of the swamp. I bet you a twenty you could lie down right now and be comatose until morning."

Well, maybe he wasn't wrong. I didn't know how I felt, exactly, other than unsettled.

"Drink up, there's more where that came from. And whenever you're ready, I'll drive you home. I'd say just crash here, but you've got to go back for your pills, right?"

My pills. *Damn.* I tried to remember the last day I'd taken my morning meds. Thursday? It was Sunday, right? Which made me also wonder, when was the last time I had talked to Max?

As I was reaching for my phone, Norman asked, "So, have you talked to Max lately? I haven't seen her online, and I was getting a bit concerned."

"About?" I asked, putting my Coke down on the coffee table and turning toward Norman, the phone in my hand.

"Her, man. I saw some of the posts on the general forums. It hasn't all been a lovefest for Maximus_Damage. She's been called names like bitch, slut, ugly, and even asked when she was going to get her surgery so she'd really be a guy. All kinds of stuff that was various shades of offensive, unnecessary, and dickish."

"Is dickish even a word?" I muttered as I fumbled furiously with the phone, unlocking it and searching for new texts or emails from her. There was one, stamped yesterday late afternoon that I hadn't read. "I should have been keeping an eye out for that kind of behavior, but since our guildies were keeping in line, I assumed that people in general were being cool. I haven't checked the game's general forums since Wednesday's raid. There's an email from her. I better read it."

"You do that," he said, getting up and crossing over the trailer to his fridge. "I'm going to throw together some sandwiches for us. You look like you could use the fuel."

I batted away the wayward thought that it was strange how everyone kept wanting me to eat sandwiches, and clicked on Max's name in my app.

From: Max Peters <maxine@mpeters.com>
To: Jonathan Owen <jonowen@supernaturalcomputers.com>
Subject: An Epic Day, Part Deux

Jonathan:

I'm sorry we didn't get a chance to Skype or connect, but hopefully you'll get this before bed, and I'll hear back from you. Today was amazing! Another giant leap for Max-kind. I set up a pull-and-hold order for my comics at the gaming shop in town, so I'll have a reason to visit without feeling like a fool. And they are ordering in a manga version of my favorite anime movie, *Wolf Children*. Have you seen it? I also played a fun game of Ticket to Ride with some teens who were finishing up their game of Magic. And what do you know, they play *League of Magecraft*! We talked about the game, and I didn't feel too much like the frumpy old outsider.

Before the gaming shop I walked to my mom's place, where she and I had a long talk about my best friend, Lois, from New York. You may remember her from *Guilds of the Ages,* she played as Peily way back in the day. Anyway, she's up against it with money, work, and general life dissatisfaction. We put our heads together and agreed that if she wanted to, Lois and her daughter, Elsa, could move in with Mom. It's a big house with one woman living in it, who happens to love kids. Mom has a huge yard, and if Elsa wants to play in the woods, she can always come to my side of town and play where we did. I really hope Lois decides to bring Elsa here and relocate permanently to Green Valley.

Tomorrow, I'm road-tripping to the malls in Knoxville to update my wardrobe. I'm always nervous about spending money unless it's on some-thing I'm passionate about, and while I'm not very passionate about clothes shopping, I am about looking both my age and having things that fit properly. So I'll be running around again tomorrow, and likely won't be online, but please write back when you get this so I know everything is cool with us. I miss you.

Hugs,
Max

SHIT. Shit, shit, *shit.* She wrote this email to check up on me, to see if she and I were still simpatico. And I screwed up by not even bothering to check my emails. I opened my texting app and messaged her.

Me: Max! I just got your email. I'm sorry, I hope you weren't worried. Everything's fine with us, as far as I'm concerned.

I got up and started pacing as I waited for her to text me back. She might still be on the road and not have gotten it, or … PING!

Max: Hey, stranger! Don't sweat it. I had a stitch 'n bitch fest with Lois and a fresh box of wine last night, and today was busy, busy. I'm home now with a small mountain of clothing and nary a single piece of corduroy in sight.

Me: That sounds most excellent. I hope you had fun!

Max: I did. How are you?

There it was. She said she wanted honesty between us. But I didn't know how to answer that question without worrying her, and I had enough people who fussed over me. And still, despite everything, I didn't want to look weak in front of her.

Me: I'm great. I'm at Deathdrop's place, and we're talking about our work schedule for the coming week. So, busy too. Hey, I gotta run. We're about to have dinner.

I could feel my pants on fire.

Max: Okay, enjoy! xo

Then I remembered what Norman had said about the treatment she was getting on the forums. *Goddammit.* Did she know what was being said? If she didn't, should I bring it up? But if she did and I didn't mention it, that would make me an even bigger ass, wouldn't it? I considered it for a moment, and then typed out another message.

Me: Hold up! I know you've been getting blowback on the general forums. I'm sorry. You don't deserve any of it.

Max: I was wondering if you'd seen it. Thank you. Just insecure people who would rather tear someone they don't know down than cope with whatever is making them uncomfortable in their own lives, I think. Well, that and a pervading culture of toxic masculinity. Don't worry, I'll be fine. I've got a thick skin. They aren't keeping me from the game. I am, for now. I've liked how it's felt, being out and about. But I won't leave *Magecraft* forever. Ttyl?

Me: Sure.

I tossed my phone onto the coffee table and felt oddly dejected, like maybe Max didn't need me in her life anymore. I mean, was I even relevant without *League of Magecraft* to bind us through common interest?

* * *

I WAS LIVING ON COFFEE, energy drinks, and mood stabilizers—when I remembered to take them—with the odd snack here and there, the days and nights blurring together. Olivia was swamped at work and didn't press me about calling Tom, so I didn't. I was gaming into the early mornings some nights, and others I would pace around, go for a run, or pass out right after dinner and sleep until Norman woke me for work. I could feel myself slipping, and I didn't know what to do.

What I did know was that I missed Maxine like crazy. The ache was how I imagined a phantom limb would feel, like she was supposed to be here and a part of me, but she was cut off. I couldn't touch her, hold her, taste her. I would lie in bed at night and try to sleep, taunted by thoughts of her lying next to me, whispering secrets in the dark and talking about a future where we built a life and even a family together.

Then reality would come crashing down around me. *How suited are you and Florida?* Momma Rose had asked. Well, considering the obligations I had here, pretty damn well-suited. Olivia worked odd hours at the grocery, and we never really budgeted for extra help for Mom. That was why I was here, working from home and not living with Norman and working at his place. And that was another thing—our business. While our customer base was in online orders, Norman was in Florida. I couldn't bail on our shared livelihood and run off to Tennessee.

173

Communication with Max was spotty at times, but she was busy with her new lease on life. How could I be anything but happy for her, even though with every step she took forward, it was like a step away from me? She came online into *Magecraft* now and then, and we would explore or quest together, talking about nothing real but having fun at least. I encouraged her to grab on to her following and make her own YouTube channel or even play on Twitch, streaming her playtime or making videos where she broke down strategy and the best mods to use. She seemed excited about the idea, so I supported her as best as I knew how, by offering to build her a new machine. She said hers was starting to overheat and couldn't handle the newer requirements for peak performance in the game. Norman insisted we only charge her for the parts at cost, and no labor, for which I was grateful. After his suspension from the guild lifted, he was far less contrary. Until one day, he wasn't.

"That's it!" Norman yelled, his voice reverberating off the walls of our small workshop. He put down the graphics card he was holding and pointed a screwdriver in my direction.

"What's what?" I asked, not used to Norman getting genuinely upset about things, at least not in the last few years.

"You, man. You're over there staring out the window like a lost puppy or something. And when you're not doing that, you're pulling at your hair or pacing around the room. I am doing everything today because your head isn't right. I don't want us to get backed up again, and I also thought you'd want to help build your girlfriend's machine." He pointed with the screwdriver to the case on the benchtop.

I exhaled sharply, almost with a grunt. "She's not my girlfriend, Norman. Hardly. We send each other emails. Frickin' emails. And when she periodically logs in to *Magecraft,* we quest together. We're questing buddies. I'm in love with her, but she still hasn't told me how she feels, so we're friends. She is most definitely not my girlfriend."

"Not the point I was trying to make, Jonathan," Norman said, shaking his head at me. "I know you bailed on your last appointment with Tom. I didn't tell Olivia because I figured it was your business, but right now, your business is my business, because it's *our* business, and it's going to tank without you participating!"

When I made no move to reply, he continued, gritting his teeth, "Fine. Let your brain turn into Swiss cheese. Moon over Maximus until you pine away to death. But know that I give a shit about you and this company we've built. So if you don't care about your own life, care about me and what we created. Care about your family. Do what you need to do to get your damn head on right, man. Can't you see that you need some help here?"

My breathing started to come in shorter pants, and I felt the familiar flicker of panic working its way up my spine. I didn't like how he was calling me out because everything he was saying was accurate as hell. Was I so transparent? How did he know I hadn't been to see Tom? Pressed up against it, I felt my fight-or-flight response kick in, and I didn't want to fight with Norman.

"I'll go for a walk," I said, "and we can get some space, cool off. I'll help with the build as soon as I get back." I made a move toward the door.

"You can't walk away from your own head, Jonathan. Call Tom, and sort this shit out with him and your doctor."

CHAPTER TWENTY-FOUR
MAXINE

"Whenever you're launching a rescue mission remember: eyes on the prize. Get distracted, and we all go down."

— *Maximus_Damage*

The pinging of my cell woke me at 7:00 a.m. on a Saturday. Several weeks had gone by since "the talk" with Jonathan, and while we had been texting and emailing fairly regularly, something had felt off. Emails at odd hours, rambling sentences, or sometimes even frantic sounding messages asking how I was. I wanted to ask him about his mental health, but I didn't know if my questions would be welcome or overbearing. I knew he missed me, and I missed him, very badly, and I felt even worse about leaving him hanging about my feelings, which were growing stronger every day. My therapist was of the opinion that I had a long way to go in my own recovery from the Wraith attack, and that even though I'd sought therapy at the time, I hadn't stuck with it long enough. Now I had to put in the work, and in her opinion it wasn't the healthiest time for me to get involved in a relationship. Especially a long-distance one with the extra pressures of rarely seeing each other. And oh, how I wanted to see him again. I felt like a piece of my own self was missing without him, and I didn't know what to do about it.

The insistent pings weren't going away. I groaned, then grabbed my phone, surprised to find messages from an unknown number. I flipped to the latest text.

Unknown: Heya Maximus, this is Deathdrop again. I swiped your digits from Jonathan's phone. Can I call you? It's important.

I was instantly awake and alert. For Deathdrop to be reaching out, something had to be wrong. I quickly banged out a reply.

Me: Yes!

The phone rang in my hand, and I picked up immediately.

"What's wrong?" I asked, my Spidey-senses tingling.

"It's Jonathan. He's not doing so good." He paused. "I've been trying to keep him going, Max, I swear. But I think he needs more help than I can offer. He's coming unglued."

"Unglued, how?" I asked, picturing a room full of newspaper clippings hung on the wall with pieces of string crisscrossing them. I instantly scolded myself for the wayward thought. I should know better than to stereotype manifestations of people's mental health.

"I think … I think you should see for yourself. I think he needs you, more than he'd ever admit. And I need backup. The more support he has right now, the better. Feel like hopping on a plane? You can crash at my place. I have a spare room, and I'll even pick you up at the airport."

I floundered for a moment, almost falling out of bed as I scrambled for pen and paper from my desk across the room. I poised the pen and said, "Give me all your info. I'll book a flight ASAP and text you the details for my arrival."

After haphazardly packing my largest suitcase, I got on the horn with Lois via Skype. If we were serious about her moving down here soon, she had to know I was skipping town for an indeterminate amount of time. I gave her the condensed version of events as she looked at me with wide eyes, nodding now and then in understanding. Then, in typical Lois fashion, she unleashed hell.

"So you're finally going to tell him, then," she said.

"Tell who what?"

"Max! Don't play dumb. You're finally going to tell Jonathan you love him."

"Love him?" I slowly sounded out the words. Did I love Jonathan Owen? My heart, so confused and torn with worry over his health, and still unsure about the nature of the connection we had forged that weekend, pounded in my chest so loudly I was sure Lois could hear it. I thought back to lazy hours in bed together, talking and touching and feeling like the only two people in the world. I remembered his kindness to my friends, the respect shown to my mother; everything right down to that ridiculous squirrel and flying melon.

I closed my eyes to stop the tears pooling in them from spilling over, and broke into a wide smile. "Holy shit," I whispered, and the chuckle I heard from my laptop made me laugh, too. I loved him. I had met my enemy and fallen ridiculously, stupidly, gloriously in love. My therapist's words echoed in my mind, that I might not be in a good place to be in a relationship. Well, that was all fine and well, but I had to follow my heart here. And it was telling me to get to the airport, stat.

"Lois, I think you missed your calling. You should be a relationship coach. Sorry, but I've got to jet. Literally."

* * *

ONCE AGAIN I found myself in an airport, looking around for the face of a stranger. Only this time they were carrying a neon orange sign that read MAXIMUS_DAMAGE. I shook my head at the overkill—Deathdrop could have gone with plain old Max—and made my way toward the tall, lightly muscled man leaning on a cane. He wore a band T-shirt and jeans with work boots, and wild blond hair with a somewhat neatly trimmed beard. During my quick assessment as I wheeled my suitcase over, I also noted that he had kind-looking eyes, so probably not a serial killer. Just a dedicated prankster who I could either thank or throttle for arranging my weekend with Jonathan.

At my approach, Deathdrop stuck the sign under his armpit and put out his hand. We shook, and the action caused me to choke up with unexpected emotion. This guy knew about Jonathan and me. He was Jonathan's best friend and probably cared about Jonathan even more than I did, and yet he needed *my* help. I had to buck up and do what I came here to do.

"Deathdrop," I said as we shook hands.

"Maximus," he replied, giving me a similar once-over.

"I think we can go by street names, yeah?" I said, breaking into a small smile. "It's Maxine, or just Max. And your name is Norman, right?"

"Yeah. But no Norm, okay? I hate that nickname," he said, taking my suitcase from me with his free hand and navigating us through the arrivals terminal.

My first instinct was to argue that I could handle my own luggage, but I got that he was helping his guest.

"Cool by me," I answered, wondering why I had packed so much crap.

I had taken a leave of absence from work, which Thuy said I was due for anyway, with so many unused vacation days sitting there. She said that the other catalogers in the region could pick up my slack for the time being as I had certainly been carrying the brunt of the workload for long enough. I was totally honest with her about where I was going and why. I told her I didn't have a firm return date, but that I should only be a few weeks. She was equally as forthright when she said that my job would be waiting for me on my return, and that I would be missed. After frantically packing and calls to my mom, Thuy, and Norman, I stopped by the library to drop off my gaming consoles. I wanted the teen gaming nights to continue even if I wasn't there to bring in my equipment every week.

We wove our way through the crowded terminal to Norman's beast of a truck, quiet settling between us.

He offered to let me use the radio, but instead I blurted out, "Tell me everything, please. I've been imagining everything from him going all *A Beautiful Mind* to … I don't even know. I should have researched bipolar disorder. I should have done some damn reading. I was so busy with my own stupid shit, I barely skimmed the Wikipedia article on it."

"Hey, stop that," Norman said, reaching out and quickly clasping one of my nervously quivering hands in his. He squeezed my hand and released it, putting his back on the wheel. "We all screw up, Max. Do I think you should've been more involved in learning about Jonathan's condition? Yes. But you can fix that now, if you are willing to put in the work."

I half-smiled and nodded. I was worried about Jonathan, and even more worried that Norman and I had decided to make this a stealth operation. Jonathan didn't know I was coming, and I hoped he would be cool with it.

"So, again. Tell me everything, please?"

Norman ran a hand over his beard and started carefully. "He hasn't been the same since he got back from Tennessee, but I think all that emotional upheaval was a trigger for underlying issues."

"So falling in love …" I trailed off.

"Oh, girl, the ship sailed on him being in love with you a decade ago. That's not what set him off. It was probably the intensity of you two hooking up and then being separated without knowing where you stood. It's not your fault, you had a perfectly normal reaction to your nemesis showing up and not knowing how to deal with the fact that he's a damn decent guy."

"I care about him so damn much, in ways I never thought possible," I confessed. "But I still feel awful about my part in this."

"Well, here's the funny thing, and I'm going to be blunt, because I always am. *It's not about you or your feelings*. It's not about me, or his mom, or his sisters. It's about Jonathan, and he's hurting. We have to help him get his feet back on solid ground and out of that hypomanic head of his, or hand him a rope so he can climb out of a hole of depression."

"Wait a minute. He's depressed *and* manic? How the hell does that even work?"

"Hypomanic. 'Hypo' meaning under, so not quite full on mania. And welcome to the joys of bipolar disorder. It's called a mixed episode, and I'm certain that's what's going on. It happened before, when he needed to go on new meds. The problem is, the stubborn ass is dodging his therapist and doctor. That's where I'm hoping you can come in, convince him that we are all trying to help him, and to go see them."

I took that all in and gazed out the window, processing this new information. "Won't the therapist come to the house if the family asks?"

"Yes, but here's another funny thing I've learned being Jonathan's friend through all this: the decisions have to be his. We can't stage an intervention and like, ambush him with his therapist. We can't haul him to the car and drag him there either. He has to take charge in the decisions about his mental health."

"But if he's too sick—"

"I know you're new at this, so you're going to have all kinds of preconceived notions and make all kinds of well-intentioned mistakes. Trust me on this one, we have to be the supporting players here. Jonathan is the one in this fight. We can't charge in headlong or force him into anything. We have to be there to listen, not judge, and to help him find the path through the dark forest of his brain. And yes, I like metaphors. I wanted to be an English major. Do you mind if I smoke? I hate it, but every now and then when stress gets me, I need one of the stupid cancer sticks to calm down. Habit I picked up overseas." Norman looked straight ahead as he drove, his hands tight on the wheel.

"I don't mind," I said, because I didn't. Before this was over, we probably were all going to cope in a myriad of ways with the situation and with our feelings. Norman pointed to the glove box, and I popped it open, finding the almost full pack of cigarettes and a lighter. I took one out and handed it and the lighter to him, and he nodded his thanks.

* * *

THE HAPPY ACRES Trailer Park where Norman lived was less than a five-minute drive away from Jonathan's home. It felt almost like an itch, being so close but unable to go to him. Norman and I had agreed the best way to break it to Jonathan that I was in Florida was for Norman to bring Jonathan to his house, instead of me knocking on Jonathan's front door. That way it would be up to Jonathan whether to tell his family I was here. While Norman went to pick him up, I set about making a salad and some wraps for dinner. I hadn't eaten much all day, and Norman had been nice enough to point out the stuff in the fridge waiting to be tossed together.

I was folding up a fifth wrap—I'd made plenty since most men I knew practically inhaled their food—when I heard the rumble of Norman's truck. I quickly placed the wrap on the pile with the others and moved to sit down on the couch. I was suddenly feeling very, very anxious about this. Why had I agreed to any scheme hatched by Deathdrop? No, Norman, I reminded myself. Not the trickster from *Magecraft*, but Jonathan's best friend who only had his best interests at heart. *Calm down*!

"You know I hate surprises, man."

I heard Jonathan's voice at the front door, and I could feel myself inadvertently shrink back into the couch cushions as far as possible. My breaths were shortening, and I thought I was on the verge of an anxiety attack as the door pushed open and Jonathan came inside, alone. Norman must have decided to give us a few minutes. Jonathan scanned the kitchen, then advanced on the plate of wraps. He hadn't seen me, but he'd sure seen the chicken salad and spinach fare. The food was in his hand

and halfway to his mouth when I stood up and coughed. He spun around, and as soon as his eyes hit me, the wrap went sailing to the floor.

"Max!" he sputtered, wiping stray chicken salad from the front of his shirt.

"Hey, Jonathan," I said, all my anxiety forgotten as we locked eyes.

I broke into a wide grin, and instinct took over. I ran to him and grabbed him in my arms. He must have been in a bit of shock because it took him a few moments to get with the program. Then he gripped his arms around me tight, burrowing his face in my hair as I sought shelter in the crook of his neck.

"Maxine," he murmured, nuzzling me gently.

I just held on, inhaling that comforting sandalwood and sunshine scent, now tinted with the odor of sunscreen and fresh-cut grass. I tangled a hand in his dark ponytail, urging his head to rest against mine, forehead to forehead. We looked each other deep in the eyes, and any bit of doubt about coming to Florida to help out was gone. This had been the right thing to do, for him and for me.

"Not that I'm not happy to see you, but why aren't you in Green Valley? How did you even find out where Norman lives? Why did he—" He paused, and then loosened his hold on me, backing up a fraction. He let out a long breath as he closed his eyes and released me, turning to pace around the kitchen. "He sent for you, didn't he?" he asked accusingly.

"If I hadn't wanted to see you, I wouldn't be here, no matter what Norman said," I answered, putting conviction in my voice.

I took a step toward him, and he took a step backward, butting up against the kitchen counter like a skittish cat. Okay, not the reaction I'd expected, but I had expected a steep learning curve. Cornering him was definitely falling into the category of well-intentioned mistakes that Norman had warned me about. I took a few steps back and made sure my arms were loose and open at my sides, palms facing toward him.

"I'm not here to force you to do anything, or to gang up on you, I swear. I missed you, and yes, I'm worried for you. But I also wanted to see you and maybe settle things between us. I think that uncertainty has been getting to you, Jonathan. I know it's been getting to me. And plus, Norman mentioned y'all have been a bit behind in the shop. Thought I might get my hands in there and help. I did build my last few systems from scratch," I reminded him.

"I suppose he also told you that we're only behind because of me," he said, crossing his arms over his chest.

I cringed inwardly at my misstep.

"He said no such thing," I replied, shaking my head for emphasis. "I asked about the business and offered to help because I want to, not because you are personally failing at something."

"Please don't try to break into any psychobabble, Max. I know it all, I've heard it all. I've been living with this thing for years and years. You think I can't see when people are getting all concerned and worried and acting like I'm a ticking time bomb or some shit? I am not my father. You do not have to tiptoe around me just because everyone seems to think I'm having a hard time." He unfolded his arms and stuck his hands in his pockets, then looked down to the floor.

"You're right. We are concerned and worried, but I know you aren't like your father, Jonathan. I know you aren't going to snap and hurt me. And that is something I have experience with."

I didn't know why I was being confrontational. I was exhausted, and I wanted to sit down and hold him, not do this right now. Norman's words from earlier echoed in my mind; it's not about me or my feelings at the moment. Right.

"I'm sorry that you might feel threatened by us trying to help you. I'm sorry if I was wrong to come here."

"Why did you?" he asked, looking up and meeting my eyes. "I mean, yes, I missed you. But I didn't want you to see me like this. I think I ought to have had some say in this whole plan you two cooked up."

"I came because even before Norman called, I realized there was nowhere else in the world I'd rather be than at your side. I was trying to scrounge up the courage to tell you that somehow."

His expression softened, and he appeared to relax, his eyes lighting up at my declaration. "It's good to see you, Max. You look good." His mouth quirked up into a smile on one side, and I took it as a win. He walked over to me, folded me up in his arms, and for that minute, everything felt as it ought to be.

CHAPTER TWENTY-FIVE
MAXINE

*"Holy hell, where was our protection for the healers in that fight? Without them,
you're toast. Remember that."*

— *Maximus_Damage*

"So we've got the pack of dragonkin cornered, and I go into stealth mode, creep around from the side, and am about to attack, when Lucille crashes, and BAM! I'm out. I reboot, relog, and I come back to find the thing snacking on the priest in my party, and everyone else is toast. Meanwhile, I've been in stealth the whole time, looking like I'm just watching everything go down. So I get a bunch of pissy messages saying that I should have stepped in to stop the carnage and that our whole guild sucks." Deathdrop—er, Norman—shared an old *Magecraft* gameplay of his as we ate our wraps and salad around his dinner table.

Norman had given us about a half hour to be alone with each other, which I appreciated. We didn't talk about much after our conversation in the kitchen, instead we sat on the couch, with me curled into his side and him touching my hair softly. When Norman came back, the easiest topic of conversation was, of course, the one passion we all shared—*Magecraft*.

So we told tall tales of epic quests and treasure hunts gone awry, and ate in between bouts of laughter or trash-talking each other's skills. It reminded me of what I missed about the game, and why I played in the first place, for that camaraderie and sense of shared fun. It was also a good diversionary tactic from answering any more tough questions about why I came here behind Jonathan's back.

"So did you ever get Lucille fixed?" I asked Norman, in between bites of the chicken salad.

"Damn straight I did," he answered, grabbing another wrap. "That little guild vacation I was forced to take? We were slammed with work, but I had spare time at night, so I rebuilt her from the ground up. I sunk a chunk of my savings into the best parts I could get for her, and she's amazing. I'll let you game on her while you're here, if you like," he offered.

"Um, I wouldn't be keen to take him up on that, Max," Jonathan interjected. "You don't know where the hands that touch that keyboard have been."

I cringed. "Thanks, Norman, but I think I'll stick to my laptop," I said, laughing.

We chatted and ate, and when we were doing the dishes, Jonathan asked, almost too casually, "So what's the plan here? I'm assuming y'all have one."

"We didn't exactly coordinate a plan of attack, man," Norman replied, putting the last plate away.

"Didn't you? You went behind my back to get her contact information, you kept it a secret that you were bringing her down here. You had to have something in mind." His tone was accusatory as spoke. He then leaned back against the counter, crossing his arms over his chest.

"It's as I told you before, Jonathan," I interjected, "I'm worried. But I also missed you, and I had it pointed out to me that you missed me too. I owe it to you to be here for you when you are having a hard time, and I owe it to us to settle what this is between us, or at least find out what it could be. That's why I'm here."

"You owe it to me," he said flatly.

"Yes, I owe it to you, as someone who has been my friend for ten years. And as someone who I care so much about that it keeps me up at night, wondering how you are doing, how your day was, and how empty that pillow beside me feels without your head on it," I answered, daring him to challenge me.

He didn't.

"And you're staying here with Norman?" He shot looks between the two of us. It was Norman who jumped in before I got a chance to open my mouth.

"It doesn't mean anything. You gotta know I'd never go after your girl. I thought that it's already crowded at your place with three people, and she'd have to couch crash or share your room. Here, she's got a whole room to herself. You can come over any time after work, and hell, I don't care if you want to stay all night. I'm at the other end of the trailer." He winked at me, and I couldn't help the snort-laugh that came out.

Jonathan readjusted his position, but kept his arms crossed. "That's all well and good. I really mean that. But I have to say, as someone who has watched a lot of episodes of *Intervention*, this has the word intervention stamped all over it in neon red. Are my mom and Olivia going to come through that door next? Elaine on Skype, perhaps?"

I took a few steps closer to him. "Jonathan, no. Absolutely, no. This isn't an intervention. We haven't even told your mom or sisters that I'm here. What they know is up to you. And no one is going to sit you down and read a letter, and no one is going to issue you ultimatums." I sighed, and ran a hand through my hair, struggling to find the right words. "What you are seeing is that people who love you are gathering around you to be supportive. To be your backup, because we think you need some right now."

He seemed to consider this, then broke into a shit-eating grin. "You love me, huh?" he asked, the smile going from ear to ear. He would happen to latch onto that slip of the tongue.

"Yeah, well, don't let it go to your head," I muttered while he gloated over me.

"You heard her say it, didn't you, Norman?"

"Sure did," he answered, being of no help at all. Okay, time to extract myself from this very uncomfortable moment.

"Tomorrow's Monday, so you'll be back in the shop all day, yeah?" I asked. At their nods, I said, "I'd like to come with, if that's okay. I can work on my own system since I know y'all are backed up with orders, if you have the space."

It was like a black cloud descended over Jonathan's head, and I couldn't figure out what I'd said wrong, but obviously it was something. He dropped his arms, stuck his hands in his pockets, and with his head down, paced around the counter. I looked to Norman, who was staring at me like I was an idiot. I shrugged, and he widened his eyes and then cocked his head in Jonathan's direction. Dammit, why couldn't I be telepathic?

I closed the distance between me and Jonathan, putting my hand on his arm. He stopped pacing and looked up at me, his eyes twin orbs of dismay.

"It's my fault," he said straight up. "It's my fault we're backed up at work again. We caught up on everything after my trip to Green Valley, and then we should have been able to fly through our orders with both of us on the job, but what he's too damn loyal to say is that I've been dropping the ball. He's been doing the bulk of the work for like, shit, I don't even know. How long, Norman? Be honest. Honesty seems to be the theme of this dinner party."

Norman bit his lip and then nodded. "Three weeks, man. You've been spotty for three weeks. It's been getting progressively worse, your concentration, but you've got to be able to feel that. I've been double-checking your work, and it's adding to the amount of time everything takes. If you don't mind your mother and Olivia asking questions, we could use her in the shop."

"I do know my way around a computer's guts," I chimed in. "And I don't mind helping at all. I think it would be fun."

Jonathan looked from me to Norman, to me again. "You do realize that you'll face an interrogation committee the likes of which you've never seen when my mom and Olivia get a look at you," he said. "But I guess we need you since I've been so useless lately." He looked down at the floor and crossed his arms again, but this time almost like he was giving himself a hug.

"Stop that," I said quietly but with conviction. "You are not useless in any way. This is your business, and you love it, and you need an extra helping hand right now. I'm honored that I can be that for you. So lean on me, okay? It doesn't make you weak."

At the word *weak*, his head snapped up and he stared at me, a quick flash of anger crossing his face, then replaced with a softer expression as he took in my smile. "Okay," he said.

"Alright, then," I replied. "So, um, what now?"

Norman coughed behind me, and I turned to see he'd raised his hand. "I have a suggestion!" he said happily, and he suddenly reminded me of an excited little kid. "Now that the three of us are united for a common good, we find ourselves in the interesting position of having possibly the three biggest badasses in *League of Magecraft* all on the same side and not bickering for once. So I say, let's join up, form an arena team, and make player versus player our bitch. We can take down any other team of three players out there if we communicate and watch our egos. I'd be willing to bet on it."

"Um, Norman, that's great and all, but you're forgetting one thing: I suck at duels," Jonathan said.

I started to nod, but then stopped. This could work! "Wait a minute! You only sucked in duels because you always fight one-on-one. This time, Deathdrop and Maximus will have your back. We need to train a little in the practice arena, so we don't embarrass ourselves the first few times we are in the real one. But I like this idea. It'll be fun."

Jonathan grinned. "Yeah?" he asked.

"Definitely, man," Norman enthused. "Come on, playing with your best friend and probably girlfriend? What better team could you ask for?"

* * *

"Holy hell, we *suck*," I said into my microphone, though the words were loud enough to reverberate around the trailer. I was currently in the guest room on my laptop, Jonathan was in the living room on Norman's laptop, and Norman and Lucille were in his bedroom. "This is all about teamwork, guys. We have awesome gear and we each know our class inside and out. I think we're not trusting each other enough. And we have to appoint someone as team lead. It's not going to work if there is no one to coordinate."

"I'm guessing you want that job," Jonathan said dryly.

"I would like to throw my hat in the ring," said Norman. "I always get overlooked. Both of you have served as guild senior officers. All the glory, and it's scrubs like me who are doing the heavy lifting."

"Hey, I take offense to that," I said, prepared to do battle over my good name. "I do plenty of heavy lifting when I'm in the game."

"Uh-huh," Norman said. "I still want to take point on this one. I think we could hone ourselves into a solid unit and dominate with some strategies I've thought up. I get that you are a great PVE and raid strategist, Max, but PVP is different. Give me a chance, boss," he joked, and I caved. He really was too impish and charming to resist sometimes.

"Fine by me," said Jonathan.

"Okay," I agreed. "You take point, Norman. We'll do what you tell us to and we'll see how far this can take us."

After a sometimes-trying-but-overall-very-fun evening, we worked out some kinks and tried our skills against other actual players. A paladin almost killed Wrath in our first match—paladins are such an overpowered class—but I jumped in and the two of us took him down. We fought back-to-back and side by side while Deathdrop stealthed around and launched surprise attacks from the shadows. After winning three matches in a row, we decided to give it a rest for the night as we had to be up early for work in the morning. Which brought us to an interesting question.

"Hey, you want me to run you back to your place? Or are you crashing here?" Norman asked Jonathan, coming out of his room in just his band T-shirt and boxers.

I emerged from the bedroom, swallowed a breath, and hoped my pride would not be on the line when I said, "You can stay with me. This is a queen bed. Not quite as good as a king to get away from my kicks, but I think we'd manage."

Jonathan suddenly looked like a cornered animal again. Shit, that wasn't how this was supposed to go. He was supposed to relax playing *Magecraft* with us, doing something familiar but also challenging and engaging, getting him out of that head of his for a while. But right now, I could almost see the anxiety seeping out of him in waves.

"Hey, no pressure," I said, going over to the couch and sitting next to him. "You know that I care deeply for you and no answer you give me about something like this will change that, right? If you'd rather go home, then go, and I'll see you bright and early at your place. Or after work, if you decide not to have that talk with your mom and sister." I squeezed his arm, and I felt some tension leave him.

"I think I will go," he said, turning to me. "But this doesn't mean I don't lo—"

"I know," I said, stopping him with a deep kiss. I knew he loved me. But right at that moment, if I heard him say it, I didn't know if I would be able to stop myself from saying it back. And in that brief moment, the thought scared me to death. I'd never said those three little words to anyone in a romantic context. I'd never felt them, before Jonathan. Could I really, truly trust my own mind and heart? I was so tired of not trusting myself that I wanted to say the hell with it and shout it from the rooftop that yes, I loved this man. And I would ... soon.

CHAPTER TWENTY-SIX
JONATHAN

"Did you ever think for a minute that I'm not the enemy? Where are you going, Maximus? Max?"

— *Wrath*

"What the hell was that?" I exclaimed when Norman climbed into the truck to take me home.

"Whoa, down boy!" he said, his hands up in a classic "Who, me?" gesture.

"Don't pull that innocent crap, you know what you did in there! That was a straight-up ambush, and I want to know precisely what you said to her to make her flake off work and come all the way down here. Now." I was starting to vibrate, I could feel anxious energy burning through me, scorching me from the inside out. I clasped my hands in front of me while Norman started up the truck and we made our way over to my trailer.

"I get it. I went behind your back. I violated the bro code or some horseshit. But you don't see you the same way I do. You may not see yourself slipping. And you may not be aware of how important you are to so many of us. So I called in reinforcements. And come on, there's no one better to watch your six than Maximus."

I sat with that for the remainder of the drive home, uncertain of why I felt so panicky when she said I could stay the night. I knew I was restless and pacing most nights, and having strange, distorted visions of tarantulas crawling on the walls or dreams of fire. No way did I want Max to see me like that. Luckily, most of the torment in my mind eased during the day when things were busy. Though apparently I'd been slacking for weeks, probably lost in my head and causing all kinds of mistakes for Norman to have to clean up. No wonder he thought I was going out of my mind. No wonder he needed backup.

"Look, man, I'm sorry if you feel ambushed or attacked. But I—"

"It's fine," I said, cutting him off. "It was cool to see her again. I had almost forgotten the way that smile makes me feel."

"She really is beautiful. You didn't lie there."

"Yeah, she is." I grinned as I hopped out of Norman's truck, wondering what I was going to say to Mom and Olivia.

* * *

"She's here? Miss Tennessee herself!" Mom said in a singsong voice, flitting about the living room as I poured milk over my cereal.

"Yes, so please, please be on your best behavior today," came Olivia's sharp tone as she entered the kitchen. "I got your back, little brother," she said, patting me on the shoulder as I quickly shoveled down my breakfast.

"I will have you know, Olivia June, that I am perfectly capable of behaving myself around a guest!"

"Well, remember she's Norman's guest, not ours. She's coming here to help work in the shop, not sit down to dinner," Olivia replied, giving me a look.

Okay, I got it. My manners where Maxine was concerned had been horrible. Time to rectify that, one step at a time. "Mom, I was hoping you wouldn't mind if I invited Maxine over for a meal and a proper introduction. I mean, she will be here today, but—"

"Today works!" she said, quivering with excitement as she moved around the living room, straightening things, refolding blankets, fluffing pillows.

"Well, don't get ahead of yourself. Let me at least text her and make sure she and Norman haven't made plans already." I tugged my cell free from my pocket and for a moment wondered who I should text, Maxine or Norman. What if Max didn't want to meet my family but would be too polite to say so? *No, stop it*, I told myself. She wouldn't even be here if that were the case. Taking in a deep breath, I forced my hands to be as still as I could make them and typed out a text to her.

"Well?" Olivia asked. "They're coming, then?"

"Yup. Mom, don't fret about having something fancy made, okay? We can always go to the diner. And Max and I will want to help if you are going to put out a spread."

"I don't get home from the grocery until four today, so if you are trying something complicated, take the help and be glad of it," Olivia broke in.

That mollified our mother, and she resumed her trip around the main room, cleaning what was already clean to start with. What neither of us wanted to say was that we didn't entirely trust her to run the stove alone in the house, and whoever was going to help her with it, be it Max or myself, would be pulling double duty as keeper of the fire extinguisher.

Norman's truck pulled into the driveway just as Olivia ran out, presumably to ask him for a lift to the grocery since she was running a bit late this morning. I heard a bubble of feminine laughter, so I guess that introduction was out of the way at least. Taking a big gulp, I said, "Mom, Maxine is here. Should I bring her in now or should I wait until lunchtime?"

"Now!" she exclaimed, her eyes wide like an excited kid on Christmas morning.

I silently prayed that Mom would also keep her prayers to herself today, and that she would remain lucid and not need to dull herself with benzodiazepines. It looked like Maxine was making tracks for the shop as Norman pulled out of the driveway with my sister, so I put down my cereal bowl and went to greet and debrief her.

I found Max as she was poking her head inside the garage, which was large and took up much of our lot. We'd divided it into two workspaces.. I was quite proud of our indoor/outdoor setup, so I watched her for a moment before interrupting her assessment. From the back, I could see her hair was loose and down, even longer than mine, and in the sun it blazed a gorgeous shade of brown that I swear had reddish highlights. She was dressed casually, in a blue flowy blouse that looked like something a hippie would wear, with jeans and those red Converse on her feet. I would prefer work boots, but she wouldn't be helping with the carpentry today, so it was okay. She started to hum a tune under her breath in that horrendously off-key yet charming way of hers. Feeling like a creeper, I coughed, and she practically jumped out of her skin before turning and flashing me a smile.

"Come on," I said, extending a hand to her and reveling in the warmth of her hand as our palms connected. This was the woman I loved, who loved me back. Whatever happened, it would be okay. "There's someone I want you to meet."

* * *

AFTER WORKING TOGETHER THAT DAY, I realized how truly diabolical Norman's seemingly innocent plan of making the three of us into an arena team in *Magecraft* had been. Norman had set us up to work as one unit, under his leadership, and he slipped into that role once again like he was born to it. We'd always had a fairly equitable division of labor and never argued over who was going to do this or that, but I guess with me not holding up my end, it was time for some decisive leadership. He assigned Maxine and I the task of finishing her build. I couldn't help but feel that she was babysitting me, to make sure I stayed on task and my thoughts didn't stray too far while I was supposed to be focused. Despite that feeling, it was a relief to have Norman step up and take charge.

What could have been a disastrous dinner with my family's ace interrogation techniques came and went with minimal incident, Maxine earning my family's stamp of approval with her kindness, cleverness, and compassion. She had indeed offered to pitch in and cook with Mom, and that alone scored her big points with Olivia. We chatted in the living room until I saw Maxine stifle a yawn and realized it was getting late. I asked Norman to take Maxine back to his place for the night, but she stopped me and said she would prefer that we walk. That was fine by me, because some things had to be done face-to-face, and finally pinning down the future direction of our strange courtship was one of them. All the uncertainty to this point was driving me up the wall.

As I led her by the hand through the moonlit darkness of the trailer park in the direction that would take us to Norman's, I struggled to find the right words to convey how I felt. I decided to leap into the deep end of it and blurted, "Having you here is amazing. But it's underscoring the fact that you live in Tennessee and I live down here. We love each other. What does our future look like to you?"

She stopped cold in her tracks, and for a moment I thought I'd made a terrible mistake. I took both of her hands in mine and leaned forward, resting our foreheads together. "We're at a crossroads," I said, jerking my head slightly to the left, prompting her to look around. We were literally standing at a four-way intersection of dirt roads.

"They say you can make a deal with the devil at a crossroads," she replied. "You know, I thought you were Lucifer himself when I first saw you in the airport. The most beautiful of the angels, and a gigantic thorn in my backside."

I chuckled and put a hand up to cup her cheek. As our hands were still entwined, this was not exactly possible, but I wasn't willing to let her go. Not when we were about to discuss something so important.

"I think," I began, "that we have to ask ourselves one simple question: Do we want to continue this relationship?"

"It's not that simple though. We might want to have one, but is it healthy for both of us to be in a committed relationship right now?"

"You mean is it healthy for me," I stated.

She shook her head. "No, I mean for both of us. Jonathan, I only started to come out of a very deep, large cocoon I had cozied myself into for almost ten damn years. I let that one attack by those asshole Wraiths define me, whether I like admitting that or not. My therapist has been great, but nothing happens overnight."

I considered this. "Okay, so maybe the world doesn't revolve around me being bipolar."

"No, *you're* not bipolar, Jonathan. You're living with bipolar disorder. It doesn't have to define you, any more than the trauma I went through needs to define me. We get to make our own destinies and choose what parts are important."

"I know what I choose. I choose you," I said simply, like it was the easiest thing in the world.

"I choose you too." She smiled. "You know, they also say that the devil is in the details, and our details are a bit much. I have commitments in Green Valley that I can't walk away from, no matter how much my heart will ache to leave here. My mother counts on me, and I can't expect Lois to just fall into that role and start doing all her outside chores for her. And there's another thing—Lois and Elsa. I think I've pretty much convinced them to move all the way across the country and then I skip town? I'm literally the only person they know in the whole South."

I felt a flicker of tension on my face, but she was on a roll, her mouth like a speeding bullet that wouldn't be stopped until it was lodged in my heart. "Which brings us to your situation. You have an entire business here, with your best friend. Then there's your mom, and I know she can be a handful. Norman and Olivia depend on you."

"I know this. I love you, and I have for years. No one else will ever measure up to a fraction of what you are to me. And I don't want to lose that. I'm willing to make sacrifices to keep you in my life and to keep you happy, Max."

"I'm willing to make sacrifices for you too. I want to fight for you, and for us. I want to put in the work. I just wanted to lay out the situation so we aren't walking into this blind. A long-distance relationship, that's what we're looking at here, right? I mean, that's what I want. I want to be it for you, whether you are physically with me or five hundred and fifty-odd miles away."

"It *is* only about an eight-hour car ride, or a short flight and a drive," I pointed out, breaking into that smile which she had once confessed made her all twitterpated.

"Wrath is my boyfriend. Imagine that." She laughed.

"Not like it took a while," I replied in a teasing tone. And with that, I took her hand and we resumed our journey, leaving the crossroads in the dust behind us.

* * *

"JONATHAN, this isn't funny. Open the damn door!" Olivia's voice punctured through the dull roar in my mind and I stopped pacing long enough to think about what she was saying.

Open the door? Such a simple thing, but … no! I needed that door locked to keep them out. Who "they" were was less clear, but I was filled with conviction that this was the only safe space.

"I can hear you in there, moving around and muttering to yourself. Please let me in so we can talk. You're upsetting Mom."

Ah, another trick, trying to guilt me into giving up my safety. Well, it wouldn't work. I looked to my window and saw lights from the neighbor's. Even they felt too close, like everything was closing in on me. So I went to the most private location I had, my bathroom, and sat down on the floor across from the vanity. I pulled my knees up as close to my chest as I could and wrapped my arms instinctively around them. I tried to bury my head in my outstretched arms so I wouldn't have to hear the noise from the hallway coming in through paper-thin walls, and so I wouldn't have to listen to that buzzing, buzzing in my head.

"… won't listen to me … to you, maybe … I don't know if … Mom, please … back to bed okay? I can …"

They all see how weak you are. All of them are secretly laughing at you. Such a burden on all of them, and they hate it.

No, shut up! I screamed internally to the sound of sick laughter.

I couldn't even tell if it was real or imagined at this point because the words felt real. And wasn't it our perception of things that make them real or not? I started to laugh, wondering why at 4:00 a.m. I had decided to wax philosophical over a voice inside my own damn head that was intent on torturing me. Or was it telling the truth? It was so hard to tell. I was tired, so tired, but I clenched my arms tighter around my legs and leaned my head back against the wall, thankful for the quiet from the hallway at least. Which didn't last for long.

"Thanks so much for coming, y'all. Between Mom and now Jonathan, I was too overwhelmed to think clearly, maybe—"

See? Burden!

I put my hands over my ears, but the voices wouldn't go away. I flopped my useless hands down at my sides, tipped my head forward, and reared it backward, meeting the wall with a satisfying crack. And again, and again.

"What is he banging in there?" a feminine voice asked.

"I think it's his head," a deeper voice replied.

"Holy shit, we have to stop him before he hurts himself."

Hurt myself? *Hurt myself!* What did they know about how I hurt? I could feel my whole body full-on rocking back and forth, hitting the wall each time, and the bursts of pain were the only thing keeping me grounded in the here and now. I was here and now, right? I wasn't lost yet … was I?

"Aside from breaking down the door, there's no way we're getting in."

"I'm not ready to go full-on *The Shining* on your door, Mrs. Owen. But I will beat it down if I have to."

"Do it. Girls, get behind me."

A loud bang, then another.

Ah, they're coming for you, Jonathan. The scared little boy can't even be trusted by his own family to handle himself. They're going to send you away.

Then, a *CRACK*, and a waft of slightly fresher air coming through the staleness of my room.

Footsteps.

"Aw, fuck, man. Max, Olivia, stay out there and keep Mrs. Owen out too. I'm going to sit with him until we can get in contact with Tom."

"Not bloody likely. I want to see what is going on." A retreat of the footsteps. "Hey, what are you doing, restraining me? You've knocked down the door. You can't keep me away from him, Norman! He was fine a few hours ago, I have to see—"

"Max! This isn't helping right now."

"But I love him, Norman!"

"I know you do. I love him too. He's my best friend, and I'm not letting his girl see him like this. Please respect that and just wait a little longer, okay?"

Footsteps moved through the trailer. Feminine crying from down the hallway, but I didn't know whose. I couldn't focus, I needed … fuck, what did I need? I buried my face in my hands until I heard someone sit down next to me.

They gently bumped shoulders with me, and a calm, male voice said, "You're having a shit night, yeah? It's okay. That girl out there? She loves you, you know. And I know you don't want her to see you like this, so let me put it another way: you cooperate with me fixing you up, or I leave." Ah, Norman.

I could trust Norman, right?

I lifted my head, which felt like a huge, heavy bowling ball, and looked up into the calm, encouraging face of my best friend since we were five. I reached out and took the tissues he offered, wiping my eyes and blowing my nose. Then, I nodded.

"Okay," I croaked, my throat dry and sandpapery. "Do I have a choice anyway?" I asked, curious about what level of cooperation he expected here.

"You do," he answered. "You can keep punishing yourself. But I hope you agree with my plan because, man, you gotta know you're not at your best right now. I can help with that."

"Okay," I repeated, and he nodded.

Norman stood and extended his hand down to me. I was so tired of looking for hidden motives and seeing enemies at every turn.

I shook my head at his hand and managed, "My lorazepam. I should have one. Make that two."

He was quiet for a moment. "I was thinking one before you can talk to Tom. If you take two, it's going to knock you out."

No fight left in me, I nodded. He turned to my medicine cabinet, fiddling around with bottles until he found the container of small white pills. He handed me one and I let it melt under my tongue, knowing it would calm that ugly inner voice still tormenting me. I pushed myself to standing, and Norman guided me by the elbow back to my bed, saying, "Man, I've got to clean up in here a little, yeah? There's like, broken door pieces on the ground and it looks like your laundry basket exploded."

I sat on the bed, and feeling tired and defeated, said, "Do whatever you want. I can't … I can't think."

"Do you want to see Maxine? She would like to see you," he said, almost too casually, as he picked up stray clothes and tossed them into the basket.

I wasn't a slob by nature, but I was self-aware enough to notice that the chaos in my environment was often reflective of the chaos in my head. I kneaded my forehead, suddenly aware of how sore the back of my head was.

"Jonathan? Do you want to see Max?"

CHAPTER TWENTY-SEVEN
MAXINE

"This game is bigger than you or I. It's about community, about friendship, and about building something together."

— *Maximus_Damage*

I sat at the kitchen table and held onto the tea Olivia had placed in front of me like it was a lifeline. I knew coming here that I would be seeing Jonathan in the throes of an episode of some kind, but I wasn't prepared for what that would feel like. The sheer helplessness that would grip me, and the way I was compelled to go to him, even though all sense said to stay back until he was ready. I looked at the empty place on the table where Norman had tossed the first aid kit when we arrived, and my gut churned. Had he cut himself? Was he back there, bleeding?

"You look like you're about to break that cup with how tense your hands are," Olivia said, sitting down across from me. "That first aid kit was a precaution. Norman likes to cover all bases." She had just helped her mother relax and get back into bed and looked like that's where she needed to be too. It was closing in on five in the morning, and we were all haggard.

"How often does it get this bad, Olivia?" I asked, almost whispering, like I didn't want her to hear the question because I wasn't sure I could handle the answer.

"That I need to call in reinforcements? Not often. Only when his meds fail and he needs to start a new one, usually. It's happened three times since he was diagnosed, and every time I've called Norman. He seems to relax around him more than with me. I think it's because Norman is better at remaining calm, Jonathan responds well to it."

I felt something in my stomach sink like a stone. "I kind of dropped the ball tonight, didn't I? By adding to the tension."

She reached her hand across the table, palm up, and I placed mine in hers. She squeezed tight and said, "This is all new for you. The fact that you are here, that you care, that you love him, all of those things matter. Of course you went Mama Bear on Norman because he wanted to come between you and Jonathan. It's okay. There's no rulebook for all this, believe me."

I squeezed her hand back. "Thanks, Olivia. I want to be useful, you know? And to see him with my own eyes, that he's okay. I—"

"I'm fine." Jonathan's voice floated into the room, and I looked up to see him standing there with Norman, looking a bit wan, but otherwise okay. He was fully dressed in a long-sleeved T-shirt and jeans, his hair combed and falling around his shoulders like a shiny curtain.

I leapt up and asked, "Can I …?"

He nodded, and I ran over to him, wrapping him in my arms. He brought his arms up around me and held on tight as we both quivered with pent-up emotion. I laid my head on his shoulder and stroked his hair, and said, "I'm sorry I was freaking out earlier. I was scared, because I would slay a dragon for you but I don't know how to stand by when you're the one who has to do it."

"I know. I'm sorry you were upset."

"Don't you dare apologize," I said, leaning up and kissing his cheek, his beard comforting as I nuzzled the side of his face. "There is something you can do, though. You can talk to Tom and your doctor, if you're ready."

He let out a full-body sigh and seemed to deflate a bit. He loosened his arms, and I took that as a sign to give him some physical space.

"You're not wrong. It's time for a new medication and for me to go back to therapy. I haven't been right for a while now, and I don't know how you all put up with me."

"No one is putting up with you, Jonathan," Olivia said. "We all love you."

"All of you? Still?" Jonathan asked. His eyes honed in on me.

"Yes, all of us," I replied softly. He reached out and we clasped hands. I noticed his hand was shaking slightly, and I wondered if that was an aftereffect of the episode, or if he was still running on high tension and anxiety.

While Mrs. Owen rested, the rest of us sat with Jonathan until he could contact Tom and his doctor at a more decent hour. We decided to have a Mario Kart tournament in the living room, and I was shocked at how good Olivia was. She consistently kicked our collective asses, and I wondered if there wasn't a gamer hidden in there somewhere. At six, she and I made pancakes while the guys played games on the Switch, and then we all sat down to a feast. Jonathan picked at the food, but did manage an entire pancake, so I was happy. He then excused himself to take his morning pills, and I asked if there was anything I could do to help. When he admitted that his room was in a sorry state, I jumped at the chance to do something, anything, so I grabbed the heaped-up laundry basket and hit up the utility closet with the washing machine. I then returned and cleaned up his room, collecting energy drink cans, stray tissues, and a few dirty dishes.

At nine, after the longest four hours of my life, Jonathan was able to get in touch with Tom, who scheduled an emergency appointment for the following day. He also liaised with his psychiatrist, who scheduled Jonathan an over the phone appointment right away. All that was left was to go to the pharmacy to pick up a new prescription and wait to see what kind of impact it would have on him.

Olivia decided to stay home from the grocery in case the night's events triggered their mother to act erratically during the day, but Norman opted to jump right back into work after making the pharmacy run. When Jonathan headed for his shoes, Norman held up his hand and ordered Jonathan to get back to bed. I mouthed a thank you and followed Jonathan down the hallway to his aired-out room, which was now neat as a pin.

"I know we need to talk," said Jonathan, pulling off his jeans and grabbing some sleep shorts from his dresser, "but I'm just so tired. Lie down with me?"

"Of course," I said, sliding onto the far side of the bed and getting comfortable. He stood there for a long moment looking at me, and I felt my cheeks turn red. This would be our first time sharing a bed since Green Valley. Though I knew sex had to be the furthest thing from his mind right now, it felt good to be in his space and to breathe in his delicious scent. I rolled onto my side, and when he climbed into the bed after me, I cuddled up to him, resting my head on his chest, tangling our legs together, and twining my fingers in his hair.

"Is this okay?" I murmured, wanting to make sure he didn't see my glomping onto him as an intrusion.

"It's better than okay. If I drift off, wake me when Norman gets back from the pharmacy?"

"And if I fall asleep too?" I teased.

"I think he'd find no problem with dousing us both with a cup of cold water to wake us."

"Yikes, you're right. I'll stay awake," I said, laughing a little.

Jonathan cupped the back of my head with his palm and brought his lips down on mine, softly and sweetly. I gasped a little as he deepened the kiss, sliding his tongue over my mouth, seeking entrance. I opened to him, and we lay like that, holding on to each other with an almost desperate edge, our mouths fused. A polite cough burst our little bubble, and as we broke apart, I looked up to see Norman standing in the doorway, a white paper bag in his hands. Jonathan stiffened slightly, but nodded, resigned to trying the new medication which, in my opinion, was a huge part of the battle.

"Don't get up, I'll grab you some water," Norman said, walking over to the small bathroom and running the faucet. "Then I'm hitting the shop for a few hours, and I'll go home to crash for a bit if I need to. Max, call me anytime if you want a lift over to my place."

"Maybe," Jonathan began, sitting up a bit, "we can both come over to your place later. Play a little arena, and I could stay over."

"If you feel up for that, I'll even buy the takeout." Norman grinned, handing off the cup of water and bottle of pills. Jonathan plucked one from the container and downed it. Satisfied, Norman headed out, his voice echoing behind him, "Call if you need anything!"

"Well, now it's just a few weeks until we know how this is going to work," Jonathan mused, putting the bottle and cup on the bedside table.

"Weeks? Is that typical?" I asked, worrying at my bottom lip, which was still a bit swollen from Jonathan's kisses. I had told Thuy I'd be back in no more than a month.

Jonathan settled back into the bed and held me as I lay half across him. "Don't worry, it takes that long to build up to a proper dose, and to come off the medication that this will replace. I know you can't stay for all of that, Max. It's been amazing having you here, but your life is in Green Valley, and no way are you throwing away your job for me."

"I think that's part of a bigger discussion we need to have when we're both not exhausted," I said, yawning wide. That set off Jonathan yawning, and within minutes, I felt the rise and fall of his chest steady, his breathing going deep and even, and his heartbeat no longer racing under my ear. I closed my eyes and planted a light kiss on his chin, then drifted off.

* * *

WE WOKE up at around four in the afternoon, and Norman's truck was gone from the driveway. Jonathan commented that he would normally jog over to Norman's, but the new med was making him feel very tired and a little spaced out. So I called up our friend and asked him to come get us. A few minutes later, we were piled into the truck, in search of a good burger joint not too far away.

Burgers and sides procured, we returned to Norman's and tucked in, falling on the food like hungry wolves. Even Jonathan was hungry, which was an improvement from this morning. He claimed the mac 'n' cheese as his own, and we let him have it because whatever tempted his appetite, he should eat. Nausea was one of the side effects of the new drug he was taking, according to the helpful pamphlet from the pharmacy, and according to Dr. Google, which I consulted on my cell phone while the guys were busy getting the food. The more information I was armed with, the better I felt.

As we devoured the meal, cracking jokes and ribbing each other over our skills in both gaming and computer-building, I looked at Jonathan's face. He looked truly relaxed for the first time since last night's seemingly out-of-the-blue disaster.

We shooed Jonathan away from the dishes, setting him with the task of finding us a movie to watch while Norman and I cleaned up. I realized how nice this was, having both of them in my life. If anyone had told me around a month ago that I would be roaring friends with Deathdrop and romantically involved with freakin' Wrath, I would have given them a verbal beating down for their rudeness. Now that I knew them, had seen them under pressure and vulnerable, I knew they were good men, and I was lucky to have them in my life, in whatever capacity.

I popped a bag of popcorn in the microwave and settled in on the couch next to Jonathan, tucking my feet under me so I could snuggle into his side. Norman sat in the recliner, and as Jonathan flicked through the movie options, Norman almost jumped out of his seat. "Dude, stop! You passed the *League of Magecraft* movie!"

"No!" Jonathan and I both said in stereo, then laughed like a pair of hyenas.

"Trust us, we're saving you from an evil that should never have been born into existence," I said, wiping a tear from laughing so hard. "Hey, Norman, have you seen *Detective Pikachu?*"

After mutually deciding on a *Good Omens* binge, I noticed Jonathan was starting to sag beside me. We made it two episodes before I decided to call it and drag him to bed. I was tired too, the emotional toll of the entire day wearing me down. I didn't realize how bone weary a person could get dealing with such strong emotions. After my attack, the emotion I felt the most was fury, and then anxiety, which I'd allowed to rule me through avoidance. But watching someone you love suffer was on a whole other level. I would take back all my fury, all my anxiety, and hold on to it forever if it would somehow free Jonathan of the things that tormented him.

We moved around the bedroom and small attached bathroom at Norman's like we'd been sharing the space for years. Jonathan pulled me into his arms and folded me into an embrace. "How much longer do we have?" he said softly, running a hand through my hair.

"I told my boss I wouldn't be any more than a month."

Jonathan swallowed hard and I saw his Adam's apple bob. He nodded and said, "We will try to salvage this train wreck and enjoy each other, okay? I'm so freakin' sorry my head is such a mess, Max."

"No, you do not apologize for this, Jonathan. You hear me? This isn't anyone's fault, let alone yours. You wouldn't choose to go through this, and the rest of us who love you are more than willing to be a support network for you. You aren't a burden on anyone, you got that?" I poked him in the chest to punctuate my words. "I am in love with you, Jonathan Owen, and that means I love all of you, including all the facets of that amazing brain of yours."

"Okay. But for real, who put Norman in charge of this operation anyway?" he asked wryly, breaking the tension.

I laughed. "We did, when he made his case for arena captain. I guess that made him the alpha of our little pack."

"Or so he thinks …" He waggled his eyebrows up and down. "He has been doing a good job of holding the fort and keeping me from tanking the business while riding The Bipolar Express."

"Mm-hmm," I murmured, listening to his heartbeat and feeling on the verge of sleep.

"Max?"

"Yes?" I replied with a yawn.

"Are you too sleepy for me to play with you a little? I'm tired, but I want to taste you. It's been so long, and you're addictive. I want a fix."

"You're serious?" I asked, feeling suddenly more awake. I looked up into his hooded eyes and felt his hardness pressing into my thigh.

"Absolutely," he replied, kissing me on my forehead, then my cheek, before claiming my lips and working the drawstring of my sleep shorts at the same time. I smiled into the kiss and wrapped my arms around him, willing the rest of the world and all of our problems away for the time being.

* * *

WE FELL INTO A RHYTHM, the three of us. Weekdays we spent at the shop, bringing the business up to schedule on their orders. More often than not, we'd stay for dinner and I would help Mrs. Owen or Olivia cook a meal while the guys worked. I didn't mind being relegated to the kitchen because I was using the time to get to know the other women in Jonathan's life, and I wanted so bad for us all to be close. Weekends the guys and I spent as a team in *Magecraft,* honing our arena skills and dominating the rankings as we learned how to anticipate each other's moves and work in sync. I hadn't asked about reclaiming the officer position, and Jonathan gave it up willingly to another guildie so he had, in his words, more time to focus on keeping himself on an even keel.

He was sleeping through the nights courtesy of his new medication and was starting to feel less lethargic during the day. His mood had elevated significantly after his appointment with Tom, and I wished I'd had the chance to meet the man who had been so influential in Jonathan's life, especially when he was a teenager and confused over his feelings for me. I would be forever grateful that he had found someone who didn't judge him for his sexuality or pigeonhole him with a label, but rather allowed him to figure things out on his own. I had been briefed on his sister Elaine's stance on Jonathan's pansexuality, and as far as I was concerned, whatever his sexuality was, it was just part of the man I was crazy about.

Time flew, and I was all too soon booking my return trip for the following weekend. I shot an email to Thuy, confirming I would be back at the library on that Monday. The days since Jonathan's medication change would have been an interesting crash course on bipolar disorder, if I didn't love the person living with it. I was so proud of Jonathan, but it was agonizing to watch him try to navigate the exhaustion and episodes of brain fog brought on by the new drug. I kept holding on to something Mrs. Owen told me the day after our first sleepover at Norman's: that Jonathan *will* eventually get better and come out the other side of this, but it would take time and patience.

Time was something we no longer had together.

CHAPTER TWENTY-EIGHT
JONATHAN

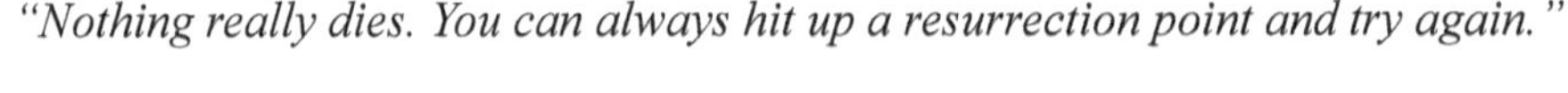

"Nothing really dies. You can always hit up a resurrection point and try again."

— *Wrath*

For the ride to the airport, we all wedged into Norman's truck, Max sitting in the middle and fully in control of our karaoke party on the way to Jacksonville. After two bouts of particularly athletic sex last night, we were both in a good mood, despite it being the day of our parting. We had no immediate plans to see each other again, but we both knew that we would. When we touched, it felt like destiny, and I was confident now that this would not be our final goodbye.

That didn't, however, stop me from becoming emotional as we faced each other, her bag checked and her ready to walk through security. She was my heart itself, and she was leaving me. No, I corrected myself, she was leaving Florida, but her attachment to me remained intact. I did some deep breathing exercises and held it together long enough to give her an epic embrace and a scorching kiss right there in the terminal while Norman whistled.

"I suppose you deserve a goodbye too, Deathdrop," she said, turning to him with a salute.

"Indeed, Maximus," he replied, bowing low.

She stepped forward and folded him into a hug, saying in a low voice that I couldn't help but overhear, "Watch his six, team leader. And by the way, did you know that a deathdrop is a dance move? It's quite popular with drag queens."

He grinned and winked down at her. "I did know that, actually."

"You're a man of many layers. Like an ogre." She squeezed him one last time and then turned back to me.

"I'm fresh out of poems fit for saying goodbye, Sir Wrath, Knight of the Beautiful Swamp Realm. But I will hold you in my heart every day and I know that you're going to keep fighting for yourself long after I've gone. And that you will call me, night or day, if you need someone to talk to. I will always take your call, no matter what. That goes for you too, Norman."

"That's great because you never know when we might need to organize a new mission. May I humbly suggest we consider a guildie trip to DragonCon?" Norman asked, waggling his eyebrows.

"That's an awesomesocks idea," she replied, looking a bit unnerved, probably because she was now so close to two people she used to loathe. Or thought she had loathed.

"I hate to break up the lovefest between you two," I said, dryly, "but Max is going to miss her flight if she doesn't get moving. And I want one more snuggle before she does." I extended an arm, and Max smiled wide as she tucked into my side, me bringing my other arm up to encircle her. I rested my head on top of hers and breathed a sigh of contentment. If I could have this every day, I would be the luckiest jerk in the world. She pulled me down for a kiss, and I met her mouth greedily, inhaling the last bit of her smell and holding it, as well as her taste, in my memory banks.

I released her and watched as she tried to be discreet about wiping away stray tears but failing miserably. "Hey, this isn't the end of us. No tears, not today, okay?"

She nodded, gave my hand a last squeeze, and said, "If I don't go now, I really will miss my flight. I love you guys. In different ways, of course, but still …" She shook her head and ran to the security entrance, boarding pass clutched in one hand.

"Norman, I need to get the hell out of here before I start to panic," I said, my façade of calm and happiness melting as I watched the love of my life walk away. I reached into my pocket and took out two of the small white pills, letting them melt under my tongue. They would relax me within minutes, and by the time we made it back to the truck, I would be groggy enough to nap for the ride home.

"No problem," he replied. "Just walk right next to me, and I'll get us through as quickly as possible."

* * *

I PICKED at my food that night, opting to go with Norman back to his place at my mom's urging. She said that sleeping in the same bed that held Maxine's scent would make me feel better, and that she couldn't handle seeing my long face from across the dinner table anyway.

"I'm sorry," I said to Norman, who had thrown some steaks on the grill while I made the salad. "I don't have an appetite tonight, I guess."

"You haven't eaten all day. Are your pills upsetting your stomach again?"

"More like not having my girlfriend around is turning my stomach. And I know, lame. I should be able to function on my own but …"

"Dude, you just left her at the airport at lunchtime. It's now dinner. Big, complicated emotions take longer to process than the span between two meals." Norman punctuated his words with his fork, talking around a mouthful of salad. "We'll wrap yours up and you can eat whenever. You know I'm not civilized enough to care about proper mealtimes."

I nodded and sat there staring at my plate until I felt a gentle shove to my shoulder. "What was that for?"

"For getting you out of your head. You know that's dangerous territory right now. If you're going to sit here and stare at your steak like it's about to leap off your plate, you might as well leave the table and do something with yourself. Pop on a console and play *Smash Bros.* or go fire up Lucille and play *Magecraft*. Or rather, since you object to the special relationship she and I have, use my laptop and play it in the living room. I don't care what you pick, I think doing something familiar will help you feel better."

I nodded, then got up from the table, making tracks for the cling wrap to put over my plate. "Since when did you become my Yoda anyway?" I asked, only half-joking. Really, since when was he the responsible one in this duo of ours?

"I hate to break it to you, Jonathan, but I've always been the Yoda."

"No way! When you got back from overseas, I was definitely the Yoda."

He considered that and said, "Okay, so maybe we've taken turns being each other's Yoda. That sit right with you?"

"Yes, much better." I stuck my plate in the fridge, and it hit me. "Wait, you Yoda'd me again! Stop using your Jedi mind tricks on me."

"And to think, Max told me that you totally used those same tricks on her back in Green Valley."

"She did?"

"Uh-huh," he said around a piece of half chewed up meat.

"Okay, we are going to discuss this more after you're done with dinner. I can't stomach watching you talk around a hunk of cow carcass right now."

"What an appetizing choice of words, man. Thanks," he continued, swallowing and belching. "I'm done. Let's get these dishes in the washer and then we can see if our third is up for some arena."

I snorted. "Our third? That girl is no one's third. She might have been gracious enough to let you take point on arena captain but that's just it, she let you. She's a freakin' force of nature. Hurricane Maxine."

We got the last of the dishes in the washer, then he posed a question in an almost too-casual tone. "About that particular storm. What do you plan to do?"

"Do?" I asked incredulously. "What can I do? You know I'm trapped here, Norman. I have responsibilities, commitments. Those didn't vanish because I fell in love and then had a mixed episode. Am having, I guess. I don't even know anymore, it's still so hard to think clearly." It really was. There were times when things stuck out in such vividness that I couldn't help but become distracted by them, and others when everything felt like I was moving through a thick mist, unable to grasp seemingly simple things.

"Well, that's obvious, man. You can't see the forest for the trees right now, because if you did, you'd know you were—and excuse the term—crazy to let that girl go."

I was stunned, literally stunned. What did he mean, *let* her go? No one made or let Maxine Peters, Maximus_Damage herself, do anything. Least of all me. Right?

"I can see the status bar loading in your brain. Whatever you are chewing on, it's wrong."

I shook my head and slammed the dishwasher closed. "I couldn't keep her here forever; her life is in Tennessee. What was I supposed to do, fuck off my responsibilities here and follow her?"

Norman banged his hand down on the counter. "Damn right you should have. And you will. I can't handle that hangdog face any better than your mother. This is bullshit, you've been through hell in your own mind for years and you deserve every slice of happiness that comes your way."

"You're not going to kiss me again, are you?" I asked, trying to inject some humor into a situation that was making me vastly uncomfortable. My heart rate increased, and I felt sweat begin to bead on my forehead and upper lip.

"Whoa, dude, sit down. Now," Norman said, pointing toward the couch. "You are shaking like a leaf. Do you need to take a pill? Or can you breathe your way out of whatever is going on?"

"I, um, I don't know. What *is* going on?" I asked as I made my way across the room and settled into the sofa.

Norman appeared beside me with a glass of water and set it on the coffee table.

"I have commitments here, not only to my mom and Olivia but to our business and to you. You honestly think it was easy for me not to follow her today? To stay here, knowing that I'm still sorting out the crap with my meds and my messed up brain without her? I know that I'm the one who has to fight this battle, but losing her after spending a month together, it's like I'm missing a piece of myself. And you have the balls to straight up say I should have gone after her? I'm doing the best I can, for everyone. Including you."

He sat down beside me and put a hand on my shoulder. "I know you think you are." He sighed, then scrubbed one hand over his face. "Look, when I got back from my deployment, I was a mess. You are the one who was there for me to put me back together, and again when my mom died. Without you, I would be lost in a liquor bottle somewhere. And I'm damn proud of the business we've managed to cultivate with our online business model. But don't you see? The answer is staring you right in the face."

I raised my eyebrows and my mouth pressed into a firm line. "I still don't follow."

"That's okay, you're still probably half whacked from that big dose of lorazepam you took on top of all your other pills. Let me do the math here. Our customers are online, not in our trailer parks. I have no family left here except your sorry ass which I've been tied to since we were playing in the sandbox as kids. I say you talk to your family about how *you* want *your* life to unfold and then we pick up stakes and relocate Supernatural Computers to Green Valley. Max might not be ready for you to live together, but we could find a rental, and maybe she would let us usurp her garage until we find a permanent workshop."

My head swam. Norman had handed me the biggest gift he ever could, and I was utterly gobsmacked. Move to Tennessee? Both of us? Actually be with Max, seeing her whenever I wanted … but could I expect that of Norman? All he had left of his mother was this trailer, still filled with her things like a museum. But maybe he needed a change as much as I did. "What about your place? You've kept it since your mom passed, are you ready to give it up?"

"Honestly, no. I mean, I'm ready to pack up my shit and start someplace new, and I think I'm ready to donate her things. But I own this place outright, and with what I have left over from her life insurance, there's no need for me to sell it. I'll keep it as our Florida base. It wouldn't be expensive to get someone around here to check up on the place for me. Maybe Olivia would do it for some spare cash. And someday I'll be ready to sell. Believe it or not, I have thought this through. I've had this brewing in my mind ever since you got back from your epic weekend in Green Valley. So the real question here isn't about me or my ability to move. It's about you and your family."

I blanched. "Well, shit."

He leaned forward. "Yeah, about that. I was talking with Elaine the other day …"

* * *

THE FAMILIAR SKYPE RINGTONE SOUNDED, and I double-checked my watch. Then, suddenly, her sunny face filled the screen, a smile shining at me. "Jonathan! I'm so sorry I almost missed you. I was chatting with Lois and Elsa and we lost track of time. They just left. I can't believe I never knew them in person before." Lois and her daughter had made the move South after all and were staying with Momma Rose, much to her delight. "They fit right into my life, like they always should have been here. Kind of like how I felt with you and Norman and your family."

"Like we always belonged together," I finished the thought, and nodded. "That's a nice segue into why I wanted to talk face-to-face, so to speak. Norman had this crazy idea, and I floated it by my family, and well, it turns out they already knew and they … I mean, this is a Deathdrop scheme, bear that in mind …"

"Whoa, slow down, Jonathan. You're talking super fast, and I can barely see your face because your hand is flying all over the place. What was Norman's idea?"

I closed my eyes and counted to ten, leveling out my breaths, and started over. "Max, we want to move to Green Valley and bring our business up with us. Norman and my family staged a bit of a coup behind my back and they're all in agreement that they want us to be happy. You and me, together. For real."

Her hand flew to her mouth, and her eyes grew wide, quickly filling with tears. "When you said you'd make sacrifices to be with me, I didn't know you meant leaving everyone and everything you know behind."

"I won't be. I'm bringing Norman, remember?" That made her laugh, and I swear, I could bottle that laugh and sell it as the sound of pure joy.

EPILOGUE
MAXINE

"Games bring people together, and those people can become your friends, and your friends can become your chosen family."

— *Maximus_Damage*

I s this the last box?" I hollered, unsealing packing tape from the cardboard box and smiling when I saw that it was full of books. Thank the gods for the extra shelving in the gaming room because fitting any more books into the main room of my cottage would be a violation of the laws of physics.

"Yes!" Lois bellowed back, unpacking things in the kitchen.

Elsa ran into the gaming room—her little six-year-old self covered in dirt from playing in the yard and garden out back—and smiled big, showing off the gap where her bottom front teeth should be. She reminded me of an adorable jack-o'-lantern, and even my mom called Elsa her little pumpkin grinner now that she'd started losing her baby teeth.

"Mommy said to tell you that the boys are back. They're bringing fried chicken, but Mommy is letting me have grilled cheese with tomato soup. She could always make you extra," she said earnestly.

Little Elsa had recently become a vegetarian after a trip to Mr. Badcock's farm to see the chicks and had become quite taken with a Plymouth Rock cock named Sampson. She'd connected the dots that the chicken people eat came from live chickens. Now she was on a crusade to recruit everyone to vegetarianism. Luckily, both Mom and Lois rolled with the punches and started cooking healthy vegetarian meals. The move from New York had been a bit hard for Lois at first, readjusting to small-town life, but Elsa was thriving, and it was nice to see Mom's big house filled with laughter and friendship. Our entire group ate over there often, almost filling out the formal dining room table.

I heard the front door slam shut, and I got up, extending a hand to Elsa. She took it, and we set out in search of our respective lunches. It had been a long morning of moving, but with everyone on board, we were doing well. *Many hands make light work*, Mom had said when she'd shocked us all by climbing into my Jeep when I'd arrived this morning to pick up Lois and Elsa. Bit by bit, Mom's anxiety and agoraphobia had been getting so much better. Sometimes she sat on the front porch of her house. Sometimes she would walk the property, and twice she had walked with me to the library and back. One time we had made it to the Piggly Wiggly in my Jeep, but she stayed in Stiles while I did the shopping. Today she was in my home with everyone, and my heart was as full as my little cottage, now bursting with both Jonathan's things and my own. A donation trip to Goodwill would soon be in the cards for us.

When we entered the main room, Elsa dropped my hand to run to Jonathan, who she had taken a shine to. He scooped her up and tickled her cheek with his beard, making her shriek in delight. She was the only person other than me permitted to play with his hair. She picked up his ponytail and pet it gently while he grinned down at her. I had to admit, seeing the man I loved with a small child in his arms was giving me all kinds of feels. I had visions of babies and picnics and big group breakfasts in our future. While those things might have frightened me back in the fall when Wrath was still my nemesis and Maximus_Damage my shield, I was definitely excited about the trajectory of my life now. Those walls I had built so high around my heart came tumbling down over the seasons, and now, in this gorgeous spring, I felt like my own spirit was becoming new again.

Jonathan whispered in Elsa's ear and he set her down, crossing the room to me and sweeping me almost off my feet in a bear hug, followed by a kiss involving tongue— in front of my mother! I pulled away playfully, wiping my mouth and gaping at him.

He bent over and laughed, a sound I would never take for granted, and said, "Sorry, Momma Rose! Got a bit carried away."

"That's perfectly alright, dear," she replied as she helped Lois and Norman set the table and lay out side dishes. "It's natural to get carried away when you're still in the honeymoon phase of a relationship."

"Not that there's been an actual wedding," I heard Norman mutter under his breath.

I was so kicking his ass in a duel later.

"Miss Maxine believes in cohabilation before marriage," Elsa said from where she was seated at the table, blowing on her bowl of soup.

"It's cohabitation, sweetie, and where did you learn that word?" I asked suspiciously. All of a sudden, Lois was very busy dishing out chicken.

"Who wants breast meat?" she asked the room.

"From Mommy," Elsa answered, looking impish.

"You little traitor," Lois said, patting her daughter's head. "Kids. You confide in them, think you've taught them to keep their mouth shut, and then boom! Out drop the truth bombs. What can I say, she wanted to know why only Mr. Jonathan was moving in with you and not Mr. Norman too, and then she wanted to know why Mr. Jonathan was moving in when he wasn't your husband. Then it was all about when would y'all be getting married because he told her that she could be your flower girl."

"Wait a sec. Lois, did you just say 'y'all'? Y'all heard that, right?"

"I definitely did," Jonathan piped up.

"I think we've heard enough from you for a while," I said, shooting him a look that said "we'll talk later" as I took my seat at the table.

We had bought a new one—our first joint furniture purchase—when it had become glaringly obvious that six would not fit around my teeny table. Even now, we had to put in a leaf and squeeze, but it wasn't bad. Not when you are squeezed in with the people you consider family. And to me, they were family, even Norman. I had no clue when or if Jonathan and I would make things official, but Elsa was right, I did believe in living together before tying the knot, even if I wasn't a hundred percent sure that marriage was something I wanted. I had thought Jonathan was on the same page as me, but now I wasn't so sure, considering he was filling our little friend's head with visions of being my flower girl.

Was Jonathan planning to propose? What would I say if he did? A drumstick landed on my plate and I stared dumbly at the potato salad, quietly contemplating that. And when I felt a nudge to my leg and looked up to meet Jonathan's gentle brown eyes looking into mine from across the table, I knew. Of course I would say yes. To hell with marriage maybe not being for me, *he* was it for me, and if he asked me to be his wife, I would gladly march down that aisle on my mother's arm, with Elsa tossing flowers over the backyard for me to step over in bare feet. Okay, so maybe I had thought about this whole wedding noise. Just a bit.

We all joined hands and said a short grace, then began to pass the sides around the table while my mind strayed to the last few months. Right after Thanksgiving, Jonathan and Norman had arrived in Green Valley and had immediately begun converting my garage into a workshop. A plan I was happy to approve of, knowing it would mean Jonathan would be at my place every day. Even if I was at work, it gave me comfort to know that he was here. More often than not, the three of us would eat our evening meal together, and Norman would drive home to their rental, leaving Jonathan and I to tear each other's clothes off.

Jonathan's switch to his new medication had been successful, and he had no further mixed episodes or episodes of mania or depression since. He kept in touch with Tom via Skype every two weeks and found a caring doctor here in town. As for me, I was still seeing my therapist. I knew that bipolar disorder was something that would never magically go away, but with careful management of both the disorder and our expectations, we could have a long, healthy life together.

A trip to Florida to visit Jonathan's family was on the radar for almost all of us— Mom still wasn't ready to travel that far. Part of the deal struck between the Owen siblings was that they would all contribute something based on their respective incomes toward hiring a part-time nurse to be with Mrs. Owen when Olivia worked or wanted to socialize. Jonathan's mother was adamant that she not be a burden on her children and only accepted the portion of the cost not covered by her husband's life insurance. I knew Jonathan and Elaine slipped Olivia more money without their mother's knowledge to help out. I was proud that he still had their backs, and I was touched that the whole Owen family was working to make it possible for the two of us to be together. As for Lois and Elsa, Lois had barely said the word *Florida* before Elsa started begging to travel down to Disney World.

We were nearing the end of our raucous dinner when Jonathan stood, clinking his fork against his soda can. "Now that we're all gathered here, I have something very important to say." I felt myself stiffen. He wouldn't! Not in front of everyone, would he? "Everyone gathered at this table is important to me. I can't count the number of ways your friendship has helped me settle here in Tennessee. You've all made Norman and me feel like family, and I'm grateful. Which is why I hope you won't take it as a sign of ingratitude that I leave y'all to do the dishes while I take my new roomie for a walk."

His pronouncement was met with groans and laughs. Jonathan walked over to where I was seated and pulled out my chair, extending a hand. "Shall we, my lady?

"I am no lady," I replied, grinning. "But yes. Let's make a quick escape before the peasants revolt."

We ducked out to some jeers and very quickly got on our shoes. Jonathan surprised me by leading me by the hand around the back of the cottage and up the path to the woods. It was the same way we'd headed on Medieval Day, and sure enough, at the crest of the small hill was the bright red tent suspended from a sturdy branch.

"What in the … are we smashing watermelons again today?" I asked, curious.

"No, no feats of strength. Maybe a feat or two of courage, though," he said, and pulled me along until we were standing in front of the tent. Inside was a bed of quilts and cushions, and a cooler. There were also two items prominently displayed. A blue tabard, and beside it, a pink head cone—which I knew was actually called a hennin— with a translucent veil.

Jonathan stared at the items, his mouth slightly agape. "There were supposed to be two matching tabards! What in the … freakin' *Norman*."

I sat down on a cushion, laughing so hard my sides ached. "Not so fast," I managed. "This has Lois stamped all over it. She plays the sweet and wise angle, but she's a loose cannon." I held the cone out, and declared, "Here's your costume, my dear."

"I'm not wearing that!" he replied, putting his hands on his hips.

"Well, I'm sure as hell not," I said, gasping for air by this point. I forced myself to stop laughing long enough to get out, "Come on, whatever you've got planned, it can only be enhanced by you wearing an excellently taped together pink head cone."

"Fine," Jonathan said, grabbing the cone from my hands. "You think I'm going to back away from a challenge just because I'll look foolish? Ha!" He plunked the cone on his head, the train reaching to about his waist.

Not to be outdone, I picked up the tabard and slipped it over my head, tying it around my middle. I glanced around for nerf weapons or any other indicator of what we were doing here.

Jonathan sat down beside me, near the cooler, and asked me if I'd like a drink. He pulled out some sparkling cider and two champagne flutes from the container.

"Now, a toast," he said, that horrendous English accent having returned. I snorted as he poured the cider, and then raised my glass.

"And what are we celebrating, Sir Wrath?" I asked, happily playing along.

"Us," he replied, clinking his flute with mine. "I am of the opinion that the joining of ourselves under one roof is a fortuitous time to declare the eventual joining of our Houses." He then stuck his free hand into his pants pocket. He withdrew a small, blue velvet box. I gasped, and a huge grin broke out on my face as I reached for it.

"Hey, not so fast," he said, pulling his hand backward. "There is something I've got to tell you about this box."

"What?" I asked, laughing with joy this time, my heart thudding so loud in my chest that I was certain he could hear it.

"Like telling you that what's inside this box is bigger than it seems. One might say it has a bit of magic, like a book," he said, trying to sound serious and failing because he kept smiling. I felt like I might faint as he opened the box, revealing an exquisite sapphire ring. He dropped the accent and said, "Maxine Peters, will you do me the honor of becoming my wife?"

My hand shook as I extended my left arm so he could place the ring on my fourth finger. It sparkled in the afternoon sunlight, a gorgeous square blue stone on a white gold band. It looked like an antique and was exactly the type of ring I would pick out for myself. I never thought I would be one of those women who freaked out over a piece of jewelry, but Jonathan was right. This ring was so much bigger than its size. It represented a promise between us, a promise to always be there for each other; to love each other even in the hard times, and to laugh together in the good.

Jonathan leaned in for a kiss, and I glomped onto him so hard that he almost tipped over. We embraced as if we only held on tightly enough, we'd become one person.

"Is it okay that I did this?" Jonathan murmured, stroking my hair with one hand. "I know you believe in 'cohabilation' before marriage."

"Of course," I replied, barely containing a giggle, I was so giddy. "We'll have plenty of time to live together during the engagement. I'm just glad you didn't do it at the dinner table." I sat back and laid a kiss on his bearded cheek.

"I had thought of that, to be honest," he replied, looking sheepish. "But I wanted it to just be us, you know?" I nodded. "Of course, everyone back at the cottage is waiting to see if I've won your hand."

"Stick with me, and at the end of the day it'll be Sir Wrath and Maximus_Damage for the win, always." I teased.

"Of that, I have no doubt."

ACKNOWLEDGMENTS AND A NOTE FROM THE AUTHOR

Just as it takes a village to raise a child, I discovered that it takes a village to produce a book. I am beyond lucky that my village was full of the kindest, most selfless, and helpful people anyone could ever hope to work with.

First, I have to give my sincerest thanks to Penny Reid for this magical creation of Smartypants Romance, which has transformed a dream I had since I was a little girl into a reality. You are an excellent mentor and an amazing human being. For Fiona and Brooke, who have helped me in a myriad of ways, from answering frantic emails to teaching me new skills, to being a rock-solid beta, I have nothing but admiration and thanks for your time and work. Michelle and Iveta, my invaluable editors, this book is far better for your investment in the story, and meticulous attention to detail. Ashley, my beta and one of my biggest cheerleaders, thanks for the awesomesauce support. The other Smartypants Romance authors, you've been at various times my inspirations, my friends, my shoulders to lean on. Thank you.

To my family for being there through all of the joys and jenga of my writing a first novel, thank you for your constant encouragement and belief in me. Pat, I love you with all my heart, and thank you for keeping my spirits up during the difficult times, and cheering me on during the good.

Carian Cole, for providing me with mentorship as a newbie writer before Smartypants Romance was in the picture, I am extremely grateful. Your guidance on writing in general is part of how I landed this gig and I am your humble fan for life. Becky, thanks for helping me in my research about Florida. Laura, thank you for your cosplay insights; any mistakes are completely my own. Jan, the brilliant mind behind the real Medieval Day, I can only say, thank you for letting our epic day in Point Pleasant inspire my story. And to all of my guildies, past and present, thank you for the memories. Particularly Pat and Chris—I don't know how we've put up with each other for sixteen years, but here we are. Thanks for the lolz, ya newbs.

Korrie, it was your Facebook group that brought me around to a love of romance, particularly romantic comedy, and I would never have discovered this passion I have for the genre without you. Your kind spirit and support have mattered deeply to me. Cassandra, thank you for recommending the heck out of Penny Reid, which started me on this strange and wonderful journey to a place called Green Valley.

<u>A note about bipolar disorder and generalized anxiety disorder</u>

In writing this book, Jonathan's experience with bipolar disorder closely mirrors my own decades-long journey living with this condition. I also informed Jonathan's experience through discussion with others with this disorder, whose names I will keep for the sake of their privacy. I also learned much from my own various mental health teams. At one point, Maxine calls bipolar a "complex disorder." She's right; it has various types and manifestations, and if you are living with this condition and reading this book, it is very possible that you might not recognize yourself in Jonathan's experience at all. My explanations in the book are hardly meant to be an exhaustive overview of the disorder, but it was my hope to show one person's journey of living with this condition, and how he is worthy and capable of loving and being loved in return.

I also wrote multiple characters with anxiety disorders, because again, I live with generalized anxiety disorder, and know many others who struggle with it daily.

I believe that the more we normalize having these types of mental health conditions, the further we work to de-stigmatize them. The more we show that these characters are people with wants, goals, dreams, with people who love them or who they love, then the closer we get to removing the veil of silence that embraces these conditions.

ABOUT THE AUTHOR

Ann Whynot has been writing books since she was a kid, and has always dreamed of becoming a published author. She is a voracious reader and book collector, and used book stores are her kryptonite. She also has a passion for video games, and met her partner in one. She loves crafting, baking, laughing, and travel. She lives with her family, dog, and two cats near a little village by the ocean on the Canadian east coast, and is inspired by both the forest and sea.

Find Ann online:
Website: www.annwhynot.com
Email: ann@annwhynot.com
Facebook: www.facebook.com/AnnWhynotWrites
Goodreads: www.goodreads.com/annwhynot
Twitter: @AnnWhynotWrites
Instagram: @ann.whynot

Find Smartypants Romance online:
Website: www.smartypantsromance.com
Facebook: https://www.facebook.com/smartypantsromance
Twitter: @smartypantsrom
Instagram: @smartypantsromance
Newsletter: https://smartypantsromance.com/newsletter/

<u>Park Ranger Series</u>

<u>Happy Trail by Daisy Prescott (#1)</u>

<u>Stranger Ranger by Daisy Prescott (#2)</u>

<u>The Leffersbee Series</u>

<u>Been There Done That by Hope Ellis (#1)</u>

<u>The Higher Learning Series</u>

<u>Upsy Daisy by Chelsie Edwards (#1)</u>

<u>Seduction in the City</u>

<u>Cipher Security Series</u>

<u>Code of Conduct by April White (#1)</u>

<u>Code of Honor by April White (#2)</u>

<u>Cipher Office Series</u>

<u>Weight Expectations by M.E. Carter (#1)</u>

<u>Sticking to the Script by Stella Weaver (#2)</u>

<u>Cutie and the Beast by M.E. Carter (#3)</u>

<u>Weights of Wrath by M.E. Carter (#4)</u>

<u>Common Threads Series</u>

<u>Mad About Ewe by Susannah Nix (#1)</u>

<u>Give Love a Chai by Nanxi Wen (#2)</u>

<u>Educated Romance</u>

<u>Work For It Series</u>

<u>Street Smart by Aly Stiles (#1)</u>

<u>Heart Smart by Emma Lee Jayne (#2)</u>

<u>Lessons Learned Series</u>

<u>Under Pressure by Allie Winters (#1)</u>

www.ingramcontent.com/pod-product-compliance
Lightning Source LLC
Chambersburg PA
CBHW021134190726
48288CB00008B/2657